Any Man I Want

(Also (with Lorelei Lovell and Cydney Rax)

The Montgomery Series

Hand in his Spice

Watch for Brothers

Any Man I Want

Published by Kensington Publishing Corp.

Also by Michele Grant

Sweet Little Lies

Losing to Win

Crush (with Lutishia Lovely and Cydney Rax)

The Montgomery Series

Heard It All Before

Pretty Boy Problems

Any Man I Want

Published by Kensington Publishing Corp.

Any Man I Want

Michele Grant

Dafina
BOOKS

Kensington Publishing Corp.
http://www.kensingtonbooks.com

DAFINA BOOKS are published by

Kensington Publishing Corp.
119 West 40th Street
New York, NY 10018

All Kensington Titles, Imprints, and Distributed Lines are available at special quantity discounts for bulk purchases for sales promotion, premiums, fund-raising, and educational or institutional use. Special book excerpts or customized printings can also be created to fit specific needs. For details, write or phone the office of the Kensington special sales manager: Kensington Publishing Corp., 119 West 40th Street, New York, NY 10018, attn: Special Sales Department. Phone: 1-800-221-2647.

Dafina and the Dafina logo Reg. U.S. Pat. & TM Off.

ISBN-13: 978-0-7582-8967-4
ISBN-10: 0-7582-8967-7
First Kensington Trade Edition: August 2014
First Kensington Mass Market Edition: July 2016

eISBN-13: 978-0-7582-8968-1
eISBN-10: 0-7582-8968-5

10 9 8 7 6 5 4 3 2 1

Printed in the United States of America

This one is dedicated to my godmother:
Rita Shirley Reddick.

I know I'm a writer, but sometimes one word
is all you need: *Awesome*

"We delight in the beauty of the butterfly, but rarely admit the changes it has gone through to achieve that beauty."
—Maya Angelou

Acknowledgments

I'd like to take this time to thank everyone who wrote in and asked, "What about Katrina? Can a sister get some sexy?" Why, yes—yes, she can! As the third and final Montgomery, I thought Katrina deserved a story of her own that also allows us to revisit characters from Beau and Roman's stories.

One thing I've been very passionate about is positive portrayals of African-American women and men in literature. Certainly, there are enough stereotypes that exist and proliferate today that warrant some contrast and debunking. Though my characters sometimes lead more glamorous lives then the rest of us, at the end of day I hope you find them relatable and real.

When you read one of my books, I'd like my characters to be people that you would hang with or invite over for dinner. Hopefully, you'll find that with Katrina and Carter.

Enjoy!

Prologue

I don't regret much

Katrina—Saturday, May 21—10:22 p.m.

"Y**ou will rue the day you ever discarded me!**" Kevin Eriq Delancey declared dramatically as he slammed his belongings into a designer suitcase that cost more than my first car. Thankfully, we were in a private villa of an exclusive resort in Barbados and no one was close enough to hear his ranting and banging around. "Rue the day! *Do you hear me?*" he repeated, punctuating each word with the hard toss of an object into his luggage.

I blinked twice and then deliberately looked back at the thumbnail I was slowly filing. It didn't seem prudent to laugh, but really—he sounded like a poorly written soap opera character. I coughed to cover up the giggle that threatened to spill out. *Rue the day?* I thought—okay, sir. I refrained from sighing deeply or rolling my eyes.

"Yes, I hear you, Kevin." I stayed still while keeping my eye on the fuming man pacing around the spacious accommodations. This trip had been successful professionally and disastrous personally. My photo shoot went flawlessly; my relationship went up in flames.

With growing detachment, I watched as Kevin railed at me, so angry that spit was literally flying from his mouth as he spoke. I had deliberately waited until tonight. I thought I'd staged this perfectly. We had a lovely dinner; I made sure he drank the lion's share of the wine. Our week here in Barbados was nearing an end. I'd hoped he'd be mellow enough to avoid just this kind of scene. True, there's never a good time to break up with someone, but seeing as how we'd only been dating a few months and neither of us were fooled into thinking this was any sort of love connection, I thought it safe to cut the ties before we headed back to the States.

I had long since given up dating models or photographers or designers. I was sick of men who required more pampering, ego-stroking, or mirror time that I ever would. I was tired of men who just wanted a trophy for their arm, a playmate for their bed, or photo op to boost their careers. Some of the blame fell on me. I hadn't always chosen my companions wisely. I was a busy woman. I didn't want to put a lot of work in and I wanted it to be easy. But I'd found that easy men were like cheap shoes: You got what you paid for, they were usually uncomfortable, and you shouldn't expect them to last long. I decided it was time to put at least as much effort into picking my men as I put into picking my wardrobe. Priorities, you know.

At first glance, Kevin seemed to be a great choice. He seemed different in a good way. He was supposed to be my anti-drama boyfriend. The grown-up, sophisticated, 'bout-his-bidness man who made the rest of them look like preschoolers. Educated, sophisticated, wealthy, and articulate; Kevin Delancey was supposed to be a step up on my dating food chain. Someone I could try and build something with for the long haul.

Yet here we were . . . again. Kevin was the CEO of a hugely successful online purchasing Web site. Serengeti was similar to Amazon.com, but the products were primarily manufactured and sold by people of African descent and targeted the African-American community. He started the company in his dorm room at Morehouse fifteen years ago, took it public for a ton of cash, and then went private again. He was now listed somewhere between Michael Jordan and Warren Buffett on the *Forbes' Richest Americans* list.

Unfortunately, those riches had not bought Kevin very much in the way of couth, class, or chill. As my nephew Chase liked to say of ill-behaved people, "Dude had zero chill." Kevin put the X in extreme everything. And I'd missed the initial warning signs. Totally my fault. Kevin rolled up on me at an event for BellaRich Designs, the fashion house I ran jointly with my future sister-in-law, Belle Richards, and my brother, Beau. Beau and Belle were also former models. Since I was phasing out modeling for anyone other than BellaRich, I'd been more focused on design and promotion. It was at a BellaRich party where Kevin came over to compliment us on the line of evening wear we'd debuted.

At first impression he came across suave, sophisticated, stylish, and supremely confident. Just a shade under six feet, he was olive-skinned, easy on the eyes, and had a smile that no doubt closed many a deal. I admit to being somewhat fooled at first. I had to dig down a few layers to find that he was all about the surface and not much else. At this moment, I narrowed my eyes at him as he continued to pace and pontificate. Perhaps he should've finished Morehouse—they generally turned out a better product.

The thing was, people met me and saw the packaging. Light skin, light eyes, long hair, proportioned body. They don't take the time to see the sum of my parts. They assumed that as a model, designer, and business owner I was all champagne, caviar, red carpets, and flashbulbs. Really, I was most at ease curled up in front of On Demand with chicken wings and cheap Chianti. Kevin didn't get to know that side of me. He had no interest in the sweatpants, T-shirt, hair-in-a-ponytail, chill-on-the-sofa side of me. We started off as arm trophies for each other and I took my time over the course of the next few months deciding if I wanted it to be more than that. Our dates were glossy: high-profile restaurants, club openings, movie premieres, charity events. I didn't like the way he treated people he didn't seem to think were his equal. Rarely did he find anyone to be his equal.

Our schedules were so crazy that I didn't

spend a lot of time with him so I thought perhaps I was judging him too harshly. After all, the man ran a gabillion-dollar business; he didn't necessarily have time for all the niceties.

I came into this week thinking that it was going to be our make-or-break week. Kevin and I had flown down to Barbados for a shoot showcasing the newest line of BellaRich resort wear. Belle and I decided to go with Caribbean-inspired colors and prints for the line. Kevin had placed a substantial order after seeing the initial drawings. Seemed like the perfect time to mix business and pleasure for both of us. If only Kevin had shown a tenth of the prowess and presence in the bedroom that he did in the boardroom—we wouldn't be in this situation. Okay, that's not fair. I wasn't breaking up with Kevin because he was terrible in bed. Being terrible in bed was the last of many nails in the Kevin Delancey coffin.

And believe me . . . it wasn't just tragic bedroom game. Wait, let me say that again: *Tragic. Bedroom. Game.* A man of his age should not only know how things work, but should at least know where to find them. I mean, this is Anatomy 101. It's just not that hard to locate a minimum of three erogenous zones. That level of ineptitude indicated both selfishness and laziness. I'm sad to say I had to fake my way through it . . . twice. Once to give him the benefit of the doubt. The second time hoping he improved his game. At my age, faking it? Ain't nobody got time for that.

Before you judge me, know this—I was not so shallow that I couldn't overlook or provide hands-on assistance to someone with subpar swerve skills.

The fatal flaw that put the dagger in whatever Kevin and I had? He treated people like crap all the time. Not just when he was stressed or busy or multitasking. He thought everyone was there to cater to his every whim. He cussed out the waiter, made a maid cry, shouted at his subordinates, threw a tantrum when the gift shop was out of the lotion he preferred, and snapped his fingers and pointed when he required something. The third day of the trip, when he pointed at the coffeepot and then to his cup, I raised a brow.

"Did you . . . need something?" I asked silkily.

He snapped his fingers twice and said, "Katrina, you know I'm better when I have my coffee."

"Is there a reason why you cannot pour it for yourself?" It wasn't that I was opposed to pouring his coffee; it was the way he expected me to respond to a double-snap of his fingers. What was I, a dog? No, sir.

He sneered. "Oh, I forgot, Princess Katrina, you are too bougie to serve your man. You've never had to lift a finger a day in your pampered life. You're too cute to pour a simple cup of coffee, huh? Never mind." While I sat there, astounded, he called the front desk and ordered a butler to be assigned to our suite. This fool could've poured four cups of damn coffee in the time it took for him to insult me, call down for assistance, and wait for someone to arrive to fetch his caffeine. After that, I was done. I played the "oops, I have my period" card and moved to the other bedroom in the suite. You would think after a week of me ducking out before he woke up and dodging him all damn day he would be a little less surprised at my declaration. I even softened the breakup by saying (cue an epic eye roll here) that he was just too much man for me.

"Are you listening to me, Katrina?" He stood by the front door of the suite, hands on hips. The much-maligned butler holding his luggage stood warily beside him. His expression indicated that he wished he was anywhere but here. I could empathize.

"Of course, Kevin," I lied smoothly.

"Well, hear this. You remember this moment. This is the moment you made an enemy of Kevin Eriq Delancey. You will regret this moment for the rest of your days."

I flung my hair over my shoulder and met his gaze directly. "I don't regret much. Life is too short for regrets."

His nostrils flared as he fought visibly to control his anger. "You *will* regret this."

Clearly nothing I said was going to make this go smoothly. "I'm sorry you feel that way, Kevin."

He swung the door open and motioned for the butler to walk out ahead of him. He stepped through and turned back. "You bet your sweet ass you'll be sorry. Also, I'm taking the jet. You can fly commercial." With that, he slammed the door shut behind him.

"Whew." I sighed and flung myself backwards on the sofa. Reaching for my cell phone, I punched a number. Belle, my business partner, best friend, and future sister-in-law answered on the first ring.

"Did you ditch Kevin Clueless yet?" Belle said in her husky southern drawl.

"Yep. He just stormed out, slammed the door for extra effect and everything."

"I guess he had his mad on?"

"Livid. He had that vein that men get in their forehead when they're agitated on full throb."

"Well, good riddance, I say, sugar. He can try and cause trouble, but the contracts he signed were airtight. If he backs out of the orders, we'll raise a stink. We're not without influence."

I let out a breath. "He says I'll 'rue' this day. Regret it the rest of my life."

She snorted. "Really . . . rue? You know I love an old-school turn of phrase, but c'mon now. What is he, a Victorian villain?"

"He's something. Best of all, he's gone. But really . . . I think we're okay. Like you said, he can make some waves, but how much trouble could he really cause?" After a bit more chatter, I wished her and Beau a good night and hung up. *How much trouble could he really cause?* I mused as I headed to the bathroom for a long, relaxing soak.

1

Not the dumbest thing,
but so damn close

Katrina—Monday, May 23—10:46 a.m.

Glancing at my watch, I had about four hours until my flight left for Miami en route home to Dallas. Since I had a little time, I calmly clicked through the photos of myself from this past week's photo shoot with detached interest. Even though I was two months from turning the big three-zero, I still looked pretty much the same as I had when I started modeling ten years ago. I cannot lie. I was genetically gifted. Thanks to Avery and Alanna Montgomery's DNA, I stood 5-10½ in flats. I had wavy, tawny brown hair that fell to my waist. My eyes were often compared to those of a lion, golden in color, slightly tilted and generously lashed. Being named Katrina and originally born in a small town in Louisiana—

people heard the name and thought of the disastrous hurricane. It wasn't that far of a jump for my nickname to be Cajun Kat. Not very original, but it worked.

As the last child and only daughter of this generation of Montgomerys, I could have been anything I wanted in life. I had the brains, the beauty, the unconditional love, and the ambition to be whatever made me happy. I had started modeling at age sixteen after graduating early at the top of my high school class. I really never wanted anything else. I loved the world of clothes and fashion. I loved creating and wearing beautiful things. I knew I wasn't going to model forever and had been slowly phasing out the modeling and spending more and more time involved in the design and business end of the fashion house. In my mid-twenties I took time to get a degree in art and fashion media from Southern Methodist University in Dallas. I thoroughly enjoyed not only the clothes but the best way to display and market the clothes across different media platforms. This shoot was the last of the artwork we needed for our next catalog.

I was deciding whether the gold bikini or the pale peach one piece would look better on the spring resort-wear catalog cover when a few things happened simultaneously. My cell phone rang, the doorbell of the villa rang, and the sound indicating that I had incoming e-mail beeped repetitively from my laptop. That couldn't be good.

I rose to move toward the door and caught sight of a photographer leaning over my balcony and pointing a huge lens at me. I snapped the curtains shut and looked down at the display on my phone. It was my agent, Fredrika Young.

"What's going on?" I answered.

"You haven't been online today?" she asked cautiously.

"No . . . but I have photographers at my windows and door and my e-mail is blowing up. What happened?"

"Kevin happened," she deadpanned.

I sunk onto the chaise lounge with a feeling of dread. "What do you mean, Kevin happened? What did he do?"

"Before or after he released the sex tape?"

"*Sex tape?*" I screeched into the phone. "I did *not* participate in a sex tape."

"He has the two of you on film, naked and in bed. Granted, it's grainy and there's not a whole lot of action, but it's definitely you, Kat. He says you offered him sex in exchange for the Serengeti business and once he'd signed the contracts, you discarded him. Discarded. He actually used the word *discarded.*"

"Yeah, he's all dramatical like that. Earlier, he used *rue* in a sentence."

"Wow. Anyway, it's total bullshit, of course. Everyone knows you aren't a sex-tape kind of girl and you've never considered pay-for-play a business tactic. If nothing else, we go after him for filming you and distributing without your consent."

"I can*not* believe this. He did say I would regret breaking up with him," I muttered.

"Do you?"

"Hell, no. I regret ever dating him in the first place." I huffed a brief and insincere laugh.

"As you should. From the looks of this tape he was a lousy bed partner."

I snorted. "To say the least."

"In addition to sucking in bed, he's a scoundrel and a liar."

"*Scoundrel* is a sexy word for someone devilish and charming. Kevin is neither of those two things."

Fredrika chuckled. "Duly noted. *Liar.* Not charming."

"Well, he did say one true thing," I admitted.

"What might that be?"

"I did discard him. I most certainly the hell did. Apparently, not a moment too soon."

"He is alleging that this is how you've closed deals for BellaRich Designs and stayed on top in the modeling field."

"Oh no, he didn't!"

"Yeah, he did. Said he has lists of other fashion execs and photographers that you've slept with. It's a slow news day, Kat. This is everywhere. They are calling you the Cajun Coquette."

I closed my eyes. Over ten years in the industry maintaining a flawless reputation in the media, playing nice with people who didn't understand the meaning of the word, smiling while half naked in rain, beach, snow, and shine and now this. . . . I was considered flirty but fun, sexy but not skanky, pretty but professional. People took me seriously. I worked hard to be more than a pretty face. I scrapped, clawed, and kicked my way into design. My designs were smart, sultry, and sought after. I carried my weight at BellaRich Designs and I'd be damned if a pompous ass with hurt feelings and no bed game was going to ruin all of that. "Thanks, Fredrika. I need to call Beau." My older brother Beau was a man who was often underestimated because he was so easy on the eyes. But of the three Montgomery offspring (me, middle brother Roman, and Beau), Beau was the one who not only knew how to play dirty, but relished the opportunity. He was sharp as a tack and knew how to think like both an angel and a devil.

Fredrika exhaled. "You're calling Beau? Good— he'll fight fire with fire. Call me when you know your next move."

"Drika?"

"Yes?"

"Thanks for believing in me."

"Katrina. You're no angel, but you don't play around when it comes to business. No worries. If you need me, I'm here."

"Thanks again." I hung up, ignored the knocking on the villa door, and dialed another number. It was answered on the first ring.

"Baby girl, how many times have I told you that your extraordinarily bad taste in men would bite you in the ass?" Beau's slightly accented voice poured out. Though we all had some Creole influence, Beau tended to lean more heavily on his than Roman and I did. "I swear, Kat, all the lovely male influences in your life and you have to hook up with the slimiest *cochon* out there. Not smart, sis."

I rolled my eyes at my older brother's rant. "Dating Kevin is not the dumbest thing I've ever done . . . but close. How bad is it?"

"Well, *chère*, I won't be playing that video at the next family reunion."

Scowling into the phone, I answered, "How is that possible? We did it twice. Both times badly. In the dark for less than fifteen minutes."

"I really didn't need details."

"I'm just saying. It was over in an instant. How in the world did that make a juicy sex tape?"

"Are you sure?" Beau queried.

"Quite. Why?"

"This tape might be doctored. The one I glanced at—and believe me, *'tite chou*, I never want to see anything like that again—has you in sunlight outside, near a beach in a hammock."

That sounded familiar and wrong all at the same time. "The only time I've been in a hammock here was for the shoot. I was topless, modeling the swim shorts. There was a male model; we did some flirting for the cameras but nothing that could be a hot sex tape. Not even close."

"This jerk must have meshed different footage together or something. Okay, I know what we're dealing with now. You need to lay low while I figure out how to go nuclear on Mr. Delancey."

All of a sudden, I remembered my team. "What about the crew?"

"We got everyone out on the first flight this morning. I'm sending someone to get you."

"What? No. That's unnecessary. I can fly home on my own, Beau. My flight is in a few hours."

"We already cancelled it," he declared.

"Oh, come on. This will blow over in a day or so."

"I doubt it. He's out for blood. Says he has proof that you've slept with half of your photographers, most of our clients. Says a lot of the BellaRich contracts were sex for signature transactions. He's claiming your entire professional career has been based on you passing out the good-good on the regular."

"*What?* I never—"

"I know that. I'm the last one you have to convince. When you think about it, it's actually kind of funny."

"In what possible way is this humorous?" I screeched incredulously.

"Out of the three of us—you, me, or Roman—which of us was more likely to be accused of using sex to get ahead?" Beau said ruefully.

My brother Roman was a straight arrow. He was happily married for the second time to a great woman named Jewellen. Beau, however, had been a notorious hound dog in his day. Not even just in his day—in everybody else's day as well. The trail of broken hearts and discarded panties he left behind was legend. He was bow-wowing right up until he met my friend Belle. We had modeled together. When she and I decided to go into design, I loaned her my condo. Beau had been kicked out of Roman's house and was trying to figure out what to do with his life and decided to stay at my place. That's how they met. After a few stumbles, they appeared to be on the path to happily-ever-after. I guess you *can* teach an old dog new tricks.

"I would say this is more ironic than funny—but hey, it's just my life imploding, laugh it up," I snapped testily. I rubbed my temple. I could feel a headache coming on. I twisted the top off of a large bottle of water and drank deeply.

"Chill, sis. Look, we all know this is ego-driven crap, but Delancey is throwing enough dirt around that we need a solid game plan before the media gets hold of you. We're releasing a statement today denying everything. In the meantime, you need to spend a few more days away from prying eyes and then come back to Dallas and stay somewhere the media can't find you for a while."

I exhaled. "How bad can it really be? I can't just step outside and laugh this off and it will go away?"

"Katrina, you're beautiful, you're rich, you're single, and you're famous. As much as people love you, they love a messy scandal more. They smell blood in the water and they're going for broke. This is going to take a little time and clean-up. But no worries, I'm on it. And I'm sending help."

I frowned down at the phone. "What kind of help?"

"Big Sexy is on his way."

I exhaled shakily. Carter "Big Sexy" Parks, super-hot former football player, one of Beau's oldest and dearest friends, currently a real estate mogul, was heading my direction. Did I mention that he's super-hot? A man doesn't get and keep the nickname of "Big Sexy" without earning it. And he really did. Even more telling, no one questioned the nickname. It fit. Everything about him oozed big and sexy. I'd thrown all sorts of "do me" hints over the years and though he never said no, he never said yes either. Never even looked all that tempted, much to my chagrin. I was a girl who was used to men wanting me and chasing me. The fact that he didn't seem to care one way or the other? Quite frustrating in a "but I can respect it" super-hot way. "Carter thinks I'm a pain in the ass."

"We all think you're a pain the ass, but we love you anyway."

I sucked my teeth in exasperation. "Carter Parks does not love me."

"Probably not, but he loves this family and he knows how to play tough. He'll keep you safe."

"I don't need a babysitter, Avery Beauregard."

"No, you don't, Audelia Katrina. You're a big girl. I know you're grown or whatever. But you do need an exit strategy and a hiding place where no one can get to you. Carter can and will provide both of those."

"Fine," I snapped out, already over it.

"I'm sorry, Kit-Kat. I didn't hear you. Was that a 'thank you' that you muttered so graciously, sis?"

"*Merci, mon frère,*" I thanked him through gritted teeth.

"That's what I thought I heard. *De rien.* Keep your head up, sis. We'll talk later."

"Later."

"And Katrina?"

"Yes?"

"Don't look at it. It will just piss you off."

"Okay," I agreed, knowing full well I planned to look soon as I hung up.

Beau used his sternest big-brother voice. "Katrina, I mean it."

"Got it. Not looking." I used my most innocent, agreeable voice.

He sighed. "I'll talk to you after Carter gets there."

"When will that be?" I glanced at the clock.

"Knowing him? Less than two hours. He was on the jet the minute after I called him."

Carter Parks was on his way, a sex tape with me on it was floating around the Internet, and it wasn't even noon on a Monday yet. "Fine."

"You okay?"

"You know us Montgomerys—we're always okay." I hung up and reached for the laptop.

2

Kevin Delancey is *not* that dude

Katrina—Monday, May 23—12:02 p.m.

I'd watched it over and over again. The first two times I was embarrassed, shocked, and ashamed. I thought about crying, but in the words of my mother, "What did tears ever solve?" I wasn't that much of a crier. All the puffy eyes and stopped-up noses just wore me out and took time away from fixing what was wrong. I moved past sadness and watched it again.

The next two times I was angry and incredulous. By the time I watched it for the sixteenth time I'd zoomed past angry to furious and had vengeance on my mind. Basically, the video had been spliced and Photoshopped to look like I lured Kevin outside to a hammock, laid back on it, took off my top, and enticed him to join me, at which point we had about five minutes of what looked like simulated sex and then the video faded to black. I realized that only the top half of the woman in the video was me; the rest of it was not. Someone with serious video editing skills put this together. And since Kevin had departed less than forty-eight hours ago, he'd either been planning this for a while or had somebody on standby waiting to make this happen.

Now, it was one thing to sleep with someone and have the world watch it, if that was your kind of thing. It was entirely different for someone to manipulate the facts to suit their revenge fantasies. Yes, I'd slept with him. Twice, in the dark, for fifteen minutes in the privacy of a hotel room. I wanted to scream that from a megaphone. Yes, I'd been topless on the beach, lying in the hammock. But those two things were mutually exclusive events. Kevin Delancey did not inspire me to get freaky or full-frontal on a public beach in midday. At all. And that pompous ass knew better.

Against my better judgment, I Googled first my name and then Kevin's: one hundred eighteen thousand new search results with my name attached. I scanned a few of them. I reached for the bottled water and drank some more, wondering if I should pull out the Advil as well. I watched Kevin give a press conference that was uploaded to YouTube, where he had the nerve to stand there with a straight face and say he felt used and betrayed. Really, though?

I skipped to another video and watched as Belle and Beau gave a brief statement on behalf of myself and BellaRich Designs. Ever so politely, but succinctly, Beau called Kevin a coward, a liar, and a crook. Brother Beau stared right into the camera with that pretty face of his and said that the truth would soon be revealed and at that time full exoneration of my good name and reputation would be restored and remedies would be sought. I had to smile—Beau had such a flair for the dramatic.

Next, I pulled up my social media sites. Scrolling through my mentions on Twitter I noticed people were taking sides with the hashtags #TeamDelancey or #TeamKat.

She is way too classy for this to be true. Delancey just mad he can't hold onto her. #TeamKat! Tweeted someone with the screen name @ModelsRock.

All models are hoes, why are you all surprised? #TeamDelancey came from @BrosB4Hoes.

Whatever really happened she didn't look like she was having fun. I would have dumped him too. #TeamKat

He is dat dude. #TeamDelancey

And so it went. I turned off my Twitter feed at that point. My inbox had blown up like an apocalyptic war zone. After an hour or so, I made it through only a fraction of the e-mails and Facebook page posts before I switched over to a popular news outlet. A headline jumped out at me: SUPERMODEL SEX SCANDAL GOES VIRAL. Ignoring the voice in my head telling me not to click on it, I opened the Webpage. A perky blonde news anchor smiled out at me.

"Katrina Montgomery, former supermodel and current designer at the hot BellaRich design house, has been paired with a legion of influential, attractive men over the years. Yesterday, one of those men came forward and accused the Cajun Kat of trading sexual favors for business deals. Kevin Delancey, of the wildly successful Serengeti Web business, affirmed his carnal knowledge of the seductress with a steamy sex tape. Katrina ascended to supermodel status at the age of eighteen as the spokesperson for La Dare Denim. Her most famous ad campaign . . ." They cut away to one of my former ads and there I stood, two years into my La Dare contract. I was in my twenty-year-old glory wearing skintight jeans, a see-through white tank top, and sky-high fire-engine red spike heels. I was all big hair, smoky eyes, and crimson lips. I strutted down a street full of men, drawing all eyes. The camera panned almost indecently up and down my body before closing in on my face. "I can have any man I want and you can too in La Dare jeans." I ran my hands up and down my body before turning to one of the men and crooking a finger at him. The commercial faded to black and the words *get what you want when you wear La Dare.* They cut back to the anchor desk and the anchorwoman smirked into the camera. "Looks like Katrina gets what she wants no matter what she is or isn't wearing."

I hissed out a breath before slamming the laptop lid shut. I stood up and started pacing back and forth. Wasn't this just a fine turn of events? I was the punch line to a bleach blonde's feeble joke, thanks to Kevin Delancey. That smarmy son of a bitch I'd dated for less than ninety days. Was I the first woman to tell him, "No, thank you"? This is what I got for refusing to bow down and just take the BS he shoveled? Oh, it was about to be on. If he wanted to play dirty, he picked the absolute wrong person to mess with.

Yep. I had definitely turned the corner back into mad. My cell phone buzzed, indicating an incoming text message. My number was unlisted and I rarely gave it out, so I knew it could be only one of a few people. Glancing at the screen, I read the message.

I'm here. Be at your door in five.—CP

Carter Parks was here. I exhaled, inexplicably nervous. I'd been around Carter for most of my adult life and this was the first time I actually cared what he thought of me. Did he think I was skanky? Did he believe anything Kevin said? Would he look at me differently? He always looked at me with a shuttered expression that bordered on indulgence, amusement, and intrigue. Would that be different? I ran my hands down the sides of my tropical-print halter maxi-dress and made my way toward the door. Security had scared away the last of the paparazzi and I wanted to make sure they let Carter through.

A sharp rap at the door told me they had. A quick glance through the peephole confirmed it. I swung the door open and waved Carter inside before closing the door behind him. Before I could say anything, he tucked his sunglasses into his pocket, pulled me into a tight hug, picked me up, and held me close.

"You all right? That guy's an asshole. I wanted to kick his ass. You want me to kick his ass? I'd really love to do it. Asses can get kicked. You just say the word, Kat."

I held on tight, burying my face in his neck.

The headache I'd felt brewing melted away. There was no explicable reason why being wrapped in Carter Parks's arms made me feel safe and like everything was going to be all right. But it did. "Hey Sexy." I let out a shuddering breath as he set me back on the ground. Everything really was going to be okay.

"Are you crying? Please tell me you are not crying over this dude?" He took a step back and looked into my face. There were no tears. "Okay, okay. Good. You look good. You always look good. You know what I mean. But say something." He ran his hands up and down my arms.

I took a moment to look at the über-eye candy that was Carter Parks. Even with my three-inch wedges on, he was taller than me. I loved that. He was six feet three and a half inches of chocolaty fineness. His body was still in football shape even though he had retired a little over four years ago. If I calculated correctly, he would be thirty-eight years old on his next birthday. He looked years younger. He had smooth, espresso-colored skin and eyes such a dark, rich brown that they appeared to be almost black at times. His eyes were widely spaced with ridiculously girlish lashes and a wide, frequently used smile that showed off his perfect teeth. He was handsome in that rugged, manly-man kind of way. Squared jaw, full lips that stopped short of pouty, angular cheekbones, laugh lines bracketing his mouth. His hair was cropped low in tight black waves. Despite the tropical temperature outside, he was nattily attired in a tailored black silk suit with a turquoise linen shirt under-

neath. Casual black boat shoes without socks com-
pleted the look. Somehow, he took an ensemble
that should not have worked and made it look like
the best idea ever. When he noticed me blatantly
checking him out, a slow grin spread across his
face and he raised a brow. "So you're all right,
then."

I grinned back with zero shame. He was a
good-looking man. It would be just plain criminal
not to enjoy the scenery. "I'm good. I mean, I'm
mad as hell. I'm tempted to take you up on that
ass-kicking offer, but I'm good. Are you going to
ask?"

"Ask what?"

"Whether the tape is a fake or not? Whether or
not I seduced a man for business?"

"Girl, please." He snorted and took his cell
phone out of his pocket. Without elaborating, he
started typing out a message.

I crossed my arms across my chest and started
tapping my foot. He had to be the slightest bit curious.

He glanced up. "Problem, diva?"

"You seriously don't have any questions?"

"I seriously already know the answers. You, that
dude? C'mon." He scoffed and then looked
around. "Pack your stuff, we're outta here."

"What do you mean?"

"I mean, princess: Open your fancy suitcases
and place your pricey belongings in them so we
can depart. Daylight's burning." He grinned at me
indulgently and went back to fiddling with his
smartphone.

The man was fine, but infuriating. "I know what packing means, smart-ass. I'm asking what you mean about me and Kevin."

He stepped close and put a finger under my chin to tilt my head up to him. "I'm not saying you couldn't seduce a man out of his last dollar if you put your mind to it, sweetheart. But that ain't you. There may be a man on this planet who you would compromise your principles for, but Kevin Delancey is *not* that dude."

"Yeah?" I tilted my head in acknowledgment. He made a solid point. I didn't realize he knew me that well.

"Yeah." He laughed and waved his cell phone at me. "I'm TeamKat."

That drew a smile from me. "Well, okay then. What's the plan?"

Carter nodded and took a step back. "You assume I have a plan?"

"You didn't hop a plane and get down here just to have conch fritters and stroll on the beach, Big Sexy. You are, among other things, a man with a plan."

"I am in possession of a plan. I do want those conch fritters, but we don't have time. You need to get packed. We're wheels up in about two hours."

"Are you going to tell me what the plan is?" I turned and headed for the closet. Most of my things were already packed; I just needed to pull the last of it together. I rolled out the last bag and started putting in some shoes. I walked to the bathroom to retrieve my cosmetics.

"Yes, the plan is to make Kevin Delancey rue

the day he ever thought to mess with Katrina Montgomery."

I, who was paid to walk gracefully, tripped over
air as I whirled around to face him. I caught myself
on the edge of the dresser. "Did you just use *rue the
day* in a sentence?"

He flashed his grin again. "Yeah, Belle told me
how much you love when guys say that to you."

I choked back a laugh and rolled my eyes.
"Adore it. Are you going to clue me in on any of
the specifics of the plan or you wanna spend some
more time cracking wise, sweet-talker?"

"Before we get on the plane, you're filming a
statement."

"Okay." I checked the dresser drawers to make
sure I had emptied them.

"Before we head back to Dallas, you're getting
a new boyfriend."

I slammed the last drawer shut and spun
around again to stare at him. "A new what?"

"Boyfriend, boo, cuddle buddy. You understand the concept. We're hooking you up," Carter
said silkily.

"Why? Who? What?" I sputtered in confusion.

"You and me, sweetheart. Our time has come."
He brushed past me, picked up two of the larger
suitcases, and headed for the door. "I'll meet you
outside when you're ready."

I was a college-degreed spokesmodel renowned
for my confidence, poise, and assurance; but in
that moment . . . all I could come up with to say
was "Ummmm."

"Close your mouth, Kitty. Time's a–wasting. We

gotta go." He let the door close behind him with a definitive *click*.

I snapped my jaw shut and sank down to the edge of the bed. In the last forty-eight hours I'd posed for pictures, designed a catalogue, broken up with a man, been immortalized as a skank on YouTube, and now acquired a new boyfriend. What was my life all about suddenly? Maybe I would take that Advil after all.

3

I can count on you to treat my baby sister with some respect

Carter—Monday, May 23—1:06 p.m.

I loaded Katrina's bags into the trunk of the jeep with a smile. I think that's the first time in our history I'd ever seen her speechless. I liked it. The best way to deal with a high-maintenance, headstrong, used-to-getting-her-own-way woman like Audelia Katrina Montgomery? Keep it simple, state it plain, and keep it moving. Katrina was the kind of woman who men went stupid for. Not just a few men. Most men. And she knew it. And used it to her advantage. I wasn't about to become one of the many.

I'd known Katrina since she was thirteen years old and watched her grow from a cute, self-confident girl to a drop-dead gorgeous, self-assured woman. I'd met Katrina's older brother Beau over fifteen years ago when he transferred into Louisiana State University at the end of sophomore year. He and I became friends immediately. He was a baseball player, I was a football player. We were both popular and outgoing, we liked to have a good time, and neither of us lacked for dates. At one time we were known on campus as the Pontchartrain poonhounds. Though I hated the name, we'd probably earned it. We were young, smart, talented, and if I may say so, handsome as hell. Beau had been the kind of guy to take everything lightly and live one day at a time. I was the guy who weighed out all the ramifications and had a plan for the future. He was flashy in a pretty-boy kind of way and I was understated and good-looking in a less in-your-face kind of way. We probably should have disliked each other on g.p. and competed for every girl on campus. Instead, we fell into complementary synergy that lasted to this day.

When Beau invited me to his house for that first Thanksgiving holiday, I jumped at the chance to see a different kind of family life. I loved the Montgomerys at first sight. They were the exact opposite of my parents. Clara and Caleb Parks split up before I could remember them being together. Caleb took off for parts unknown two weeks after my birth. My mother, never one for responsibility, fled not too long after. For years I had been shuffled from aunt to neighbor to kindly teacher until my grandfather stepped in around the time I turned twelve. Collin Parks became both mother and father to me. He was stern, but fair, and always stressed the importance of living up to your word, getting an education, and facing situations like a man.

A few years later, he went away for a weekend and came back with an infant who he introduced as my younger brother Chris. I loved that kid at first sight. Collin and Chris made up my family unit. It was just the three of us until the day I signed my first NFL contract. That was the first day I ever laid eyes on my father. He and my mother appeared from God-knows-where with huge smiles on their faces, apologies on their lips, and their hands out. The minute I wrote a check, they disappeared, not to be seen again until their accounts ran low. The first time it hurt. The second time it stung. Then I became immune to it. I came to understand that not everybody who gives birth is a parent.

In direct comparison, Avery and Alanna Montgomery were solid, straight-shooting parents who only wanted the best for their kids and were willing to work to get it for them. Beau may have taken some time to come into his own, but there wasn't a mean bone in his body and he was deceptively smart. Roman, Beau's younger brother, was serious and ambitious with a wicked sense of humor. And then there was Katrina. At age thirteen, she was already a looker. Whip-thin and witty with a precocious attitude and smart mouth that only the spoiled baby girl of a family could pull off.

She went from cute and thin to pretty and willowy to jaw-droppingly stunning and curvy in the blink of an eye. Beau had gone into modeling after our junior year of college and Katrina followed him into the industry when she turned seventeen. We had been around each other for years. She and I had easy camaraderie from the beginning. Over the years, our interactions grew a bit more charged. Women like Katrina Montgomery were rare. If she hadn't been the younger sister of my best friend, I would have asked her out the minute she was legal. About eighteen months ago, she started throwing not-so-subtle hints that she was interested in turning the friendship into something more interesting, but as much as I wanted to . . . I wasn't ready to go there quite yet. Watching her come into her own as she stepped further away from the catwalk and more into the corporate side of design had piqued my interest. She'd developed additional depth and she wore the mantle of maturity well. I broached the topic of dating her with Beau briefly last year and he had sounded so appalled that I backed off.

But when this Delancey fool broke bad, Beau called me to ask for my opinion and assistance. Near the end of the conversation he said, "You know what, CP? If this is the type of asshole she's gonna be hooking up with, I'd just assume she'd date you."

"Wow, ain't that a ringing endorsement?" I teased.

"Carter, you know what I mean. My only concern was that the two of you would get together, burn hot and fast, and then flame out, leaving all of us in an uncomfortable situation."

"Could still happen," I replied honestly.

"Yeah, but you won't put a damn sex tape of her up on effing YouTube. No matter what happens, I can count on you to treat my baby sister with some respect."

I was momentarily stunned silent.

Beau laughed. "What did we always say?"

"We may be scoundrels, but we're gentlemen." I recited our motto.

"Exactly so, *mon ami*."

"So what are you saying?" I wanted him to spell it out.

"You think I didn't notice the two of you dancing around each other all these years?"

"I never laid a hand on her," I swore.

"Of course you didn't, but you looked plenty."

"Still looking," I admitted.

"We Montgomerys are nice to look at. If you want to do more than look, Big Sexy, you have my blessing. She turns thirty this year and you aren't getting any younger."

"I'm six months younger than you, bruh, and neither of us are ready for a rocking chair on the porch," I reminded him.

"But you must admit," he sniffed, "I'm better maintained."

"Oh, there you go." He may have mellowed, but his ego had not diminished.

"I'm just saying, if you ever wanted to give it a try, this is your shot."

"Pardon me while I check and see if snowstorms have hit hell." I honestly never thought I would see the day when Beau gave me the green light to date his sister.

"I know, I know. It just seems like a good time for her to get into a stable relationship with a well-respected man. A good man who is strong enough to deal with her without taking advantage, you know?"

"Wow. Not sure if you are complimenting me, dissin' her, or pimping me out."

"*Mais oui?* You expect me to believe that it's gonna be a real hardship for you to date my gorgeous sister and have her on your arm? Do recall that I have been around for your revolving door of semi-relationships with a bevy of random beauties. Now that you're ready to close the revolving door, you know my sister is an upgrade."

"You're assuming she'll go along with this?"

"Parks, all that time you were looking at her?" Beau mentioned.

"Yeah?"

"She was looking right back."

"Well, all right then." I nodded in satisfaction.

"And Carter?"

"Yeah?"

"You break my sister's heart, I'll break every bone in your body."

I coughed to cover up my scoffing snort. "You wish you could."

"Let's not find out. *C'est vrai?*"

"Agreed."

That brought me back to right now. I was here to get Katrina off this island and sequestered someplace safe before we went back to Dallas to face the music. I figured now was as good a time as any to let her know that the days of her dallying around with the Delanceys of the world were done. As if on cue, she came strolling down the steps of the villa as if she hadn't a care in the world. She slid large sunglasses on her face and smiled at the bellhop as he carried the rest of her bags forward. I leaned against the side of the car to enjoy the view.

Her long, light-brown hair fell in soft waves past her shoulders to the middle of her back. She wore a long dress with big flowers all over it. Her shoulders were bare and she looked like she'd gotten a little sun in the last few days. She caught my interested perusal and peered at me over the sunglasses. "What are you looking at, Parks?"

"Good-looking woman walking toward me."

"I've no doubt that you've seen one or two or those before."

"There's no one quite like you, Katrina," I countered honestly.

She whipped her sunglasses off and squinted at me. "What's all this now?"

I held open the door for her. "We'll talk on the plane. You need to look over your talking points on the way to the airport."

"You already wrote my talking points?" Her voice was inching towards screechiness, but I was determined to be patient with her. She was having a hell of a day.

"Not me. The new marketing person, I forget her name."

"Danila. I met her when I was taking night classes at Southern Methodist. She's a good friend and very savvy. We brought her on a few months ago."

"Yep, her. She wrote them up. I'm just the messenger." I held my hands up.

"I'm not an invalid, you know. I'm not without brains. I don't need people spiriting me away and writing words to put in my mouth."

"Understood." I waved toward the open door as I caught sight of a photographer, who had clearly evaded security, trudging across the beach in our direction. "Can we get going?"

She put her hand on her waist. "Carter, I'm not one of your floozies. I want answers and I want them now."

Patience gone, I stepped to her, crowding into her space until she was pressed against the car. I placed a hand on either side of her and boxed her in. I leaned down to whisper in her ear. "Katrina, you're possibly the hottest woman I've ever seen and I like you. A lot. On various levels. But I'm not one of your flunkies. You won't be talking to me any old kinda way. I'm a man. All right? No one would ever mistake you for a floozy, diva. You want to have this discussion out here in open while the paparazzi hovers with telephoto lenses, or can we go?"

She blinked up at me as if trying to gauge my mood. I held her gaze while she decided what to do next. A small smile lifted her lips. Her hands slid under my jacket to bracket around my waist. "I know you're a man, Carter. Believe me, I know. We can go."

"Well, all right then." I nodded, backed off, and aided her into the car. We exchanged a loaded glance before I pulled out and headed toward the airport.

4

A two·inch, two·minute, two·faced bastard

Katrina—Monday, May 23—3:41 p.m.

"I'm not saying this." I sat in the airport lounge and scrolled through the prepared statement on my tablet and shook my head. "It's very professional and classy and I get why it was written this way, but I'm not saying that."

Carter let out a full-bellied laugh. "You just won me twenty bucks."

"I beg your pardon?"

"I bet Beau that you would not go for that sugary-ass statement."

"Yeah, no. If I'm speaking, I'm doing it my way and damn the consequences."

"My girl. Do you."

I glanced over at him and then looked out the window at the small plane sitting on the tarmac. "Is that the same plane Beau and Belle used last year?"

"Yep."

"What's a former football player and current real estate developer doing with a plane?"

"It's a shared resource. Six of us went in on it. Are you trying to ask me something?"

It occurred to me that I didn't know that much about Carter. He went to school with my brother, he owned real estate, he did something involving venture capital, and he had some charities. I knew he had a younger brother and that his grandfather raised him. He was from a small town in Louisiana. I knew he was popular with the ladies. But that's about all I knew. "What's your middle name?"

"Evan."

"How did you get the name Big Sexy?"

"By being big and sexy, probably," he teased.

"Seriously, there's no story behind it?"

"There's a story behind it, but if I tell you, I'd have to kill you."

I rolled my eyes. "Uh-huh. Do the people you work with call you Big Sexy?"

"No, the only people that call me that knew me from my football days."

"Your wild and wicked days?"

"I didn't attach any adjectives."

"So you're not wild and wicked anymore?" I probed.

"I don't know about all that," he answered cryptically.

"I'm just saying. I can imagine." I could only imagine.

"Can you?" He grinned. "I'll just let you do that then."

Getting information out of him was like pulling teeth. "Where do you live?"

"Dallas."

I almost stomped my foot in frustration. "I *know* that. I mean what part?"

"Highland Park." He named a very prestigious and traditional tree-lined neighborhood where the uber-rich, old money, and power brokers live.

"Highland Park?" I arched a brow.

"Highland Park."

"I would have pegged you for a loft in Uptown. Or a townhouse near Legacy." Legacy was a new live-work-play area north of Dallas with corporate headquarters, night spots, planned communities and upscale eateries. It was a haven for up-and-coming professionals.

"Four-bedroom house in Highland Park."

"Seriously?" That was the home and neighborhood of someone planning on settling down and having a family. Carter had some hidden depths I knew nothing about. But . . . I was quickly thinking I wanted to learn.

"Seriously," he confirmed, grinning as if he knew what I was thinking.

"So are you rich?"

"You need a loan, Kit-Kat?" he drawled.

"Nope, I'm just asking."

"I can afford you, princess."

I sent a side-eye his way. "I can afford myself, thank you very much."

"You're welcome very much. You know, we actually have a lot in common."

"We do?" I wondered what.

"We do. We both became successful in careers that require spectators and look a lot more glamorous from the outside looking in. We're both originally from Louisiana. We both put family above all else. We both get underestimated when people don't look beneath the surface with us. And we both like doing things for ourselves, hate to admit weakness, and won't back down from a fight."

"Huh." I let all of that sink in. He got me. Probably better than anyone else I could think of. I wasn't sure what to do with that.

"And of course, we both look good. Any other questions before we film this?"

"Actually, yes. Has that plane been sterilized since the last time Beau and Belle were on it? I heard they tried to christen every surface."

He laughed. "It's been thoroughly scrubbed. You ready to do this?"

"Now's as good a time as any."

He motioned to a young guy standing over to the side clutching a small video camera. "Katrina, this is my assistant, Shawn. Shawn, Katrina Montgomery."

Shawn almost tripped over his feet hustling forward. "Ms. Montgomery, I'm delighted to meet you. Pictures don't do you justice." He looked to be in his early twenties and was dressed in a pink polo shirt and khaki pants. I stood up as he approached and—just because I could—when he extended his hand to shake I took it, held it, and leaned in to kiss his cheek.

"*Enchanté*, Shawn. I hope you're referring to pictures in which I'm clothed?" I teased in a sultry voice.

If it was possible for a dark-skinned black man to blush, Shawn did just that. "Oh. I—well—now." He shot a panicked, awed look over to Carter.

Carter shook his head and stood up. "Katrina, have mercy on the young'un. We still have a two-hour flight ahead of us."

"Where are we headed?" I queried.

"Punta Cana." He named a popular resort town in the Dominican Republic.

"Another beach?"

"Problems, diva?"

"I'm just wondering what the point of taking me off one beach to deposit me on another one would be?" Shawn's head swiveled back and forth as he watched the byplay between us.

"I'm borrowing a house there. No one will know how to find you. Maybe I need a few days off. You can scout locations for the summer catalog. The Dominican Republic is lovely this time of year. Need any other reasons?"

I sighed. "Fine."

"So glad you approve."

I dug into my purse, pulled out a small makeup kit, and touched up my lipstick, added some drama to my eyes, and brushed a sparkly bronzer across my cheeks and forehead. I bent over and ran a brush through my hair before flinging it back and teasing it on the ends. "I'm ready for my close-up."

Shawn's jaw dropped as he took in the results of my quick makeover. "Wow."

"Close your mouth, Shawn, and pick up the camera."

"She's like a goddess or something," Shawn stammered as he fumbled to get the camera operational.

"Or something." Carter shot me a look. "See what you've done? You've fried Shawn." He reached over, patted Shawn on the shoulder, and took the camera. "You wanna practice or just go on three?"

"We'll go on three."

He held up the camera, aimed it, fiddled with the setting, and then motioned *one, two, three* with his other hand.

I took a deep breath, exhaled, and flashed my runway smile. "Hi everybody, it's Katrina Montgomery here. You've been reading and watching a lot of things about me recently. I wish I could say that everything Kevin Delancey said wasn't true. But, unfortunately, I did make the disastrous error of sleeping with him twice, indoors, with the lights out. It lasted about fifteen minutes. It wasn't noteworthy. And it certainly wasn't worth trading any favors or risking my reputation over. In fact, sometime after the first three minutes of the awkward episode, I would have paid *him* to cease, desist, and leave. Imagine my surprise to see a fabricated video that in no way resembles the truth. Just to be clear, I have never and would never offer my body as payment for anything. I'm a designer, a business-woman, and a model—not a hooker. Or at the prices he's quoting, that would be more like a call girl or escort? Pardon me if my terminology is off. I'm not as acquainted with the seamy side of life as Kevin appears to be. The only errors in judgment I'm guilty of involve an unfortunate obsession with neon lace leggings in my early twenties and having the audacity to break up with a mega-maniacal multimillionaire who has never heard the word *no* or thumbed through *Sex for Dummies*. Really, Kevin, just a passing acquaintanceship with female anatomy? Would do you a world of good, sir. An entire world."

Carter cleared his throat.

I got back on track. "But that's neither here nor there. In the meantime, it seems that I'm a lit-tle too popular for my own good right now, so I'm going off the grid for a while. A family friend is whisking me away. Love and appreciation to those of you who have supported me and continue to see me for who I truly am." I raised my hand in the peace gesture. "Team Kat!" I winked.

"That's a wrap," Carter said before handing the camera to Shawn. "Upload it and send it to Beau before we take off, will you?" Shawn nodded and ran off. Carter swept me up in his arms and swung me around. "You rocked it."

I wrapped my arms around his neck and gig-gled. "I kinda did, didn't I?"

"Oh, yeah. Neon lace leggings? Cease, desist, and leave? *Sex for Dummies*? Instant classics." He set me back on my feet and I stood loosely in his em-brace.

I snickered. "That was the nice version. The first draft in my head had a line about him being a two-inch, two-minute, two-faced bastard."

Carter winced. "Harsh."

"But true."

"I'm curious. What did you see in the dude?"

"I was trying to date a grown-up. And he masqueraded as one for a little while."

"You need to upgrade your taste in men, girlie."

"Got anyone specific in mind?" I peered up at him through my lashes.

"Only one possible candidate." He yanked me back up against him and kissed me with precision, purpose, and power. I immediately caught fire and my head started spinning, thoughts scattering like grains of sand swept out to sea. His lips moved against mine as if he had been kissing me for years. He knew exactly where to slide his tongue, where to nibble, where to soothe. My hands gripped the back of his neck and I was tempted to climb him like a tree and cling for dear life. His hands grazed my rear before he broke off the kiss. "That's addictive," he muttered in a gravelly voice that indicated he was no less affected than I was.

"Wow," I whispered.

"Yeah."

"I mean . . . whoa." I licked my lips and tried to get my bearings.

He ran a finger along my jaw and dropped a quick kiss on my lips. "Let's go, diva, we're due a conversation."

"Naked conversation?" I asked hopefully.

He smirked. "We talk with clothes on first and then we see what comes next."

I blinked at him in amazement. As much heat as we just generated and he wanted to spend time talking? Like, actually talking? "You're not planning on getting me naked soon?"

Shawn had walked back in on the last half of that sentence and stopped dead in his tracks. "Uh, do you want me to come back later?"

Carter shot me another look and waved him forward. "Video transmit okay?"

"Yes, we got confirmation that Mr. Montgomery received it. He said it will be up shortly, safe travels, and not to forget what he said about your bones. I'll see you back in Dallas in a few days. Great to meet you, Ms. Montgomery."

I smiled and waved at Shawn before I raised a brow in Carter's direction, "Your bones?"

"Yeah, Beau threatened to break them if I break your heart," he announced casually as he glanced at his watch.

"My heart? You talked to my brother about my heart?"

"Problems, diva?"

"One, I'm about tired of you calling me a diva. Two, you talked to my brother about being with me?"

"Three, I'm not getting you naked fast enough?" he added with a knowing smirk.

I didn't know whether to slap him, kiss him, or storm off. I contemplated the wisdom of doing all three. I was a little insulted that he didn't seem eager to consummate what we started. Most men wanted to get to that part right away. One of the reasons I had been semi-impressed with Kevin was that he seemed (in the beginning, at least) willing to wait for the naked part. Now I found myself frustrated that Carter was applying the brakes.

He reached out, picked up my purse, and handed it to me. He took my other hand in his and started walking toward the tarmac. "I'm a different kind of guy. One, you *are* a diva. It's fine, I'm cool with it. Part of your charm. Two, I talked to your brother about dating you and your heart came into the conversation. He's cool with us exploring whatever there is between us. Provided no heartbreak occurs. Three, part of this exploration involves getting to know each other. With and without clothes on. You didn't even know my middle name thirty minutes ago."

"I don't need to know your middle name to sleep with you. I've known you for over ten years. Do we really need all the foreplay and seduction after all this time?"

He pointed toward himself. "I'm Carter. Not the other guys you've had falling at your feet. I'll respect your brain, worship your body, cherish your company, enjoy your conversation, indulge some of your whims, and honor your wishes as much I can. Okay? I know you, Kat. I got you. But I'll do these things on my terms. Not yours. Are we clear?"

I drew to a stop at the bottom of the stairs leading up to the plane. My eyes locked with his. It was a battle of wills that he clearly intended to win. I was not this girl. The girl who lets men—this man—tell them what to do. The girl who lets a man take her by the hand and lead her along. I was strong, independent, and self-sufficient. I was a Montgomery. We stood up. We pushed back. We made ourselves heard. We made up our own minds, forged our own paths, and damned anyone who didn't like it.

But seriously, what's a girl supposed to say to those words that rolled off his tongue, those words that came effortlessly out of his mouth in that sexy baritone? This man flew to my rescue just because my brother asked him to. Maybe because he wanted to be there for me. I didn't know, but either way he got in a jet and came for me. For me. This man who had intrigued me for years. When this man who also made me weak from one kiss took me by the hand and told me he's got me, what's left for me to say? "We're clear."

"Thanks," he said quietly.

"For what?"

"Not fighting me."

I flashed a smile. "I'm not always easy."

"You're never easy. Again . . . part of your charm."

"As long as you know what you're getting into," I warned him.

"Oh, I know. Do you?"

"Not a clue."

"All right, then." He nodded and escorted me onto the plane, greeting the pilot. "We're ready to go, George."

"Right away, sir. The weather is clear and the winds are on our side. We'll be there in about an hour and thirty-five minutes. Welcome aboard, Ms. Montgomery."

"Thank you, George." I opened an overhead compartment and noticed my laptop case was already there. I slid my purse in beside it and sat down. Carter settled next to me and buckled in.

"You still wanna have that talk?"

"How long are we going to be in Punta Cana?"

"Four or five days at the least."

"We'll talk there. I just wanna—"

"Do nothing and stare out the window at the water?" he asked.

I stared at him in amazement. "How did you know that?"

"You once said it's one of your favorite ways to unwind, to fly over the water and think about absolutely nothing."

I racked my brain, trying to think of when I'd said that. "I don't even remember saying it out loud."

"It was the year you all came out and watched me play the Pro Bowl. You were griping about how long the flight was. You had on this tiny pink bikini with the sexiest gold sandals." He shrugged and looked away.

I placed my hand on his arm. "Carter, that was like five years ago."

"The bikini was memorable," he joked.

"You remember what I said. You've been paying attention for a while, haven't you?"

He shrugged again. "I watch."

"You watch me."

"According to Beau, you've been watching me right back."

I sniffed in exasperation. "Beau talks too much."

"You'll get no argument from me on that point. If I had a dime for the times his mouth wrote a check his ass couldn't cash."

"Do tell?" I prompted. I knew some of Beau's scandalous past, but none of Carter's. I found myself rabidly curious.

"No, ma'am. I'm already trying to date his sister; I can't break any more of the bro code for at least a decade," Carter teased as he keyed some text into his cell phone and turned it off before tucking it into his jacket pocket.

An older woman walked down the aisle from the front of the plane. "Hi Carter, would you and your guest like anything before takeoff?"

"I'm good, Sheryl, thanks. Katrina?"

"No. Maybe some water after we get in the air?"

"Same for you, Carter?"

"Sounds good. Thanks for coming out on short notice." He flashed a smile.

She laughed delightedly. "Sure, it's a real trial to hop a plane to spend a week in the Caribbean. How will I ever escape these oppressive working conditions?" She giggled again as she set about readying the plane for departure.

I sighed. That right there would have never happened with Kevin. He belittled his staff and rarely had a kind word for them. Not once had I seen a worker giggle with joy at performing their job. Carter was an actual grown-up and a gentleman. Just when I was starting to wonder if those type of men still existed, here he was.

"What's the deep sigh and deep thought about?" Carter asked quietly.

"How do you know I'm thinking deeply?"

"You get this line in the middle of your forehead when you're deep in concentration."

"A *line*?" I shrieked.

"Barely visible to the naked eye, princess. I think you're safe from Botox."

"You mention lines and Botox to a model who turns thirty in a few months? That's like sixty in model years." This was a man who was not worried about tiptoeing around my feelings.

"Like you care. You only model for your own design company anymore. Besides, you know you still look good. Lock down the divatude."

"Lock down the—" I couldn't think of the last time a man pushed my buttons like this.

"You were reflecting on something deep before we got sidetracked?" He reached over and buckled my seat belt, brushing the back of his hands across my chest as he retreated.

I narrowed my eyes. "I was thinking that you are a gentleman and an actual grown-up, but I may have been hasty in my assessment."

"Because I keep you off-balance? Challenge you? C'mon, now. At least be truthful."

"What do you mean?" I frowned at him.

He leaned over and took my hand in his, tracing lines from my wrist to the tips of my fingernails and back again. Such a simple touch, but it sent tingles along my nerves. He lowered his voice.

"You like it. You like not knowing what I'm going to do next. Wondering when I'll touch you and where. Anticipating how good it will feel when I do."

He was right. I did like it, but I'd be damned if I let him know. I snatched my hand back and closed my eyes. "I believe I'll nap."

He chuckled softly. "Sweet dreams, Kitty."

5

You may be a scoundrel,
but you're a gentleman

Carter—Monday, May 23—8:32 p.m.

I sunk onto the chaise lounge overlooking the infinity pool and the ocean beyond before releasing a pent-up sigh. The modern, tropical-style villa was four bedrooms and four baths and backed onto a stretch of private beach. The entire place was styled in muted blues and greens and added to the ambiance of much-needed relaxation. My schedule had been unusually hectic of late, but today had been an especially long day.

Beau called me last night when he got the heads-up on Kevin's plan and I'd set things in motion before flying out early this morning. Between flying and plotting and dealing with the diva, I was ready for some downtime. After landing in Punta

Cana, Katrina disappeared into her suite of rooms and I had fired up my laptop to get in touch with the office. Contrary to the events of the day so far, I had other concerns beyond Katrina Montgomery's sex life.

Shortly before retiring from the NFL, I had the good fortune to meet a businessman, Stavros Carmichael, who bought and sold casinos and nightclubs worldwide. Though I had no interest in entertainment real estate, he taught me the ins and outs of developing, managing, and selling commercial properties. I worked with him in my spare time, learning every aspect of the business from the ground up until I retired from the league and then went out on my own. Business was a lot like football. The team with the better players, the better strategy, and the better focus on the big picture won. It was highly competitive and every once in a while, you just had to go with your gut and gamble on the outcome. I loved it. More so than football, Parks Properties was challenging and satisfying. It also gave me the financial freedom, so my grandfather retired in comfort, my younger brother Chris didn't worry about his college tuition, and allowed me to indulge my charitable foundation that aided young athletes needing a little help to get to the next level. I also set up small trusts for my mother and father, which paid out yearly. If they ran through their yearly allotment before the twelve months was up, that was just too damned bad. I'd learned the hard way that I was little more than an ATM to both of them. Even ATMs set a limit on withdrawals.

Earlier today, I had checked in on a shopping mall project I was working on in the Phoenix area and two office buildings in Toronto that I'd planned to sell, but decided to keep because I made more on the leases than I'd originally projected. I returned a few e-mails and instructed Shawn and Gina, my second in command, on how to handle things over the next couple of days before signing out.

After changing into shorts and a T-shirt, I followed my nose to the kitchen where Katrina and Sheryl put the finishing touches on dinner. We made small talk over fish, vegetables, and rice before Katrina disappeared back into her room. She was hiding. I decided to leave her be. We were here for at least four days and nights. She couldn't hide forever.

That brought me to this tranquil moment. I raised the tumbler of spiced rum and soda to my lips and leaned back with another sigh. My peace and quiet was disturbed by the ringing of my cell phone. I flipped it open. "Carter Parks."

"Chris Parks." My younger brother's voice came across the line. Chris was the result of my parents' doomed attempt to reconcile shortly after I went to live with my grandfather. He was sixteen years younger than me and finishing up his senior year at LSU. Smarter in his classes and faster on the field, Chris was the best that the Parks DNA had to offer. He was graduating magna cum laude and as a four-time all-American middle linebacker. I was alternately proud of him and terrified for him. He was twenty-two years old with his whole life ahead of him and I was determined to make sure he got to wherever he wanted to go. He had been drafted first round by Dallas and also accepted into the Stanford MBA program.

"What's up, bro?" I asked with a smile.

"You tell me! You're the one cavorting about with hot models and whatnot."

"How do you know that?" I wondered.

"Man, they already got pictures of you two all booed up next to some car on the beach somewhere."

That damn photographer in Barbados. "Yeah, well . . . you know."

"I don't know, that's why I'm calling. It's not like you to cut out in the middle of business deals to chase skirts."

"I don't chase skirts and you need to show some respect. Katrina is a lady," I chastised.

"Is she ever!" He whistled in admiration. "You gonna get with that or what?"

"What did I just say about respect?" I repeated.

"Aw man, you serious about this one. Okay. Okay. When are you coming back?"

"A few days, a week tops."

"Good, 'cuz I gotta make a decision and you gotta help me make it."

Chris had to decide whether he was going to play professional football or go to business school. I could see the pros and cons of each, but ultimately it was his decision to make. "Which way are you leaning?"

"I'm not; I keep swinging back and forth. And Grandpa's no help. Keeps telling me to pray on it and listen when—"

"—God whispers in your ear. Yeah, that's one of his favorites."

"What does that even mean?" Chris puzzled.

"It means you'll know what to do when the time is right. But I'll be back and we'll talk it all out, okay?"

"Thanks, bro. And hey?"

"Hey?" I prompted.

"Don't do nuthin' I wouldn't do. I mean, if you get in over your head handling a woman that fine, you can fly me in for reinforcements. Katrina's only what—three or four years older than me?"

"Seven years. But don't you worry your knuckle-headed self about it. I got this." I hung up on his laughter and shook my head. Youngsters always had jokes. I switched the phone to vibrate and leaned back to relax once more. I had drifted into a peaceful state between sleep and wakefulness when Katrina stormed outside. I raised one eyelid. Oh hell, she had her mad on. I closed my eyes again.

"Why don't you have a woman? What's wrong with you?" she asked without preamble.

"Who says I don't?" I teased.

"Oh, come on. I've heard you and Beau say it often enough. You may be a scoundrel, but you're a gentleman. No way would you be hugged up on me if you had a woman at home."

"That's true. You might know me better than I thought you did." I raised my glass to toast in her general direction.

"So what's wrong with you? A man doesn't get

to be your age and unmarried unless he's a dog or he's damaged or both."

My age? Ouch—that hurt. She and Chris had me fitted for a walker already. "Wow. You *don't* know me. Generalize much?"

"Something's holding you back. And please don't tell me you haven't met the right woman yet." Her tone was snarky.

"I'm selective," I explained.

"You mean picky."

"I mean discerning," I clarified, amused by her not-too-subtle attempts to get to know as much about me in the shortest time possible.

"Oh, really?"

"Really."

"What does it take to make the cut?"

"What do you care? You're at the front of the line," I countered.

"There's a line?" She sounded offended.

"A short list," I amended.

"Do tell. What magical powers must a woman possess to make it to Carter Parks's short list?"

"Look in the mirror, diva. You're the total package."

She was silent for a minute. "Dammit."

"Beg pardon?"

"I was trying to be mad and you had to go and say something sweet."

I opened my eyes and took another sip of my drink. "You're trying to be mad?"

She flounced over and perched beside me. "What are the rules here? Are we doing this for real?"

"You lost me, Kitty. Speak it plain."

"This whatever between me and you. Is it just for show, is it just for kicks, is it just until whenever? What?"

"What do you want it to be?"

She reached over, took my glass, and downed the contents. "Carter, you drive me to drink."

I took the empty glass from her and stood up. "Back 'atcha, beautiful. Listen, stop trying to make everything a thing. You and me, exclusive, dating. That's all. Let's just ease into this and see where we go. You just got out of a relationship forty-eight hours ago."

"That wasn't a relationship."

"No?" That gave me pause. How exactly did she define a relationship? I would not have been huddled up on a beachfront villa with a woman I wasn't in some sort of relationship with.

"No, it was a . . . temporary lack of sanity." She gestured vaguely with her hands, waving them in the air. "An attempt to—as you say—make a thing a thing."

"Hmm." I set the glass down in the outdoor sink and ran water over it. "Do you want to go over the plan tonight?"

"Not really. I'm beat. It's been a long day." She came up behind me and slid her arms around my waist. "Carter?"

"Yeah?" I turned to face her.

"In case I forget to say it—thanks for coming for me." She kissed my cheek and waltzed back into the house.

I touched my cheek and smiled. She was going to be the death of me.

6

Then we battle

Katrina—Tuesday, May 24—10:50 a.m.

I waved to Sheryl as she headed out to see some of the island. I didn't know where Carter had found her, but she was wonderful. She did a little bit of everything. Organized the house, answered phones, ran errands, and cooked like a dream. I considered myself to be a pretty good cook, but she whipped up delicious meals effortlessly. I should have resisted this morning's cheesy shrimp and spinach omelet, but it was too savory to pass up. I turned back to the laptop in time to answer a question.

"How bad was it really?" my sister-in-law Jewellen asked me as she played with her hair. Jewel was one of my favorite people in the world. Like me, she was a sheltered suburban girl. Unlike me, she was patient and sweet and generally saw the good in everybody. She owned a staffing agency based in North

Dallas and had just recently opened a second office in Frisco. A few years back, my brother Roman literally ran her over on a basketball court and after one heck of a courtship, they got married. She treated Roman's son Chase like her own and was a seamless part of the family. We called her *Bijou*, French for "jewel." Jewel was a cute little thing at a shade under five-seven, with a bright, clear complexion and reddish-brown hair that usually fell to just under her shoulders. Recently, she had cut it into a wavy bob that stopped at her eyes. She'd been fiddling with it ever since.

We were on a video conference. Jewel was sitting with Belle, Fredrika (my agent), Danila (our PR person), and another friend of ours who worked in the New York offices of BellaRich, Yazlyn.

"*Bijou*, your hair is cute. Leave it alone. How bad was what really?" I set down my second cup of coffee of the day and tilted my head in curiosity.

"The sex, Trina, the terrible, awful sex between you and Kevin. You announced to the world that he had never thumbed through *Sex for Dummies*!" Danila clasped her hand over her mouth to stifle a giggle.

"You said you wanted to pay him to cease and desist!" Fredrika gasped out as they dissolved into laughter. She almost slid off the edge of her chair she was so tickled.

Yazlyn caught her breath. "On a scale of 'gee, I could have had a V-8' to 'make the lambs stop screaming'—just how bad was it?"

I giggled at her *Silence of the Lambs* reference. "It wasn't serial-killer bad, more like lazy and unfocused, but blessedly over soon."

"Oh, all right. So you won't be appearing on an episode of *I Survived* to tell the tale. Good to know," Belle joked.

"I don't want to be on television anytime soon," I said with all earnestness.

"No one feels bad for you, Audelia Katrina," Jewel piped up. "You are sitting in paradise with fine-ass Carter Parks. That is not bad living."

"Okay?" Belle high-fived Jewel.

"What are you two doing noticing the fineness of Big Sexy when you are sleeping next to Roman and Beau Montgomery every night?" Yazlyn eyed them teasingly.

"A woman can look and appreciate a fine form when she sees one. Is the man not nicknamed Big Sexy, for goodness sake? I appreciate things that are beautifully designed." Belle shrugged with a guiltless smile.

"It's not a hardship spending time with a man who looks like that in a place like this." I gestured to the view behind me.

"I hate you all," Yazlyn said. "You're supposed to be in crisis, Kat. Instead, you've landed on rose petals."

"Sure, if you overlook the fact that fake, naked videos of me are all over the place, life is a rosy dream." I leaned back and crossed my arms with attitude.

"Well, there is that," Fredrika agreed.

"At least you look good, sugar," Belle said. "Even the paparazzi pics have you looking right."

"We can always count on Belle to see the sunny side of things," Jewel teased before turning serious. "The guys are coming in. Is Carter there?"

"One sec." I paused the sound and video feed and walked to the entrance of the den. "Carter? You got a minute?" I hadn't seen or spoken to him yet this morning. By the time I got up and spoke to my mom and dad, Carter had been behind closed doors in the room he was using as an office, buying and selling stuff or whatever mogul-y stuff it was that he did these days.

"For you, always," he announced as he came around the corner and into the room. He was dressed casually in a T-shirt and knit shorts. Dammit, he looked good. He dropped a light kiss on my forehead as he brushed past me and sat down at the table. He patted the seat beside him.

"Coffee or vitamin water?" I offered as I walked toward him.

"Vitamin water sounds good. Thanks, Kitty." He smiled as I handed him the cold beverage, a napkin, and a coaster.

I paused and frowned. Not three days ago I wanted to slap the mess out of Kevin for inferring that I should pour his beverages and here I was fetching refreshments for Big Sexy.

"Problem, diva?" He twisted the top off and took a sip.

"I just got you a drink," I said slowly.

"And I appreciate it." He responded and raised a brow.

I laughed at myself. "It's just irony." When someone didn't expect things of you and was genuinely grateful for small gestures, it was a completely different thing. Carter was right; I'd been dating the wrong damn men.

"Okay. Am I missing something?"

"Just an *aha* moment. You're welcome, Carter."
I grinned at his confused expression before sitting
down next to him and taking the camera off pause.
"We're both here. What's the latest?"

"Do I even want to know what took you two so
long to get to the computer?" Roman asked with a
brow raised and a mock glowering expression on
his face.

"Don't start with me," I admonished, shooting
him a look.

Beau snickered. "I for sure do not want to
know. Let's just move on. We have good news and
bad news."

"Give us the bad news first," Carter said.

Danila spoke up. "First, there are some naked
pictures floating around."

"I've never posed nude," I affirmed.

"Doesn't look like you posed at all. The pics
are more like someone hid cameras in your house
and clicked when you walked around and got out
of the shower," Roman said through a clenched
jaw.

"What the hell?" Carter exclaimed. "Who did it?"

"We don't know for sure. We sent our security
guy over to sweep her condo. He got them all, but
we couldn't trace where the feed was going."

"This is getting nasty." I shook my head in
amazement.

Fredrika spoke up. "Sad to say, it gets worse.
Looks like Kevin is up to some new tricks. He's got
a swimsuit distributor saying you offered to do him
regularly if he got your orders out the door first. A
Harry Jamison out of New York."

"To *do* him?" I shouted.

"Yeah. Like sexually. Must we spell it out?" Beau winced.

"Oh, for Christ's sake. I talked to him on the phone once. Once! He made a half-assed pass, I laughed it off, and we moved on. I didn't even handle his order; I sent him over to Inez in sales. I never even met this Harry guy face-to-face." I snapped, slamming my palm down on the table.

"Isn't Jamison a notorious ass-grabber?" Yazlyn scoffed.

"And a loudmouth to boot. No worries, though, *chère*," Beau said gently. "We already have three other designers that will attest to Harry's bullshittery."

"I like the usage of *bullshittery* as a noun. Was that the good news?" Carter asked.

"Actually, no." Beau continued, "The good news is that we've started digging into Kevin's past and his business dealings."

I leaned forward. "How's it looking?"

"Not good for our friend Kevin. Seems he's a flagrant asshole."

"I could've told you that with no special investigative skills." I rolled my eyes.

"As could we all, sis," Roman added. "But we found out he made some enemies on the way up by taking shortcuts and stepping on a lot of feet. We won't go into details until we have all the facts, but if he wants to sling mud, looks like we'll have plenty of our own to launch."

"Other good news: Your video statement was well-received. The more salacious aspects of Kevin's original claims are still circling the newswires, but we haven't lost any clients yet. And sad though it may be, the nude photos have actually upped our orders," Belle said.

"My bare ass is glad to be of service," I huffed.

"We have to have a pretty good criminal or civil case for fabricating the video and the stalker-y pictures by now, right?" Jewel asked.

"We will when we can prove that Delancey's behind it," Carter said.

"Something about this, though," Beau pondered. "I can't put my finger on it, but it feels like more than just a jilted dude with a big ego getting some revenge."

Belle nodded. "It does. But anyway, Kit-Kat; it's up to you. We can let this thing die naturally or we can go to war."

"If it was just him calling me a ho, I could let it go." I shrugged.

"Could you really?" Carter quirked a brow.

"Maybe. But him coming after the design house like this, trying to muddy up all of us? The Montgomery name and whatnot? I can't let that slide." I glanced over at Carter, who nodded in agreement. He dropped his hand to my thigh and gave an encouraging squeeze. Who knew? Carter Parks was touchy-feely and I liked it.

"Then we battle," Beau said, rubbing his hands together.

"You don't have to look so excited about it," Roman scolded.

"Hey, he came after one of us, besmirched the family name. This I do not forgive," Beau said with dramatic gestures.

"Is that a *Godfather* impersonation, bruh? If so, it was pitiful," Carter drawled.

"Is that your hand on my baby sister's thigh, bruh? If so, it is disturbing," Beau returned.

"What's that about?" Roman frowned, squinting into the monitor.

"Boys, can we focus?" Jewel intervened, sending both Beau and Roman a stern look.

"Thank you, Jewellen," I piped up. "What's the next step?"

Danila suggested, "I think we should send something out to all our clients. Get some preventative statement in front of them, especially since it looks like Kevin is going after them one by one to see if any has a grudge. And then we need to start leaking Kevin's dirt to the media. Let's make him the story."

"That sounds solid." Carter tipped his head in admiration.

"We need you back stateside by Saturday," Beau announced.

"What's on Saturday?" I asked.

Beau and Belle exchanged sappy grins. "We're eloping to Vegas."

"What?" we all exclaimed.

"The wedding kept getting bigger and we kept shifting the dates and really—it was too much. We're just going to gather up immediate family, some of the BellaRich staff, and let the Bellagio do the work." Belle said.

Roman smirked. "Have you told Madere and Pops yet?"

"Actually, with all the upset over Katrina's troubles . . ." Beau began.

"Oh no." Carter shook his head. "Don't even try it, pretty boy. You are not using this to get out of telling Madere that you are depriving her of a big church wedding."

Jewel chuckled, "Man up, Beauregard."

Beau sat back with a sigh. "Fine. Belle and I will call them in a second. Check your e-mails for details on the wedding this afternoon."

"Looking forward to it." I beamed. "God knows I'm ready for another sister. Even-up the odds at the family gatherings."

"Indeed." Jewel nodded.

"Whatever." Roman cut eyes at me and Jewel. "Anyway, do you all need anything down there or are you good?"

Yazlyn choked on her cup of coffee. "I doubt there is anything we can do for them to improve their current circumstances. I mean—look at her, look at him, look at where they are!"

"Hate is so unbecoming on you, Yaz," I said, preening. "If you need us, you know how to find us." I reached out and slammed the lid of the laptop shut.

"So . . ." Carter started in a silky voice.

"So . . ." I purred in answer.

"Do we . . . need anything?"

"I think we're good right here." I put my hand atop his on my thigh and threaded my fingers through his.

"I do believe you're right." He leaned in a little closer.

"We can still hear y'all!" Belle's voice boomed out from the laptop speakers.

"Yeah, if you're gonna get it on at least let us have video to go with the audio," Yaz implored teasingly.

"And that's enough of that," Roman's voice snapped out before the musical tone indicating that the conference had terminated sounded.

I laughed shortly. "Anyway . . . blue skies, great climate, excellent company. What more could a girl want?"

We smiled into each other's eyes.

"You still have work to do today?" I asked him.

"I could, but I don't have to. You?"

"Ditto. We should do something," I murmured.

He took another sip of his water and I watched the muscles in his throat convulse as he swallowed. My eyes fell to his torso and I sat, mesmerized, watching his chest rise and fall slowly as he breathed. A vein at the side of his neck pulsed and I observed it all with fascination. I wanted to know how every single thing, inside and out, of Carter Evan Parks worked. I noticed his lips moving and realized he was talking to me.

"I'm sorry, what?" I asked breathlessly, licking my lips in sudden thirst.

"I asked, Katrina, if you had something specific in mind that you wanted to do. Right now." His lips curved upward in an indulgent smile.

I smiled back and met his eyes: They kind of glowed. Was this the first time I'd ever looked Carter in his eyes and paid attention? I remembered he was waiting on an answer. "Yeah. Yeah, I do."

"What?" He squeezed my hand.

"Beg pardon?" I was so unfocused and distracted. It was like Carter was a shiny new puzzle I had to possess and solve immediately. I couldn't recall feeling quite like this before. Did he feel this way? Where had it come from? Where would it lead? *Oh shut up, Katrina!* I scolded myself and tried to stay present in the moment.

"What do you want to do, princess?" he asked softly.

Besides jump your bones until we both scream for mercy? I blinked the thought away, but not before he saw it in my eyes. The air around us went up about ten degrees. I blinked again. "Let's go swimming."

He blinked twice and then stood up, pulling me with him. "That's one way to get wet."

My jaw dropped. "Did you just say—"

A bad-boy grin spread across his face. He raised my hand to his lips and kissed the knuckles. "I'll see you by the pool in ten. I don't suppose you still have that pink bikini, do you?"

Giggling, I shook my head. "That's long gone. Something similar, though."

"Surprise me," he challenged, dropping my hand and backing away.

"I'll see if I can find a l'il sumthin'-sumthin' to impress."

"You impress just by breathing, diva. Just by breathing." With a lingering look, he turned and headed to his room.

Whew! I braced myself on the table and took a few deep breaths. That was a whole lotta grown and sexy man right there. Contrary to what I had thought, he wasn't just a cute guy who used to play football and dabbled in real estate. He was a serious businessman; he had plans and dreams and aspirations that I wanted to hear all about. He wasn't the lightweight superficial men I was used to dealing with. He was grounded and not to be played with. He knew how to say the right things and send the right looks and I, the woman who never had to work for a man in her life? Had to step my game up.

7

Sex is easy; it's the rest that gets twisted

Carter—Tuesday, May 24—noon

Swimming lap after lap in the refreshing blue water of the pool accomplished a few things: I got in some exercise for the day; it helped me burn off some of the tension and cooled me down after that exchange with Katrina. I wanted to take things slow between us, but she seemed determined to go to full boil right away. Katrina was a beautiful woman with an engaging spirit and I had been "in like" with her for a long time. There was only so much a man could resist. A rustling sound near the shallow end caught my attention and I stopped to stand up in the middle of the pool and take a look. And then I did a double take and made sure my tongue was not hanging out. Katrina was prowling (yeah, I do mean prowling) toward the pool wearing a barely-there white bikini held together by tiny silver chains and a sheer flowing thing over it with four-inch high sandals with crystals sparking on them. Very little was left to my very vivid imagination. It should've been illegal for anyone to look that good ever in the history of womankind.

"Woman, you are going to be the death of me," I muttered and started toward the steps.

She sent me a sultry smile and slid the cover up off her shoulders before tossing it to the side. The sun shone on her bronzed skin, highlighting every gorgeous feature and curve. She rested her hands on hips and held the pose. This was not my Kit-Kat. This was the model that had adorned many a magazine page and for good reason. "We wouldn't want that. I prefer you alive and breathing."

"Funny, I prefer me that way as well."

"How's the water feel?" She squatted down and ran her fingers through the water slowly.

I wanted some sort of award for my restraint in the face of overwhelming temptation. "Come on in and find out for yourself."

She stood, kicked off her heels, and twisted her hair up. "I do believe I will, Mr. Sexy." With innate grace, she strode to the deep end of the pool and executed a perfect dive into the water. A few underwater breaststrokes later and she emerged next to me with a huge grin on her face. "I love the water, it feels awesome." She leaned back and floated in circles around me.

I grinned back at her. "You're a water baby. I did not know that."

"I adore water. You don't know *everything* about me, Carter Parks."

"No; no, I don't. But I'm aiming to find out. I'll tell you one other thing. . . ." I scanned her form.

"What's that?"

"I'm learning a helluva lot more with that bikini you are halfway wearing. Did you know it's see-through when it gets wet?"

Her grin turned salacious. "Is that right?"

I shook my head, reached out, grabbed her around the waist, pulled her upright and up against me. "So you waltzed your fine ass out here in four see-through pieces of material and swam right up to me, huh?"

"Yeah, I did." She wrapped her arms and legs around me. "What're you gonna do about it?"

"Woman, you are really asking for it," I warned.

"Why, yes I am. Are you going to give it to me?"

"Ha!" I barked out a laugh and turned with her in my arms. I pressed her against the side of the pool and leaned in. I nuzzled her neck and bit lightly on her earlobe before whispering in her ear. "You're not going to move me anywhere I don't want to go, princess. Hot as you are, smart as you are, you don't have to give me the hard sell, babe. I'm already on the hook."

"Then take a bite already!" She squirmed up against me.

"When we're ready," I said through gritted teeth while holding her hips still.

She rolled her pelvis once more. "I think we're both ready."

"And that's your problem, princess." She was too used to getting her own way. Probably every guy she dated got wrapped up in her looks and her body and didn't look any deeper. I wasn't that guy. I wasn't going to be the guy who hit, quit, claimed the trophy, and moved on.

"What's my problem?" She quirked a brow.

"You're thinking below the waist instead of above the neck. What's wrong taking our time? There's a lot at risk here. We've been friends for years. Your brother is my best friend. I spend half my holidays with your parents. My grandfather fishes with your dad. If we implode and things get ugly, the fallout will be uncomfortable for so many people we care about. Is it really that big of an issue if we take it slow and get a little more comfortable with each other?"

Her eyes were wide. "Good God, you are serious! This is really happening? After years of dancing around each other, I'm offering myself up on a platter and you want to get to know me better? Really? You sound like a girl." She sulked.

I slid my hands from the indentation of her waist down to her rear and pressed against her once more. "Do I feel like a girl?"

She exhaled shakily. "You most definitely do not feel like a girl."

"All right, then. You already know when we do this it's going to be thermonuclear. We don't have to rush it. We can take our time. Sex is easy; it's the rest that gets twisted."

She unwound herself from around me with a

dramatic sigh. "Let's race. Two laps lengthwise. I win, we do the easy stuff. You win, we do it your way."

"You're thinking I forgot you were on the swim team in high school?"

"You were a professional athlete; doesn't that give you an edge?"

"Katrina, everything's not a competition. We do this my way or we don't do it. We can race, but we do it for fun."

She squinted at me. "I don't recall ever working this hard to get laid before."

"Maybe 'cuz I want to be more than a lay to you."

"You're a different kind of guy."

"I keep telling you that."

"I'm starting to believe you. So what do we race for?"

"Scrabble or Monopoly tonight," I said. We had a history of wickedly competitive marathon board game sessions in the past.

"You suck at Scrabble," she teased.

"You suck at Monopoly," I parried.

"Let's get it on," she challenged.

"Prepare to get your ass kicked, Cajun Kat."

"Bring in on, Big Sexy."

8

A fancy gun with shiny bullets

Katrina—Friday, May 27—6:23 pm

You know how people say that someone is driving them crazy and you nod sympathetically even though you know—absolutely know—that they are not being steered toward insanity by another person? Yeah, this was different. I firmly believed that messing with Carter Parks would have me seeking therapy before long. We had spent the rest of the week in Punta Cana getting to know each other. Or rather, he got to know me and I struggled to keep up.

I could not figure him out. He engaged in deep conversation, he snuggled while watching TV, he took my hand for long walks down the beach. Who was this guy? I had it on good authority that Big Sexy was a player . . . no pun intended. Not just a ballplayer but a relationship player. He was known as a guy who landed, but didn't stick; someone who made no promises, enjoyed himself, made sure a woman enjoyed herself, and was onto the next. In all the time I'd known him, he never had the same woman on his arm twice and never for any lengthy period of time. So I didn't think I was that off-base to think that Carter and I could scratch an itch for each other and go back to being friends. Carter Parks, professional itch-scratcher. That's what I thought I signed up for.

I saw no evidence of that man this past week. This was a man who asked me questions so probing that I had to ask, stop, and think about what I believed and dreamed before answering. This was a man who was not afraid of challenging me, didn't mind pampering me, but did not allow me to get away with anything less than a genuine response or reaction.

I was intrigued and aroused every moment I was in his company. He saw too much. It was the most uncomfortable feeling ever. When we were ironing-out accommodations for this weekend in Vegas I almost opted to stay in a room by myself on the other wing of the hotel. Just so I could get some space and perspective. This was the first time in recent memory I was shying away from a relationship because I felt out of my depth. Usually I fled because I was bored or felt smothered or used. But this was an entirely new situation. Only the knowing, smug glint in his eyes as he waited for me to agree to share a suite with him or sleep on the other side of Bellagio kept me from fleeing.

He might have had me second-guessing myself, but I didn't have to advertise it.

We'd landed in Las Vegas a few hours ago and I was never so glad for the company of my family and friends. My mother had brought me a suitcase full of fresh clothes and I gratefully had her meet me in the suite. I needed the buffer. Alanna Montgomery, lovingly referred to as Madere, was a tiny, long-haired, cocoa-skinned beauty who brought warmth into every room she entered. When she arrived, I stood back and watched while Carter picked her up and whirled her around. She flung her head back and laughed joyously.

"How's the only woman to ever steal my heart doing?" he asked and smacked a noisy kiss on both her cheeks, still holding her aloft. I held back the urge to clear my throat and roll my eyes.

My sixty-plus-year-old mother giggled like a schoolgirl and took his cheeks in her hands and kissed him back. "If I was twenty years younger, *bel homme*, you wouldn't have to ask!"

Carter kissed her again and hugged her tighter before setting her back on her feet. "If Pops didn't own so many guns, I'd have to fight him for ya."

"You may have to dodge a few bullets yet." She slid a glance from him to me and back again.

He held his hands up. "I've been a perfect gentleman with his baby girl."

"This is true. He has kissed you more in the last thirty seconds than he has kissed me all week." Yes, I was a little testy about it.

Alanna looked slowly between us again and her smile widened. "*C'est vrai?* How noble of you, Carter.

And how very disappointing for you, *ma fille.*" She turned toward me with arms outstretched.

"Hi, Mommy." I was almost a full ten inches taller than my mother, but I still loved being wrapped in her arms. Somehow, getting the hug from Madere brought back all the stress and drama of the week and tears sprang to my ears.

She pulled back, looked into my face, and patted my hands. "None of that now. You've had a long week. Not your best. Name in the papers, face on the television, and for all the wrong reasons. But you're a Montgomery and we weather storms, yes? Come out stronger on the other side. Consider this a wake-up call."

"A wake-up call?" What did she mean?

"Not every pretty man with a fat bank account and a bucket of degrees is worth your time, *bébé.*"

I slammed my hands on my hips and scowled down at her. "I break up with a guy and he decides to make up lies about me and it's my fault?"

"Shouldn't have been with him in the first place. You give an *imbécile* a fancy gun with shiny bullets and you're surprised when you get shot?" she asked matter-of-factly and gave a classic Madere Gallic shrug. Carter choked back a laugh and disappeared into his room on the far side of the suite. The door closed behind him with a decisive *click.*

"Am I the gun or the bullets, Mom?"

"Don't get smart with me, Katrina. Own up to your lack of judgment and let's talk about what's going on with you and Carter." She turned toward the other bedroom in the suite. "Separate rooms, eh? That boy's no fool."

I sighed, picked up the suitcase, and followed her into my room. I kicked the door shut behind me and collapsed onto the bed. Madere sat down beside me and stroked my hair. "I'm tired, Madere."

"Chile, you been sunnin' and surfin' for a week, whatchu tired from?"

"Mentally tired," I clarified.

"Why?"

"Too many thoughts crowding my brain." I sighed wearily.

"Let's take it from the top, 'tite chou.'"

"Are you and Pops ashamed of me?" I asked the thing that weighed most heavily. "For the sex thing?"

She gave me a tender, but rebuking, look. "Trina, you know better. We know you. We know what you would and wouldn't do. You're a beautiful woman and people don't always deal well with that. You've never caused us a moment's shame in your life. You are almost thirty years old; we know you've had sex before. From now on, maybe you pick a man a l'il more worthy of your favors?"

Well, she certainly had a good point there. "Yes, ma'am."

Her expression turned fierce. "Dat Delancey boy better hope I don't see him in the streets."

I did not laugh because she meant it. Alanna Montgomery was tiny, but formidable. I'd spent the majority of my life taking care to stay on her good side.

"What else is on your mind?"

I shrugged.

"Maybe you spend a minute or two thinking

'bout that beautiful man across the way who can't keep his eyes off of you?"

"Hmpfh. He looks; he doesn't touch."

"What does he do?"

"He watches and he talks and he beats me in Monopoly."

"That makes him a bad guy?"

"That makes him a bit of a mystery to me. I'm used to men who are interested in the packaging."

"Isn't it nice that a man sees more?"

"I guess. It's just unnerving. Different." Frustrating, infuriating, and aggravating, but I didn't want to overshare.

"Based on your track record, *ma fille*, I can't help but think that's a good thing. I like him for you, I always have."

I sat up in shock. "What do you mean, *always*?"

"There's always been *quelque chose* special between you two. A mother knows," she said cryptically.

"I think he thinks we could be special. Like happily-ever-after and all of that."

"You don't think so?"

I took a deep breath and then admitted, "I'm not sure I believe in all that stuff."

Her brows rose. "All that stuff? Really? You sit here with a woman still in love with her man after forty years. You say this on the eve of the wedding of your oldest *frère*—did any of us believe he'd ever settle down? You see Roman and Jewel. And still you wonder? What made you this way?"

"I believe in it for everybody else. I'm not sure it's for me," I said in a small voice.

"Why do you think that?"

"Because I've never felt that for anybody. I've never been in love, never got my heart broken. Maybe I just don't feel things that deeply? Maybe I'm just not that deep a person."

Madere pushed up from the bed and glared down at me. "Are you not my child?"

"Yes, ma'am, I am," I answered quietly.

"Isn't Avery Montgomery your father?"

"Yes, ma'am, he is."

"Then you should know better. We cry often, we trust sparingly, we laugh long, and we love hard. You just need to meet someone you're willing to let down your guard for."

"How will I know when someone is worth it?"

"You'll just know."

I really hated it when people said that. *You'll know it when you see it*—what if I don't? What if I miss it? What if I let down my guard and the wrong person takes advantage? That would suck. I gave her a look full of skepticism.

"Look at it like 'dis, *chère*. Your ex is calling you everything but a child of God, your naked hind parts are over the YouTube. In my opinion, your life can only go up from here."

"Mom!" I exclaimed. We exchanged glances and then burst into laughter. We fell onto the bed, rolling with mirth.

The door swung open and Carter entered with Pops and Beau. The three men stood with arms folded. My father remained a great-looking man, over six feet tall, honey-brown skin with salt-and-pepper hair. Avery "Pops" Montgomery reviewed the scene in front of him with a twinkle in his eye. Beau stood an inch or two taller. Though Roman, Beau, and I favored each other a lot, looking at Beau was like looking at the bulkier male counterpart of myself. Carter stood in the middle of them with brows raised.

Pops smirked. "I guess I don't have to ask if you feelin' all right, *mon enfant?*"

I pulled myself together enough to hop up and fling myself into my father's arms. "Hiya, Pops. I'm good."

He gestured to Carter with his thumb. "This one taking care of you or do I need to get the shotgun?"

"Get the shotgun, Pops!" Beau egged him on.

"Man . . ." Carter warned, looking uncomfortable for the first time all week. So uncomfortable that I left my father's arms and turned to Beau.

I kissed him on the cheek. "Behave, brother." I stepped to Carter and threaded my arm through his. "Don't shoot him, Daddy, I'm getting kinda fond of him."

"Is that right?" Beau, Carter, and Pops said in the same breath and same tone.

Madere grabbed Beau with one hand and Pops with the other. "*Allons,* gentlemen. Let the children have a moment. Katrina. Carter. We'll see you at the restaurant in twenty minutes."

"Yes, ma'am," Carter and I intoned.

"We have guests. Even your Aunt Yo-Yo and her latest husband showed up. We've got a lot to do. I'm telling you, not twenty-two minutes, not twenty-five: twenty."

"Not a scintilla of a second past twenty minutes," I repeated, holding back the urge to roll my eyes.

"If I gotta come looking, I'm bringing my gun." Pops slanted a look at Carter as Madere pulled him toward the door.

"You tell him, Daddy," Beau said. The minute his back was turned, I took off my shoe and beaned my eldest brother in the back of head. His hand sprang to his neck. "Hey! Ma, Kit's throwing things at me."

"Throw something back," she called out over her shoulder as she swept out of the room.

Beau picked the shoe up and tossed it back. Carter and I ducked. It flew past us to land harmlessly beside the coffee table. I walked over and picked it back up, holding it in my hand.

"Didn't you used to play baseball? What kind of throw was that?" Carter teased.

"I'm getting married tomorrow, my aim is off."

"Already blaming the little woman." Carter sucked his teeth.

"Did you just say *the little woman* up in here?" I asked incredulously.

"Woo, bruh!" Beau laughed. "I'm going to leave you to handle that. See you at Emeril's over by the MGM in eighteen minutes. You two be good," he joked and ran out the door before the shoe could pop him again.

I tapped the shoe against my hand and caught Carter grinning at me. "What?"

Carter noted, "That's a wicked throwing arm you got there, Kitty."

"Growing up with those two, I had to develop some special skills."

"I'll just bet you did," he murmured and glanced at his watch. "We have seventeen minutes, you want to change?"

I exhaled. "This dinner should be a hot mess. Four uncles, three aunts, who knows how many cousins. At least I like the bridesmaids."

"Who are the bridesmaids again?"

"Well, we're down a few. Belle's two sisters couldn't make it. One takes her medical boards today and the other is eight months' pregnant. So now there's me, Jewel, Yazlyn, and an old friend of Jewel's that we've all gotten close to, Veronica."

Carter nodded, "Yeah, I know Roni. Greg the banker's wife."

"Gregory Samson is your banker too?" Roman met Gregory when he started dating Jewel. At the time, Greg had been dating Renee, another friend of Jewel's. I knew Renee from when she was the marketing rep for Royal Mahogany Cosmetics and I was their spokesmodel. Long story short, Beau and Renee hooked up. Greg found out and turned to Veronica to get over his trauma. Gregory and Veronica worked out in the long run; Beau and Renee did not. Renee and Beau had an ill-timed one-night stand just shortly after he started working with Belle, but that ended before it even started.

Veronica had been a friend of ours ever since, Renee was kind of like our mortal enemy. She hated Jewel for finding happiness with Roman. She resented Beau for being Jewel's brother-in-law and not wanting her anymore. And she disliked me because . . . well . . . I took every opportunity to make her life hell at Royal Mahogany Cosmetics. I just plain didn't like her conniving ass. Ironically, Gregory and Beau had become good friends.

"Yeah, Beau introduced us a while back and he's brokered some deals for me. He and Roni are good people."

"Yep. So you ready for all this?" I asked him.

"To stand up for Beau while he marries the perfect woman for him? Yeah, I'm ready for that." He smiled widely.

I studied his face. "You are genuinely excited about this."

"I am—why is that a surprise?"

"I don't know. Most guys don't love weddings." Actually, most of the guys I knew thought they were a waste of time and money.

"I usually don't, but this is Beau with Belle. I mean, let's be real here, it's Beau . . . and God knows I never thought I'd see the day. Aren't you excited?" he wondered.

"I am delighted. Like you said, this is Beau we're talking about. But he's my brother."

Carter shrugged. "He's my brother too."

"On the one hand, that's really sweet. On the other hand . . . ew, what does that make us?" I scrunched up my nose.

He ran a finger down my nose. "Don't over-think it, princess. You and I are . . . close."

Backing up toward my room, I smiled at him. "Close, huh?"

"Close like gonna get closer."

"Yeah, yeah . . . promises, promises," I crooned and then pointed at my watch. "Fourteen minutes, baller—we can't be late."

"We most definitely cannot. I'll see your gorgeous self by the door in about five minutes."

I whirled away. "See you then, handsome."

9

I like a woman with a devil dancing a jig on her shoulder

Carter—Friday, May 27—11:23 pm

"I'm too old for this shit," I announced to the group at large as I waved off the topless chick gyrating in front of me, offering a bottle of champagne. It was me, Belle's father, Percy Richards, Beau, Roman, Pops, Greg, Belle's two brothers, Davis and Dalton, along with a Louisiana guy Beau and I knew from way back in the day, Batiste Landry.

"We all are, son," Pops agreed, watching as a rail-thin woman with surgically enhanced boobs and buns twirled on a sparkly pole.

Beau stood at the edge of the booth and squinted around, "Is it me or are all these girls really, really—"

"—Surgically enhanced?" Roman offered.

"—Young enough to be jailbait?" Greg shook his head.

"—Limber?" Davis offered.

Percy smirked. "Boys, I don't want to act like the old dude in the club, but since I am probably the oldest cat in this place, could we just—"

"Find someplace quiet to have a drink and a cigar? *Mais oui*, that sounds like a plan," Beau said and we all stood up with varying degrees of relief.

"My bad," I apologized. "I asked the concierge to make us VIP reservations at a lounge for a bachelor party and she automatically assumed this is what we wanted. And when no one said anything when we walked in, I decided to suck it up for you guys."

"It's not that big of a hardship watching naked women shake their booties, but I have to admit, some of the appeal is gone," Batiste said, shrugging, as we slid out the booth.

"Wait," Beau said. He and I exchanged looks. "*Mon ami*, for old times' sake?"

I chuckled, "Oh, why the hell not?" I reached into my pocket and pulled out a money clip. "Ladies?" It was almost comical how the sight of a stack of bills caused a ripple of energy to run through the place. I stepped over toward the stage and shuttled the bills up in the air, making them rain down in increments. I backed out of the way as girls and customers alike scurried over to grab up what they could. With a gesture, I led the fellas out of the club and back to the limo. I leaned over and gave instructions to the driver. He nodded and held the door while we all climbed in.

"I wonder what the girls are doing?" Roman asked and all heads swiveled toward him.

"You whipped like that?" Davis laughed.

"Have you seen my wife?" Roman asked him with a raised brow.

"Not just his wife, mine too, all those ladies. Not a one of them is hard on the eyes. You think they went the male stripper route?" Greg wondered.

"Naw, Belle's too classy for that," Dalton said.

"I know my daughter and she goes toe to toe with Beauregard. I wouldn't be so sure," Percy said, smiling.

Pops snorted and pointed at Dalton. "Son, that's your sister, so I mean no disrespect, but any woman hooked up with Beau is no angel."

"Amen," Beau agreed.

"Isn't your wife with them, Pops?" Batiste asked.

"Ain't no angel married to me either. I don't know about you boys, but them angelic women bore me to tears. They wouldn't want me and I sure wouldn't know what to do with one. I like a woman with a devil dancing a jig on one shoulder while the angel sits on the other, *tu comprends*?"

"Makes sense to me," I agreed. Not that there was anything wrong with a saintly woman, except when you're the kind of man who knew regular intervals of holiness were not realistic for him. "I like a woman with a little more naughty than nice."

"This explains Katrina's appeal to you then," Roman said drolly.

"Right, 'cuz without that she's such a troll otherwise?" Greg asked.

"Own money. Drop-dead gorgeous. Brains. Well-raised. Sense of humor." Dalton looked at Pops. "Any nieces or second cousin's daughters you'd like to introduce me to?"

Pops gave him the stink-eye. "This one hung around for fifteen years and I'm still not sold on him with my *bèbè*. You ain't been round but a minute, youngun."

"Whelp, you tried it," Beau teased his future brother-in-law.

"He is a whole lotta try," Percy teased his son.

The limo pulled to a stop in front of the Mirage hotel. "Gents, inside if you will." I got out and led the way. We cut through the casino and headed toward the south entrance. We entered Rhumbar and a hostess came over to greet us immediately.

"Parks, party of nine," I announced. Rhumbar was an upscale cigar lounge and cocktail spot with a laid-back vibe, grown-ups, and no loud music.

Her smile widened. "Welcome sir, we have an area reserved for you out on the patio."

We cut through the leather seating and widely spaced aisles to head outside. A grouping of sofas and chairs overlooked a water feature and low-key jazz filtered in quietly from hidden speakers. We chose seats around the table and stretched out easily. A uniformed gentleman set out an ice bucket, glasses, three different bottles of scotch, and opened up a humidor. "Your choice, gentlemen."

"This is nice." Percy nodded, pulling out his cell phone. "I'm gonna post this to the Facebook. You boys smile like you got good sense."

Obligingly, we all huddled in and smiled while

Percy figured out how to click and post a picture. Batiste sloshed a small measure of a single-malt scotch into a tumbler and picked a cigar out. "Now this is more my speed." He raised his glass. "To brother Beau on the eve of your nuptials, which none of us thought we'd live to see."

"Amen." Pops raised his glass.

"Brother Beau," Roman toasted.

"And his beautiful bride," I added.

"*Mais oui.*" Beau nodded with a smile.

"I have a question," Dalton announced.

"Boy, are you waiting for permission to ask?" Percy shook his head. "Go head on."

"All right then, no disrespect to you or my sister, but what turned the tide for you, Beau? What made you decide to become a one-woman man?"

"Why don't you ask the other married fellas?"

"The other married fellas weren't notorious stick men." Dalton side-eyed him.

"Hold on now, I had some moves back in my day. Shoot. Still got a move or two now. You youngsters just don't know. Old school is the best school." Pops stood up and did some little hip-swiveling jig that got the tables around us to send up a cheer. Pops bowed, smirked, and sat back down. Roman topped off his glass with a grimace and passed the bottle to Beau.

"Okay?" Batiste high-fived Pops. "Just because a bear only sips from one honeypot, don't mean he still can't growl."

I cringed. "I will pay all of you not to take that metaphor any further. Answer the man's question, Beau."

Beau beamed. "It's a cliché, but it's true. When you meet the one woman you don't want to lose, you commit. Period."

"But how did you know she was that one woman?"

"I just knew." Beau shrugged. "There was a specific moment when I was in a bar with Pops, Roman, and Carter. This beautiful woman came over and asked if we would join her for drinks. I had no interest. Not even the slightest temptation. I knew what I had at home was better. That's when I knew."

"That's deep," Davis said.

10

I need two Tylenol, a gallon of water, and six more hours of sleep

Katrina—Saturday, May 28—8:07am

I cracked one eye open and squinted against the obscenely bright light coming in through the window. Rolling to my left, I encountered a hard, warm male body. Very hard. Very warm. My other eye flew open. In front of me was the chiseled, bare chest of a man. This was not a bad way to wake up. My eyes scrolled up and met Carter's amused gaze head-on.

"Wait . . . what?" I sat up, realized I was naked, and slid back down under the sheet. "*Mon Dieu, qu'est-ce que je fais?* What did I do?" I glared at Carter. "What did *you* do?"

He looked at me drolly. "Really, you think I waited for you to be drunk and sloppy to have my way with you? I'm that guy?"

I reached out and raised the sheet to see that he had boxers on. "Apparently not. I was drunk *and* sloppy? One other question for you . . . why am I the only one naked?"

"Diva, you came in here and tossed your clothes off. When I brought you a nightgown, you stuffed it under the mattress."

I rolled over and sure enough, there was a flimsy piece of purple cotton peeking out from in between the mattress and box springs. I fell back against the pillows with my eyes closed. "I wish I could remember why I thought those last two glasses of champagne were a good idea."

"Champagne always seems like a good idea at the time," Carter answered agreeably, propping up against the headboard.

"Is this . . ." I looked around again. "This isn't even my room."

"No ma'am, it is not."

"Don't be charming," I admonished. "I sense I made a fool of myself last night."

"I don't find a beautiful, naked woman climbing into bed with me foolish at all. It was quite endearing," he intoned calmly.

I winced. "Oh, lordy—it's starting to come back to me. Was I dancing and singing?"

"Most of Justin Timberlake's greatest hits, I believe."

"No."

"Yes, you even broke out some nostalgic *NSYNC to round out the catalog. You have a pretty nice, smoky alto singing voice. Another Kit-Kat hidden talent." He seemed unnecessarily amused.

"Why didn't you stop me?" I complained.

"Sweetheart," he sighed. "I tried. You were a woman on a mission."

Hell if I knew. I remembered leaving dinner and heading to the Thunder Down Under Male Revue with the girls and having champagne. I remembered stopping at the Paris Hotel where Veronica got on a hot streak at the roulette table. She was buying novelty drinks for the table. I know I started drinking something fruity out of a large plastic replica of the Eiffel Tower. (This, in hindsight, was not a good idea.) I remembered Mom and Aunt Yo-Yo leaving and the rest of us going to a club. I remembered ordering more bottles of champagne. Everything else was a blur. I sat up, sobered. "I hope I didn't do anything stupid that's going to end up on YouTube. I can't afford any more negative publicity." I couldn't believe I'd let my guard down.

"When Jewel dropped you off last night she said the security guys we sent with you made sure that didn't happen," Carter assured me.

"What security guys? I didn't see any security guys."

"Well, if you saw them, they wouldn't be doing their jobs now, would they?"

I slapped my hand to my forehead and fell back against the pillows. "Whew, I'm an idiot. I know better. I never drink like that."

He quirked a skeptical brow. "Uh, princess? I've seen you drink champagne like that a time or two before."

I grimaced. I kept conveniently forgetting that

he's known me for a long, long time. "Probably. Champagne is my kryptonite. I try and stay away from it unless I'm around people I trust. It tends to make me reckless."

"I'll remember that." He leaned over and kissed me on my forehead. "As much as I've dreamed of lying next to your fine naked self in bed, we gotta get moving." He rolled out of bed and stretched his arms over his head, showcasing all that smooth skin stretching over rippling muscles. That was too much chocolate temptation for my blurry eyes this early in the morning. "Stop ogling and get it in gear, Kitty."

I closed my eyes, groaned, and rolled over. "I need two Tylenol, a gallon of water, and six more hours of sleep."

He smacked my left butt cheek as he strode past on the way to his bathroom. "I can't help you with the sleep thing, but check the nightstand."

Sure enough, sitting on the nightstand to my right was a large bottle of water and two tablets. I sat up and reached for them gratefully. "Carter Evan Parks, you are so much awesome."

He called out over the sound of water running. "Yeah, you told me last night right before you started singing 'SexyBack' but after you did a decent video reenactment of 'I Want It That Way.' "

"But—" I stuttered and tossed back the Tylenol, "that's the Backstreet Boys."

He snickered. "I tried to tell you that you were mixing your pop playlist. You said you didn't care."

"What can I say? I like pop music and boy bands," I admitted and drank some more water.

"Clearly. I actually don't have a problem with them per se. Admittedly, by the time the pink bra flew off on the second chorus of 'SexyBack,' I decided to sit back and enjoy the show. I didn't care what you were singing." He started the shower running and I climbed out of bed. He'd already seen it all anyway so I ambled naked into the bathroom just in time to watch him step into the stall.

Water sluiced down his form and I plunked down on the marble vanity to unabashedly watch as he grabbed a washcloth and soap and started cleansing areas I was itching to touch. He washed shins, thighs, and buttocks before soaping the cloth back up. I licked my lips while he cleaned his shoulders, neck, chest, and abs before moving the washcloth lower. Lucky washcloth. Literally, my palms were itching and saliva was pooling in my mouth. For the woman who was supposed to get any man I wanted, I stayed losing with Carter Parks. I needed to get me some of that and quickly. This peep show was tortuous. I crossed one leg over the other as a needy sound bubbled up from my throat. He glanced up and caught me watching. He stroked the washcloth slowly up and down his hardness while never taking his eyes off mine. It was, without a doubt, the hottest thing I'd ever seen. It was easily apparent how he earned the name Big Sexy.

"I can't decide if you're a saint or a sinner," I murmured, folding my arms across my chest in hopes of easing the ache in my nipples.

"Like you," he growled, growing larger and harder with each stroke, "I'm a little of both."

"Do you need some help with that?" I offered, wishing with every fiber of my being that he'd say yes.

He ducked under the water to rinse the suds off and switched the temp from warm to cold. "Rain check?" He looked up and saw the irritation and frustration cross my face. It was starting to feel like he was playing games and I didn't like it. Not one bit.

Tossing the washcloth to the side, he strode out of the shower and stood in front of me. He unfolded my arms and uncrossed my legs, opening them wide before stepping in between them. His hands bracketed my rib cage and his thumbs stroked the underside of my breasts. I rested my arms on his shoulders and arched into his embrace, craving more.

He murmured against my temple. "Katrina, I'm hard enough to cut glass right now. You can't possibly doubt that I want you. But your brother, my best friend, is getting married in a little over four hours. You really think that if I do what I'm dying to do, what you want me to do at this moment, we're going to want to leave the room anytime soon?"

Heedless of the icy drops of water falling off of him and onto me, I ran my hands down his body and dug my fingernails into his taut ass, pulling him closer. We both moaned as his erection slid against my wetness. I was so open and he was right there. So close to exactly where I needed him. His shaft twitched involuntarily and I shuddered in reaction. His breathing was serrated and rough in my ear. I knew he was hanging onto his control by a thread. I also knew I didn't want our first time together to be a rushed hit-and-quit with one eye on the clock. "If we're gonna get out of this room, you need to get back into that cold shower and I need to head back to my side of the suite," I whispered.

"Okay then." He released his hold on me and clenched his fists as he took two steps back. I slid off the counter onto shaky legs.

The tension between us was thick. We were on the edge of something. Good or bad, I didn't know, but it was definitely something. I tried to joke it off. "All this unfulfilled hotness and me without my vibrator."

His gaze sharpened and his hand reached out to grasp my wrist. "Don't."

"Don't what?"

"Don't take the edge off. Keep a lid on all the unfulfilled hotness. Save it for me."

"What about you and your washcloth games, you gonna keep that bottled up?"

"Yeah." He nodded.

"Why?"

"We're worth the wait."

Dammit, he always said something that I couldn't argue with. We stood there facing off, naked in every single way in front of each other. No artifice, no guile. Part of me wanted to get an attitude, part of me wanted to walk away, part of me wanted to push him down onto the bathroom rug and hop aboard. Instead, I nodded slowly. "Okay Carter, I'll see you over in the villa later?"

"I'll be there," he said.

"Worth the wait," I repeated.

"Absolutely," he reiterated.

I sighed, turned on my heel, and marched away. On my way back to my room I picked up articles of my clothing I'd flung off at some point last night. I yanked a pump encrusted with pink Swarovski crystals out of the potted fern by the love seat and glanced around for the mate before shaking my head. I swear to God, I'd spent more time naked and half naked in front of Carter with very little return for my efforts. We'd only been "dating" for a week and already Big Sexy was the biggest pain-in-the-ass boyfriend I'd ever had. And the best. That said something about me that I was in no condition to explore. Catching a glance of myself in the bathroom mirror, I stifled a shriek. *Not a good look, Katrina.* I had less than an hour to pull myself together and get over to the Bellagio private villa to help Belle get ready to marry my brother. I twisted my hair atop my head and secured it with a clip. I'd start with a cold shower and go from there. It was going to be a very long day.

11

Send out my damned bride already

Carter—Saturday, May 28—11:48 am

The 2500-square-foot villa had been transformed into a rose-laden wedding chapel. Belle had chosen gold and blue as her colors and her coordinator went all the way in with it. The ceremony was being held in the living areas of the two-bedroom villa. Fabric, flowers, lights, and candles adorned most surfaces. White roses were arrayed in large bouquets and petals were strewn along a carpeted walkway leading to the newly created altar.

Beau and I stood with the preacher waiting for things to get started. I slid a questioning look at Beau as he shifted nervously from foot to foot under the flowered arch some creative person had placed in front of the windows overlooking the private infinity pool deck. It was the fifth time in the last minute and a half that he fidgeted around. Beau was not a fidgety kind of guy. Particularly not in Armani formal wear. He loved how he looked in a tux and hated to ruin the line. All this shifting about was worrisome.

"Dude. You straight?" I asked in a low voice, keeping my face neutral. About fifty friends and Montgomery family members sat staring at the two of us. I'd overheard his Uncle August taking bets on whether Beau would really go through with this or not. I put a hundred on my boy Beau going the distance. We were about five or ten minutes away from the ceremony starting. Reverend Moss had been flown in from Dallas and stood beside us. At my words he lifted his eyes from the Bible he was holding and gave us a speculative glance. We both waited for Beau's answer with much anticipation.

"*Je suis bon, mon ami.* I'm fine. It just hit me, you know. I'm here. We're in tuxes. There are more flowers than I thought humanly possible scattered every freakin' where. I'm about to do this thing. The whole forever and always, death-do-us-part thing."

"Uh-huh." I nodded slowly. "That generally goes hand in hand with the matrimony thing."

"This is real-life serious grown-up-ness, you know?" He looked like a man who just woke up from a dream and realized where he was and what he was doing.

"Yep. It had to happen sooner or later. Even Peter Pan stopped flying around with Tinkerbell, left Neverland, and settled his ass down." I had no idea what I was saying . . . just something—anything—to calm him down and keep this moving.

He turned to look at me. "Is that how the original story goes? I thought in the book he never grew up, ditched Wendy, and flew around playing the flute."

I put my hand on his shoulder. "Bruh, I am not standing up here on your wedding day debating the origins and evolution of Peter effing Pan. Im'a need you to get your head in the game and make this woman your wife already. It's not only what you want, it's what you need. Let's do this, all right?" This best-man business was tricky. I had to straddle backing his play if he decided to bolt with keeping him grounded and here to do what I knew he really wanted. I gave Beau my sternest "don't make me kick your ass up in here" glower.

He put his hands up in surrender. "Stand down. I know, I know. I needed a moment to take it all in. Just had to get my bearings. You know, I really never thought I'd do this."

I decided not to tell him that no one ever thought he'd do this. On a need-to-know basis right now? He didn't need to know that. "Man, you're almost forty. Your oats been sown years ago."

Beau pointed at me and then himself. "Which of us is the pot and which is the kettle? I'm just taking a breath."

"Breathe already, bruh. Exhale or whatever. You are never gonna find a woman that perfect for you who also puts up with all your trifling ways."

"I'm less trifling than I used to be, but I take your point." Beau grinned at me and clapped his hands together. He inhaled deeply and exhaled slowly. "All right, let's get this party started." He raised his voice. "Send out my damned bride already!"

"Oh no, you didn't!" Belle's voice rang out from down the hallway. "I will be there when I get there and you will damn well wait."

"You tell him, girl!" a voice rang out from the second row.

"Man, is your Aunt Yo-Yo already lit?" I asked Beau.

"I assume she's still boozy from last night." He shrugged. "I don't know what all the girls got into."

I pressed my lips together and looked off into the distance. Some things an older brother didn't need to know about his little sister.

"It's like that?" Beau asked.

"Like what?" I asked innocently.

"You already keeping Katrina's secrets instead of sharing with your boy?"

I shrugged. "She's prettier than you."

"Whipped already," Beau teased.

The entrance music started, saving me from any kind of response. What would I have said anyway? *I wish I was whipped, but I'm trying to do right by your sister and it's killing me?* No, some thoughts you just kept to yourself.

The rest of the wedding party filed in wearing navy and gold: Davis with Yazlyn. Dalton with Veronica. Roman with Jewel, Batiste with Katrina. Katrina glided down the aisle in a skintight gold dress that left her shoulders bare and clung everywhere a man wished it would on its way to the floor. Her hair was pulled back and fell in curls down her back. She winked at me and put some extra wiggle in her walk when she saw me staring. "Jesus Christ," I muttered, concentrating on not sporting wood on this reverent occasion.

Beau elbowed me in my ribs. "For God's sake, get some dignity about yourself, man. Put your tongue back in your mouth. That's my baby sister and this is my wedding day."

"Uh-huh," I said absently, not taking my eyes off of his baby sister. He jabbed me again with his elbow, harder this time. And I pulled my eyes forward to see Pops wagging a finger at me from the front row. "My bad," I mouthed.

The party reached the altar and lined up. The music paused for a moment and then the wedding march began. Belle floated into view on the arm of her father, Percy. Belle was a tall beauty who looked like an all-American cross between Halle Berry and Iman. Her hair was short and layered. She had wide brown eyes and a smile that had sold many tubes of toothpaste. Today, she looked incandescent. I nudged Beau. "Look at that beautiful girl you're about to claim."

Beau stood up straighter, with eyes only for his bride. "Damn straight, I am. Step it up, babe," he called out. "I need to make this legal before you realize I'm getting the better end of this deal."

"Oh, I was already knowin', sugar." She winked.

He stepped forward to shake Percy's hand and shifted Belle's hand into his. "If you don't look like a sexy-assed Disney princess."

She grinned up at him. "You know I had step up my cute to compare with your pretty ass."

"If both of you cake-topper-looking idiots could

get on with it, we could get out of these monkey suits and have a party already," Roman stage-whispered.

"Right?" Katrina said. "Some of us have other things to do today."

"Other things or other people, Miss Hot Pants?" Veronica teased.

"Whichever," Katrina said, sending me a heated look.

"I see you, princess." I gave her a head nod.

"Ain't nobody trying to see dat," Beau groused.

"Children!" Madere scolded. She looked at Reverend Moss. "They were really raised better than this. You can go ahead, Reverend."

"But, um . . . we do want the short version, rev," Belle said, smiling. "We're really more about the honeymooning."

"One would think you two had that part perfected by now, sis," Davis teased.

"Delaney Mirabella and Dalton, if I have to come up there!" Percy called out.

"That was actually Davis, Dad." Dalton corrected him.

"Maybe if you hadn't given half of us names that start with 'D' you could keep us straight." Davis grinned.

"I've got you straight enough to come up there and whip all y'alls impertinent asses in front of these fine folks," Percy announced. Everyone in the church smothered their laughter since Percy looked like he meant business.

Reverend Moss cleared his throat. "Why don't I just take it from the top, shall I?"

I patted him on the arm. "Do your thing, sir."

He nodded. "Dearly beloved, we are gathered together here in the sight of God—and in the face of this company—to join together this man and this woman in holy matrimony, a commendable institution to be honored among all men; and there-fore—is not by any—to be entered into unadvisedly or lightly—but reverently, discreetly, advisedly, and solemnly. Into this holy estate these two persons present now come to be joined."

I relaxed as the ceremony got underway, Beau and Belle staring into each other's eyes; friends and family smiling and nodding; Katrina giving me the tonight-is-the-night look. This was how the day was supposed to be.

12

I'm sneezing on your four-tier white chocolate wedding cake

Katrina—Saturday, May 28—1:49 pm

I kicked my shoes off and reached forward to help Belle remove the glittery tiara from her head. I smiled at her. "You really do look like a Disney princess." Her strapless white gown was layers of crystal-encrusted whisper-thin silk that wrapped around her torso and tapered down to her waist before billowing out to a full ball gown.

She beamed back at me. "I know. Can you believe it, honey? All this time I was so positive I was going to go sleek and modern, but when Yazlyn brought me this designer's dress, I had to have it. Was it too much?"

"Not at all. Is it bad that I'm wondering who

the designer is and if we should launch a line of wedding dresses at BellaRich?"

"Ha! I thought the same thing, sugar," Belle drawled in her Georgia-peach voice.

"Good, we'll talk about it when you get back from your honeymoon. Now, what are you changing into for the reception?" I looked around the bedroom.

"Remember that white suit you designed for resort wear?"

I tilted my head in confusion. "That was a man's suit."

"It was. Beau had the idea to nip in the waist, put sheer material on the sleeves, turn the pants palazzo, and make it out of jersey and silk." She pulled it out of the closet and showed it to me.

I flipped open the jacket to look at the altered, more feminine design. "That brother of mine, who knew, huh?" The material it was made with was white, but shot through with iridescent threads, making it look like it was glowing. "That's pretty genius."

"Beauregard has his moments." She gave a secret smile and turned so I could unzip the dress and assist her out of it.

"He was smart enough to seal the deal with you." I handed her a robe to slip on.

"He sure 'nuff did, didn't he?" Her smile turned tremulous.

"You sound surprised."

"I have to admit there was a part of me that wondered if he would cut and run at the last minute."

I slid my arm around her waist for a quick hug. "Oh, Belle."

She shrugged. "He loves me. I know this. He shows me in so many ways. I love him back, but he was deeply committed to playboyism for a lot of years. I had to wonder if he could let it all go."

"Playboyism?" I repeated with a smirk.

"Sounds nicer than *rampant man-whoring*."

"True. But that was then, this is now. All it took was one good woman, the right woman, and he got his head on straight," I declared with a nod.

"Hmm. Funny you should say that," she murmured as we headed over to the small room behind the bath where the mini–beauty salon was set up. I waved the makeup artist and stylist in so they could refresh Belle's face and hair before the reception.

"What's funny about that?" I raised my brows.

"You know, sweetie, you and Beau are so much alike in so many ways."

I shot her a warning look. "Wedding day or not, if you're about to call me a ho, I'm sneezing on your four-tier white chocolate wedding cake."

"Classy." She rolled her eyes. "You know I'm not about to call you any such thing. I will say that for some reason, you both tend to think that happiness—true happiness—is meant for someone else, not yourselves. And if all it took was one woman—me—to get Beau to where he is today, can't you open yourself up to the possibility that all it will take is one good man—Carter—to get you there, too?"

I settled in the chair opposite hers and crossed my arms. Five minutes as a wife and suddenly she had all the answers? "This is because you're married now, right? Because you are Mrs. Beau Montgomery—whoa, the sound of that just freaked me out a little bit. Moving on—you think everyone else is ready to be Mr. and Mrs. Somebody?"

"No, Miss Snarky. When I first saw you and Carter together at that bar, the one where Renee showed up and . . . you know what, let's not go there on my wedding day. You know when I'm talking about. You'd had too much champagne . . ."

"Apparently a recurring theme in my life, but yes—I know what night you are talking about."

"I thought then that there was something between you." She looked over at me, daring me to deny it. I didn't.

"There is. It's called *sexual tension* and we're going to take care of that this evening." I resisted the urge to do a fist pump into the air. It was going to be tonight, it was going to be epic, and I could not wait. Okay, I was probably too excited, overly anticipating the event. I'd been with guys before and in my experience, they always talked a big game and delivered very little. I had a feeling, a gut feeling that this time would be different. More than a feeling, a foregone conclusion. This was Carter. He was not the kind to overpromise and under-deliver; it just wasn't him. The fact that he wasn't bragging about his sexual prowess made me want to find what he was working with even more.

"Katrina, you think Big Sexy was waiting on you to grow up to scratch an itch? Like he can't have any woman he wants, whenever he wants?"

"You think he was waiting on me to grow up?" I liked the idea more than I thought I would.

"I definitely think he's been waiting on you."

"He has never said a word about long-term. We've only been officially dating for a week. We haven't even slept together yet. Everybody needs to just calm down."

"You've known each other for years. More than foreplay, it's like you've been in pre-relationship status for years."

"This is different. It's me and Carter. We don't know exactly what we've got yet. It might take some time to unravel it all."

"I knew the weekend after I met your brother that it was going to be serious."

"I think you've got some revisionist history going on there, but I'm going let you have that on your wedding day." To my recollection, she held him off for about three months and then they spent another three months bouncing naked whenever the whim struck them. Then they decided they might want to get serious between all the naked time. But, hey, I was on the outside looking in, so what did I know?

"Girl, please wake up and smell the happily-ever-after. If you could just be open to it . . . that's all I'm saying," Belle implored me.

I waved her concerns away with my hand. "I have too much going on to think long-term right now. I have to find out who is making my life hell, we're behind on the summer line, and I want to talk about designing shoes."

"Shoes and wedding dresses. We will. But let me say this last thing."

"It's your day, sister. Say whatever you want."

Her eyes turned dreamy and she reached over to squeeze my hand. "Sister."

I squeezed back. "I know, right? Can you believe you married my brother?"

"Can you believe he married *me*?" I thought it was cute that she thought he was such a catch. I loved my brother, but he was high maintenance.

"He would've been a fool not to. My brother is many things, but a fool is not one of them."

"You got that right. But back to you."

Clearly she wasn't going to let this go. "Oh, jeez. Okay. Speak your truth, married lady."

"Carter is the real deal, okay? I want you to give this an honest try. If you don't think you can do it, just walk away now and save everybody some unnecessary drama."

"That's what he said."

"He's right."

"Okay. I hear you. And I'll take it under advisement. Now, let's get you in that gorgeous suit and back by your husband's side before he comes looking for you."

She glanced down at the band of diamonds that joined the chocolate diamond solitaire on her hand. She gave me a smug grin. "Husband. I am Mrs. Beau Montgomery."

"Um, um, um. May God have mercy on your soul."

13

We could use a little boom·chicka right now

Carter—Saturday, May 28—4:03 pm

Katrina crossed her leg, curled into the cradle of my arm, and spoke softly in my ear. "My feet are killing me, I want out of this tight skirt and I am so over the reception of it all. How much longer until we can get out of here, you think?"

I smiled at her ruefully. "Let's see . . . I'm the best man. You're the maid of honor and the bride and the groom are still here. We can't go until they go."

"We've danced, we've eaten, and we've given speeches and toasts. We've done the cake and photos. You and I have chatted up everybody here. I answered every nosy cousin's questions about why my bare behinds are all over the Internets."

"Yes, and the questions as to why you tried to

dive for the floor when the bouquet came your way?" I teased her. Belle had tossed the bouquet straight to her and there was no gracious way not to catch it. When Beau tossed the garter my way, Percy stepped in front of me and caught it. It was a hilarious moment, made more so when he turned and tucked the garter into my jacket pocket, saying I'd have far better use for it than he would.

Katrina shrugged. "Anyway, Beau and Belle are married up right nice, I say we make a break for it."

"I can't decide if you are eager to get to bed for me or for sleep." I looked down into her eyes.

"First one and then the other." She grinned and shook her head when the waiter tried to top off her champagne.

"You've been nursing that half glass of bubbly for hours," I noted.

"I want to be clearheaded for tonight and it's important that I hydrate." She winked and took another sip of water.

I squeezed her shoulder. "Planning on sweating this evening?"

She gazed up at me through her lashes. "I expect you'll put me through my paces."

"Girl, you keep talking that talk and see what it gets you."

"Please show me. As soon as possible, please and thank you," she whispered.

I had really wanted to give us time to get to know each other on a different level before we got into all the sex, because I didn't want it to be all about the sex. I already knew it was going to be a lot of very, very spectacular sex. But I wasn't going to make it one more night without having her.

Walking away this morning had nearly crippled me. Watching her go soft and wet while watching me in the shower was the absolute last straw. The chemistry that had always been there between us had been bubbling up all week and it was about to boil over. "You know why I wanted to wait, right?"

She nodded. "Yeah, it's gotta be different."

"Right." She got it. We were making progress.

"But it is. I've never felt quite like this before. It's not just physical. I get that. But Carter, I can't wait any more. I want this. With you. And you have to know by now; it's not going to be any other way between us. We lit a match and it's about to burn out of control. I sound like an idiot saying these things, but I have to tell you how it feels. It's hot and urgent."

It was great to know that she felt the same way. "I know, baby. Believe me. I almost said something about being on fire for you until I realized how *boom-chicka-wah-wah* that sounded."

"Woo . . ." she exhaled slowly, "We could use a little boom-chicka right now."

"We could use a lot." I looked around and located Beau and Belle in their own little world. "Let me nudge your brother and his bride on up outta here."

"Hurry." She breathed with those flames we discussed flaring up in her eyes. Her skin was flushed and she looked so damned doable in that moment that I had to dig deep for control and force myself to walk away.

"Hey Montgomerys!" I approached the newly-weds and put an arm around each of them. "I think you two have earned an exit. You've got an early flight to Bali in the morning and I don't even want to know what you're trying to get into tonight. Since these folks are going to stay until every last drop of booze and grilled shrimp is devoured, how about you tip on out? Officially."

Beau nodded. "My man, we were just wondering how much longer we were required to entertain folks."

I clapped him on the back. "Your credit card will do the rest of the entertaining. Go enjoy being man and wife."

Belle kissed me on the cheek. "You ain't slick, Parks, but since I'm cheering for you, we'll let it slide."

I elbowed Beau out of the way and gave her a bug hug. "Thanks, I'm going to do right by her. Listen, this one gives you any trouble, the upgrade is always available."

"Hey!" Beau snatched her out of my arms.

"Everybody, Mr. and Mrs. Avery Beauregard Montgomery are departing to begin their honeymoon. Let's clap them out the door, shall we?" I announced. I ducked out of the way as the crowd converged on Belle and Beau. With a smile, I turned and met the knowing glint of Pops Montgomery's regard.

"We expect to see you and Katrina over to the house when you get back to Dallas next week," he called out.

"Yes, sir," I agreed.

"And I expect your grandfather taught you to treat a lady like a lady." He stepped closer to me.

"Yes, sir."

He stood directly in front of me. "All right.

Don't make me get the shotgun, boy. I'm too old for jail."

"Yes, sir." I squelched a smile.

He opened up his arms and gave me a big hug. "Gotta good feelin' 'bout you two. Just remember, she's a thoroughbred. Beautiful but high-strung, used to getting her own way and quick to run. You need a firm hand, an open heart, and a soft voice, ya hear?"

"Sir, did you just liken your only daughter to a horse?"

"Look here boy, I ain't 'bout all dat political correctness. I know you take my meaning."

"I do indeed, sir."

"Go head on then and take care of my girl. Get up outta here. I got this."

I nodded and backed away before anybody changed their minds. "Thanks, sir. I will, sir. Good night, sir." I motioned to Katrina, who almost tripped in her haste to meet me by the door. I pushed the door open and shut it behind us quickly. We stepped into the bright Nevada sun and back across the bridge to the private hotel entrance.

"What was that?" she asked as we walked inside, briskly heading toward the elevator bay.

"I think I just got the all-clear from your father."

"What?"

I decided to keep the horse analogy to myself. "He told me he had a good feeling about us and told me to take care of you."

She stopped dead in her tracks. "For the last damned time, I can take care of myself."

I drew her toward me slowly and leaned down until my lips were a hairsbreadth away from hers. "Yes, but do you really want to . . . take care of yourself? Tonight?"

"Well, when you put it like that. . . ." She licked her lips and I could not pass up the invitation. I meant to drop a light kiss on her lips, but the moment our mouths touched, it was a whole different ball game. Her mouth fell open needily and my tongue plundered inside. We battled to taste each other, nipping and lapping in the rawest, least sophisticated ways possible. We were too hungry for finesse; it was all about feeding the sensations.

"Get a room, Big Sexy!" a voice called out and we broke apart, remembering where we were.

"Woo-hoo, get some, Kit-Kat!" another voice called.

I couldn't believe I'd been so careless. The last thing we needed were any more revealing photos of Katrina out there. "I'm sorry, I forgot. You went straight to my head."

She looked around. "We're still by the villas. This area of the hotel is by invitation only." She glanced over my shoulder. "That was Greg and Roni giving us shit, by the way."

I turned to see the couple grinning at us. I shot them the finger. "We have a room; we're headed to it now, thank you very much."

"Not a moment too soon!" Roni called out and they waved at us as they disappeared down the opposite hallway.

Thankfully, there was no one on the VIP elevator and we made it to our room without incident. I put out the *do not disturb* sign, closed the door behind us, and slammed the second lock shut. It was finally time and I wanted no interruptions.

Katrina kicked off her shoes, unzipped her dress, and let it fall to the ground. She stood there in a strapless gold bra with the tiniest panties I had ever seen. "For the record, Carter Evan?"

"Yeah?" I tossed my jacket to the side and pulled off my tie and cuff links.

"No, I don't want to take care of myself tonight. I'm all yours for the taking."

"You ready for me, Kit-Kat? I mean, really ready?" I watched her intently.

She stepped to me and started taking the studs out of my dress shirt. When it was completely unfastened, she pulled it off of me and started working to undo my pants. "Why don't you try me and find out?"

"I'll take that as a *yes*. Let me ask you something," I muttered as I toed off my shoes.

"Anything," she responded, kneeling in front of me to pull off my socks.

The sight of her on her knees in front of me derailed my thoughts for a moment.

"Carter?" she breathed, looking up at me as my pants hit the ground.

"Huh?"

"You were asking me something?"

"Yeah, I got distracted." I reached into my pants pocket and pulled out a foil packet.

"You want me to do anything for you while I'm down here?" She reached for my boxers and dragged them down, freeing the foil from my hand, ripping open the package, and sheathing me quickly. I hissed out a breath, grabbed her underneath her arms, and lifted her up. If she kept her hands on me, we'd be done before we got started.

"You're gonna be the death of me. I was going to ask if you're a sweep-you-off-your-feet-and-carry-you-to-bed kinda girl or a drop-down-and-do-me-on-the-floor kinda girl, but shit just got urgent." I carried her over the sofa and set her down.

She unfastened her bra and I put my hands over hers.

"I wanted to do that."

"Carter, I promise next time we can do it all romantic on a bed of rose petals and we can take four hours to lick chocolate and strawberries off each other by candlelight if you like, but right now can we just—"

"I got you, babe. Hold on, it's not going to be pretty."

"But it's going to be good."

"Damn straight."

14

That was definitely worth the wait

Katrina—Saturday, May 28—4:31 p.m.

Carter picked me up and set me on my feet, flipping me around so I was bent over the high back of the couch. Something about being placed into the position of his choice flipped all my triggers. It was hot. I both felt and heard him rip the flimsy g-string panties off of me. I found myself breathless with excited anticipation.

"Breathe, baby," he whispered from behind me and I shuddered. "Brace." He positioned my arms. "And hold on. Ready?"

"More than."

He thrust inside of me in one powerful stroke and I shrieked. "You good?" he ground out through gritted teeth.

"So damn good." Jesus, he was huge. He filled me up and stretched me deliciously as his powerful hips drove against me again and again. I strained back against him, eager for all he had to give. His hands slid up my torso and his fingers plucked at my nipples, rhythmically in sync with his impossibly deep strokes. "Don't stop."

"Trust me, I won't," he promised, running his tongue along the back of my neck. "Stay with me." He wrapped his hands around my waist and pulled me up and back as he sat on the chaise lounge so that I was sitting on his lap with his shaft deep inside of me.

I undulated on top of him and we both groaned. "I like this."

"I thought you might." He closed his thighs and opened mine over his and began pumping up into me with short, sharp strokes. His hands gripped my hips and he bounced me against him so I felt truly taken. There was no nerve he didn't rake against, no pulsing folds that escaped the imprint of his hardness. I was helpless to do anything but ride. I flung my head back against his shoulder. I'd never been like this. He'd barely put his hands on me and I was desperate. The feel of him stroking inside had wetness seeping out of me. And it wasn't enough. I made an agitated sound and writhed against him.

"Problem, diva?"

"I need—"

"I know what you need." He took one of his hands off of my hips and slid it through my seeping wetness. He pulled my left hand off his thigh and guided it between my legs. He stroked, using my own hand with his covering it, directing the pressure and the motion. His thumb flicked my sensitive nub once and then twice before he replaced his hand with mine. "Touch yourself, baby."

"Oh Christ," I moaned, doing as he asked. I caressed myself and he grew harder inside of me.

He watched me over my shoulder. "That's so damn hot, Katrina."

"Uh-huh," I panted, my hand moving faster between my legs as his strokes sped up. I felt the convulsions starting deep inside of me and I began squirming on top of him. "Oh God, Carter."

"That's my Kitty, take what you want."

I squeezed around him and arched violently as I trembled on the edge. His teeth bit lightly into the side of my neck as he bounced me harder along his length and I exploded over the precipice, crying out in pleasure. I twisted my pelvis, grinding against him, drawing out the waves as they continued to singe my nerves and steal my breath. Finally I slumped forward and sighed. That was definitely worth the wait. He ran his hands up and down my arms in slow, languid movements. It took a moment or two before I realized he was still pulsing rock-hard inside of me. I wiggled my rear and looked over my shoulder at him. "Hey you."

"Hey." He grinned. "Welcome back."

"Yeah," I said, grinning and stretching luxuriously against him. "I was gone there for a second."

"I'd like to send you there again," he growled.

I climbed off of him and pushed him onto his back before straddling him once more. "Perhaps you'd like to come with me this time?" I reached between us and guided him back into my core. I closed my eyes as he slid home. I stretched out on top of him so we were plastered against each other. I inched my hips up, down, and around in tiny increments, torturing the both of us.

"Don't mind if I do." He watched me under lowered lids while I continued my languid rolls against him.

"Can I call you C?" I asked, swirling my hips in a slow figure eight and running my hands along his shoulders. He was a beautiful man. I started to heat up again just looking at him.

"You can call me whatever you want right now."

"C?" I groaned as he tilted his hips up and to the right, hitting just the right spot deep inside of me.

"K?" he replied in a tight voice.

"You make me really hot," I purred while he rubbed that spot inside me with the tip of his shaft. It wasn't the deepest thing I'd ever told a man, but it was the unvarnished truth.

"Then we're even."

I slid my hands behind his neck and lifted his head up to mine. I attacked his lips with a swell of passion. His lips were ridiculously soft and he was an amazing kisser. He sucked lips and skimmed teeth and licked every crevice and allowed me to do the same. It was like he wanted to learn every nook and cranny and then come back around for more. His tongue reached out and we played thrust and parry until I couldn't breathe. "Shift up," I said and leaned back to watch his abs ripple as he rose to a sitting position. "A man who looks like you should be banned and only brought out on special occasions."

He barked out a surprised laugh. "Have you looked in the mirror lately?"

"I'm obviously pretty," I said matter-of-factly, "but you're like a lethal weapon with hidden layers of hotness."

"If you say so." He matched my unhurried pace with equally deliberate moves of his own.

"I do say so," I affirmed and brought my knees up on either side of him. "You have the most amazing stamina. Can you stay like this all day?"

"Much as I'd love to, I doubt it," he said, smirking.

"I was going to do this whole thing where I crawled on top of you and rode you until you screamed out my name," I confessed.

His nostrils flared and he flexed inside of me. "Is that so?"

"Um-hmm," I murmured.

"What's stopping you?"

I paused. We'd been pretty honest and upfront with each other, but I always struggled between what I thought people expected of me and what I really wanted. I wanted to ask for something, but I didn't want to be judged for it. Especially not by him. He was too important. I cared too much what he thought of me.

"Katrina," he said sternly.

My eyes flew to his and I shook my head. "Never mind."

He looked at me contemplatively for a moment, as if trying to figure out the answer to a puzzle. After a long gaze, he nodded. "Okay then."

"Okay then?" I moved to push him backwards again and he resisted, shaking his head slowly.

"Carter—I . . ." Thinking I had ruined the mood, I scrambled around for something to get us back on track.

"Shhhh." He wrapped an arm around my waist and stood up with me in his arms.

"You're going to have to stop carrying me around like I weigh nothing," I admonished, though secretly I loved it.

He wrapped my arms and legs around him. "Yeah? Who's going to stop me?"

He had a point. "Where are you taking me?" I asked.

We entered his bedroom and he laid me down on the bed. "Where you want to go," he answered and climbed on top of me. He spread my legs with his thighs and put my hands over my head. He held each of my wrists in his hands and lowered his hips onto me so I was pinned between him and the mattress. I was completely open to him; completely vulnerable. The feeling should have scared me. Instead, I was thrilled.

My breath hitched in my throat and my eyes fluttered closed when I realized he knew what I wanted without having to be asked.

"K?" he whispered, running his tongue along the pulsing vein in my neck to just under my ear.

"C?" I tried not to whimper.

"Open your eyes and look at me . . . now," he commanded in a low voice.

I looked up at him helplessly, so enthralled with what he was making me feel.

"I'm going to take you now." His voice was a vibrating baritone in my ear.

"Please," I pleaded and canted my hips upward so he could slide back inside of me.

"Oh, God, you're soaking wet," he grated.

"I know. I can't help it."

"Good." He began to ride me in earnest, driving into me with unchecked carnality. He pounded with such power and authority that I began climaxing instantly. My inner folds fluttered around him as we pumped against each other, joining in a cadence as if we'd done this a million times before. He was pressed so tightly against me that each thrust of his body against mine scraped my nipples across his chest.

"Harder," I rasped out. I wanted more and strained against his hold, loving the fact that he was in charge, but giving me everything. He grunted as my sex clenched harder. He let go of my wrists to grip my hips, tilting them up so he could reach that much deeper. He unlocked something inside that unfurled and broke loose and suddenly I was all sensation.

"C!" I screamed as it became too much. Too much feeling, too much pleasure.

"I got you," he soothed as his hips twisted, taking me to a whole different level. "I got you. I've always got you."

Raw screams erupted from me as another orgasm stronger than I'd ever felt ripped through me. I have no idea what I was screaming as I tightened and arched against him over and over again. I wrapped my arms around him to hold onto something solid.

He threw his head back as his release flowed from him in a heated rush. His body pulsed over mine for long moments before he slumped to the side. He unsheathed himself and dropped the condom in the trash can by the bed. He pulled me over to him with a deep sigh of satisfaction.

We lay wrapped in each other for a few quiet moments. I was thoroughly satisfied, slightly stunned, and only a little bit embarrassed.

"How did you know?" I whispered and traced patterns on his chest.

"I guessed. You're a together woman, on your game twenty-four-seven. I wondered if maybe you wanted someone else to take control sometimes."

"Not someone. I couldn't do that with just anyone."

"Good." He kissed my forehead. "I'm glad you trust me enough to be yourself. You don't have to be anyone but who you are, that's who I want. I don't need all sorts of bells and whistles. I just want one hundred percent pure Katrina."

"That's enough for you? I'm not all stilettos and see-through bikinis and champagne."

"Girl, I want you in a T-shirt eating buffalo wings and drinking Kool-Aid. You are more than enough for me. You're a gift, Kitty, no matter how you're wrapped."

My emotions welled up and I blinked back tears. "So you're not expecting a stripper pole in the living room?" I teased.

"You stripped just fine without it last night." He nuzzled my forehead.

"I have put you through a lot this week," I admitted.

"You're a little high-maintenance. Lucky for you, you are more than worth it."

"Kevin didn't get me," I mused out loud. It occurred to me that none of the men I had ever dated understood me, not the real me. Maybe that's why they could never give me what I needed. In or out of bed.

"He was too self-centered to care. And he's a fool. Can we not talk about him while we're basking in afterglow?"

"Are you an afterglow kind of guy?"

"Hell yeah. Foreplay, multifaceted bed game, afterglow with cuddles? I'm here for all of it."

"With everybody or just me?"

"After you, there isn't an anyone else."

"You do say the right things."

"I speak the truth."

I sighed and snuggled closer. "I'm just saying. Thanks for knowing what I need."

"Thanks for letting me give it to you. Feel free to ask for anything you want."

"Anything?" My eyes lit up as I let my imagination run wild. The freedom to be myself in every area of my life with someone I trusted? That was just as addictive as the sex.

"Within reason." He smacked my ass and then rubbed away the slight sting.

That was the great thing about Carter in a nutshell. He was willing to let me be myself, but made sure I knew I had boundaries. If you had told me this morning that I wanted a man to place boundaries on me, I would have laughed. Thinking back to this morning gave me an idea. "This morning when you were in the shower with the washcloth?"

His eyes went smoky. "Yeah?"

"Can I watch?"

"You just wanna watch?"

"I might want to assist." I slid my hand down and wrapped around him. "How in the world are you getting hard again?"

"What can I say? You inspire me. But I'm feeling kinda dirty. Want to help me clean off in the shower?"

I licked my lips. "Oh yeah. If you miss a spot, I might need to lick you clean."

"Did I mention that you're going to be the death of me?"

"Only every day for the past week." I grinned as he stood up and pulled me into the bathroom with him.

15

Boy, your business is in the streets

Carter—Monday, June 14—11:40 a.m.

I'd been back from my trip to the Caribbean and Vegas with Katrina for two weeks and I was still playing catch-up at work. The eighty-hour work-weeks I was used to putting in didn't hold the appeal they used to. My vice president Gina and I were already talking about bringing on extra help at the executive level to take up some the slack. The company was stable and profitable enough that I didn't need to have my hands on the wheel every second of every day.

Watching Beau settle into married life as he and Belle balanced work and home had opened my eyes to a few things. I'd spent so many years concentrating on getting to where I thought I needed to go that I hadn't taken a moment to sit and reflect on the end game. I spent high school and college working my ass off to be the best athlete I could be, knowing that was my ticket to some level of security for me and my family. Not saying I didn't have some good times along the way, but I never played as seriously as I worked.

I was 75 percent talent and 30 percent raw hunger and ambition. That extra 5 percent was my saving grace. I was only a year or two into my professional football career when I realized I was going to need a fallback plan. I watched guys who were more talented than me getting hurt or cut or traded—out of the league with no idea what to do next. The average pro football career is three years. The average life expectancy for a black male is sixty-seven years. If your playing career was over at the age of twenty-five, that was a lot of retirement to deal with on very little income. I wasn't going to be that guy.

I'd put the same dedication and drive into making Parks Properties a success as I had in my ten-year playing career. I considered myself a combination of blessed, lucky, and smart.

The only area where I hadn't really put in the effort to be successful was in my private life. Family I kept close. Friendships I cultivated. But focusing on one special lady and giving her all I had? This was the first time I was with someone who even inspired those kinds of thoughts.

As expected, the physical aspect of my relationship with Katrina was enthusiastic, energetic, and intoxicating. Put plainly, we were combustible in bed. Physically compatible in every way. Sexually, we brought out the best and wildest in each other. Katrina had a deep pool of stored-up fantasies from the simple to the seriously sexy and I had both the desire and innate ability to bring those fantasies to life. It was chemical synergy.

The surprising thing was the way we seamlessly integrated into the other areas of each other's lives as if we'd always been there. When we got back from Vegas two weeks ago, we swung by her place, picked up some of her stuff from her condo, and she'd been at my house ever since. No discussion, no drama.

I bought the large, remodeled Tudor a few years back, hoping to fill it with a family someday. I felt a jolt when Katrina walked in my door and set her bags down. She instantly belonged. Clearly, I'd underestimated just how much I wanted someone—her—there. It was like finding the last piece to a puzzle. She waltzed in and took in the open-concept first floor with its mixture of dark antiques, light hardwoods, traditional furnishings, and muted walls, and nodded.

"I like it. The blues and greens are little too Carter Parks corporate, but I can work with it. Bring in a stronger shade of that ocean color here, maybe wine-colored accents over there." She gestured. I wondered if she realized she had started redecorating my home without being asked.

"Carter Parks corporate?" I asked.

"Yes, buttoned up. Grown-up. Smooth. Deceptively easygoing and congenial."

I crossed my arms and raised a brow at her. "As opposed to?"

"My Carter Parks. A little untamed, deep thinker, still with a few rough edges, down for whatever, and doesn't mind cutting a little loose from time to time."

She had been paying attention. I reached out and pulled her to me. "All that, huh?"

"Ya know, so far, so good. For all I know, you could have a dungeon with whips and chains in the basement," she teased.

I leaned down and brushed my lips against hers. "You would love that, wouldn't you?"

"Don't start. We have things to do today that require us to be clothed." She pushed away from me and backed up a step or two.

"I could work around that." I crooked a finger.

"I'll just bet you could." She shook her head and narrowed her eyes. "You don't really have some sort of bondage room, do you?"

"No. But I can scare up a thing or two to get your freak flag flying," I promised and took a step toward her.

"Carter!" she shrieked and whirled away running.

"Bedrooms are upstairs," I called out, giving her a head start before I took off after her.

Don't get me wrong: In the two weeks we'd been living together it wasn't all slap, tickle, and giggles. Katrina and I were two strong personalities, so we bickered and we battled. We were two people who were used to getting our own way. Neither of us liked to concede a point, but at the end of the day we either agreed to disagree or deferred and moved on.

Katrina was a high maintenance woman and I was a hands-on kind of guy. If the relationship was to move forward, I had to steer us there. That sort of relationship upkeep required dedicated time and attention. Not to mention patience. And sometimes my patience ran short. I knew Katrina was worth it in the end. Getting there was going to take the best I had to give.

I stood at my office window near the Galleria in Dallas and watched the noonday traffic on the Tollway. I was considering calling Katrina to see if she had time for lunch when the intercom buzzed on my desk phone.

"Mr. Parks, your brother is on line two and your grandfather is on his way up."

"Thanks, Shawn. Are you ever going to call me Carter?" I teased.

"Maybe, one day," he declared before putting the call through.

"What's up, Chris?" I switched the call to speakerphone and leaned back in my office chair.

"I am calling to say thank you!" he chirped enthusiastically.

I frowned down at the phone and waved my grandfather in as he appeared outside my door. Collin Parks marched into my office like the former military man he was. Back straight, salt-and-pepper hair trimmed low, looking fit in a pair of khakis and a polo shirt with a lightweight jacket over the top. I pointed at the phone and mouthed,

"Chris." Gramps nodded and sat down in one of the two chairs I had placed in front of the desk. "Thank me for what?"

"Sending your girlfriend and some of her friends out to practice today. They definitely brighten up the sideline." Chris had decided to defer enrollment to business school and pursue football instead. He signed with Dallas and was attending minicamp in the facility across town. He was renting an apartment in Las Colinas and I enjoyed seeing him regularly.

"Katrina is out there?" I realized I had no idea what her schedule was today.

"Oh, yeah. We are definitely TeamKat around here."

"Doing what?"

"She and some of the models she knows brought lunch out for the team and staff. They are also wearing some league gear that's been designed for women."

I knew BellaRich had turned in a bid to create clothing for the NFL for Women line but I didn't realize it came through. "Oh, yeah? What's for lunch?"

"Mexican. Turn on NFL Network; your girl is doing you proud."

"I hope you are spending as much time working as you are looking at models," Gramps cautioned his youngest grandson.

"Of course, Gramps. You know how I do," Chris said.

"Yeah boy, I do. That's why I'm reminding you of what you're there for."

"Yes, sir. Um . . . later Carter." Chris hung up.

I picked up the remote and aimed it at the TV hanging on the far side of the room. When it powered on, I punched in the channel number for the NFL Network. They were showing a commercial.

"What brings you down, Gramps?"

He crossed his arms. "We gotta do the speech over at the First Chance Foundation."

Gramps ran two of my charitable foundations. One worked with businesses across Louisiana and Texas to provide jobs and scholarships to young teens who may not have the opportunity otherwise. We also offered some tutoring and counseling to the kids. I'd named it the Carter First Chance Foundation. The other worked to reintegrate returning vets into the workplace. We also offered advanced training and counseling for the vets as well. That one we named the Carter Second Chance Foundation. "What's up?"

"We've got a couple of knuckleheads in there talking mess. Stuff like they don't need to worry about their grades because they're going pro." In order to participate in the First Chance programs, we held all the kids to a grade-point average. If they dropped below the average two grade periods in a row, we had them leave the program. Education was stressed as a cornerstone for advancement.

Every year we had a few kids come through with so much real athletic talent they thought that was going to be enough to see them through. They didn't think about what might happen if they didn't make it or got hurt. Those were the ones I worried about the most. "Okay, I'll come out after-hours in a week and bring some of the fellas with me. We'll serve a dinner and get the real story told." I had a few former players who came out with me and we did our own version of Scared Straight.

"Bring your shiny new girlfriend with you, she'll make an impression," Gramps joked and pointed at the screen. "Ooo-wee boy, she is looking fancy."

Sure enough, there was my shiny new girlfriend looking fancy in a sparkly tank top and tight hot pants with sky-high heels, smiling widely into the camera. I turned up the volume.

"Miss Montgomery, you've been in the news a lot lately. In light of some of your recent troubles, do you think it's a good idea for the NFL to partner with your company to design sexy clothing?"

Katrina smiled even wider. "First of all, I don't have recent troubles. I have an ex-boyfriend who plays dirty, which reflects poorly on him, not me. Secondly, what is wrong with sexy clothing as long as it's well made and flattering?"

"You have to know that your ex is going to say that you slept with someone to get this contract. Are you sleeping with someone affiliated with the NFL?"

Gramps and I exchanged a look. A mischievous grin crossed Katrina's face and her eyes twinkled. She tossed her hair over her shoulder in a gesture I was familiar with. "Uh-oh, this means trouble," I muttered.

She leaned in closer to the interviewer. "Actually, Mark, I am."

Mark's mouth fell open and the other reporters standing around scrambled to get closer as they sensed a story brewing. "Um, I beg your pardon? You are admitting to sleeping with an NFL official?"

She shook her head. "That is not what I said."

"What are you saying?"

"Mark, I don't know why it's any of your business, but I am exclusively enjoying the favors of Carter Parks, retired NFL player and current real estate mogul. He has nothing to do with sexy clothes unless you count the fact that he loves taking them off me. And I don't mind letting him. Hey, babe." She blew a kiss from her glossed-up lips into the camera.

Gramps snickered. "Boy, your business is in the streets."

"Yeah. It is." I couldn't stop my grin from spreading if I tried. I knew I should feel some sort of way about it, but I was kind of proud she claimed me.

"You gonna keep this one, son, or throw her back like the others?"

"C'mon now, I don't do that."

"Sure you do," he scolded me.

"Does that look like a woman who gets thrown anywhere she doesn't want to go?"

"Son, I raised you since you were a puppy. You think I don't know when you're ducking a direct answer?"

"I don't know, Gramps. I'd like it to work out for us, go the distance. I don't know if she's ready for that. Either at all or with me. I don't know."

"You know what? You've fought for and won everything you ever wanted in life. This is no different. You make a plan, you execute, and you win. That's who you are."

I'd never heard my granddad talk to me like this. It was quite a day of revelations. "Well, thanks."

"Don't thank me for telling the truth. Now what's your plan?"

"About that . . . I don't really have one yet."

Gramps got up and sent me a disapproving look. "Get on it. Woman like that doesn't come on the market but once in your lifetime. If she recognizes you for the good man you are, you need to do like that singer says."

"What singer?"

"That hot number from Houston that never wears pants, married to the rapper, sings pretty good."

"Beyoncé?"

He nodded enthusiastically. "That's the one. She says if you like it, then you need to put a ring on it. That's what you need to do, Carter, you put a ring on it."

He'd been watching VH1 again. "All right, Gramps. A ring on it. I'm going to work on that."

The intercom on the office phone buzzed again. "Ms. Montgomery on line two," Shawn announced.

"Tell her I'll be one second." I got up and went around the desk to hug my grandfather.

He slapped me on the back. "I'm going to head out, go to that pretty townhouse you bought for me, and watch your life unfold on *SportsCenter*."

"You're having a little bit too much fun with this, Gramps."

He threw back his head and laughed. "Yes, I am. Gonna get me some great-grandkids before too long. I'd like a girl the first time out if you can manage it."

I was at a loss for words. "You might be getting a little further down the road than Kit-Kat and me. But I'll keep that in mind."

"You do that, son. You do that. Your girl is waiting on line two." He smiled and walked out.

I sat back down and pressed the speakerphone. "Exclusively enjoying my favors, are you?"

Katrina's laugh rang out over the speaker. "You saw that, did you?"

"Indeed I did. You were looking right. I like the new designs."

"I thought you might. Listen, I'm thinking about cutting out of here early."

"You've already had quite a full day."

"Haven't I, though? Maybe you've got some ideas on how to fill in the rest of my day."

"Are you propositioning me, Kitty?"

"Trying my damnedest to get more of those favors of yours. Think you can help me out?"

I opened up my calendar on my laptop. I had two meetings this afternoon. Neither one was crucial. "I can be home in half an hour."

"See you there," Katrina purred.

"Bet." I started looking for my keys.

"Oh—and Carter?"

"Yeah?"

"Hurry." She put so much heated inflection into that one word.

"Already there." I slammed the phone down. "Shawn!" I called out as I stuffed my laptop, tablet, and cell into my messenger bag.

"Yes?" He stood at the door and watched in surprise as I shoved my arms into my jacket and pulled my car keys out of the top drawer.

"I need you to have Irene sit in on my two o'clock meeting today."

"Okay." He jotted a note.

"And I want you to sit in on the four o'clock."

Shawn paused in surprise. "Me?"

"Yep."

"You want me to go to a meeting in your place?" The kid looked terrified.

"Shawn, all you have to do is listen and offer an opinion every now and then. Don't sign anything."

"I wouldn't!"

I clapped him on the shoulder on my way to the elevator. "I know, Shawn. That was a joke. I have the utmost faith in you."

"Is something wrong?" he asked.

"No, why do you ask?" I pressed the down button and wondered what Katrina had on under those tight pants that she didn't have a visible panty line. I pressed the button again. She had told me to hurry. I did not plan to disappoint.

"I don't think I've ever seen you leave the office early," he said in confusion.

"Well then it's high time, don't you think?" I flashed him a grin and stepped onto the elevator.

He put his hand in the door as it was about to close. "If something comes up, can I call you?"

I thought about it for a second and then shook my head. "No. I'll see you in the morning." The door closed on his stunned face. I jingled my keys in my hand, watching the descending numbers. Getting a life felt pretty damn good.

16

It's time to pull out the big guns

Katrina—Tuesday, June 22—8:50 a.m.

"**K**atrina, one second," Danila requested as I swept past her office on the way to mine at BellaRich. The offices were near the fashion district and took up two floors of a converted manufacturing flat. Downstairs were our sales and display offices. This floor was designed like an open loft, with a wall of windows across the back wall that housed our conference rooms, larger offices to the right, and cubicles to the left. We'd recently updated the break room and made it into a small, full-service kitchen, break room, and lounge. I waved to a few people hovering near the coffee machines as I neared.

I pretended that I didn't hear Danila calling me.

"We have a small problem," she announced, clearly expecting me to pop in there.

"I'm not trying to hear it!" I tossed over my shoulder, lengthened my stride, and kept moving down the hallway. I was in a happy place and planning to stay that way. My hot new boyfriend had me feeling good, our NFL designs were sold out, and there had been no more Kevin drama. Life. Was. Good.

We had filed suit against Kevin for defamation of character and we demanded that any other accusers either show proof or retract their statements. The only thing we hadn't been able to do was prove that Kevin planted cameras in my condo or determine if he was acting alone. I was content to ride out the last of the snide comments and questions to make the whole thing go away. The other night, I'd run into some people who I'd thought were friends of mine, but they were downright nasty and a little too thrilled that some dirt had been thrown in my direction.

I considered it a wake-up call. Not everybody who you are friendly with is necessarily your friend. This whole experience with Kevin let me know that for too long I'd let what other people thought of me define me. I also realized that there were very few people in the world who truly knew me. My family, my sisters-in-law, Yazlyn, and Carter. They knew the real Audelia Katrina. They'd seen me at my best and my worst and they were okay with me either way. So if Kevin being a complete dick meant that I was able to weed through fake friends to figure who was genuine, it was a small enough price to pay. So, yes, life was good and I was aiming to keep it that way.

"Katrina!" she called out again, leaping out of her chair to catch up with me. I smiled at Tara, the summer intern who was assisting me while my regular admin was on maternity leave. I pushed open the door to my corner office and set my laptop case down on my glass-top desk. I walked over to the small Keurig on the credenza and programmed my second cup of coffee for the day. Living with Carter had many, many privileges, but sleeping in was not one of them. Not that I was complaining. He had the most delicious ways of keeping me awake at night and waking me up in the morning. I languidly stirred creamer into my cup and reminisced over the amazing way he'd woken me up this morning. It involved an ingenious use of cherries and scarves and napkin rings.

Danila came running in behind me. I whirled around and flounced down into my chair with a sigh. "Fine. What's today's drama?"

"Just a second, Beau and Belle are coming."

"Aw hell." I kicked my feet up on the desk.

"Exactly." She sat down at the small round table in the corner and flipped the cover open on her iPad.

I heard Belle and Beau coming down the hallway.

"Delaney Mirabella Montgomery, that is not what I said." Beau's heated voice rose beyond polite levels. "All I said is that you might have mentioned that twins run in your family before we decided to scale bareback mountain."

"Oh jeez," I muttered, wondering not for the

first time if working this closely with family was such a good idea.

"And I said that not only have you met my twin sisters, it was your damned idea to throw both caution and condoms to the wind. Literally," she snapped back and pushed past him into my office. She gave me a kiss on the cheek, took a sip of my coffee, and sat down on my sofa with her arms and legs crossed. Beau stood in the doorway, looking slightly ill.

"Good morning, family!" I trilled with a wide smile. "Are we going to be designing a line of baby clothes?"

Beau blanched. "We don't wanna talk about it."

"Then perhaps you shouldn't have been shouting in the middle of the workplace about scaling bareback mountain," I suggested.

"Tacky ass." Belle shot him a look.

I glanced back and forth between the two of them. This was not the first time I was stuck in between the two of them and their flare-ups. It didn't bother me. When two people were passionate about each other, it spilled over into a lot of different areas. Poor Danila, who was new to this, shifted uncomfortably in her seat, clearly wondering what side she was supposed to be on. "Newlyweds, chill. You both want kids. Whether it's two now or one later, you'll be great parents. Now, let's allow Danila to break the bad news. You're freaking her out."

Beau went to sit next to his wife and slid his arm around her. He kissed her on the forehead. "Sorry, babe. Go ahead, Danila—what is it now?"

"Renee Nightingale."

We all groaned. "What about her?" Belle asked with a frown.

"In addition to her public relations firm, she contributes to an online magazine about beauty and fashion."

"Okay . . ." I prompted.

"Her article from last night is being picked up by the major media outlets."

"Danila, you don't have to ease us into it. Just speak it plain," Beau coaxed her.

"Okay, in the article she talks about how the Montgomerys are sexual predators."

"*What?*" Belle shrieked.

"She said Roman corrupted Jewel, Beau seduced and discarded her, and Katrina only got and kept the Royal Mahogany campaigns because she was sleeping with the CEO."

"Oh, for Christ's sake," Beau cursed.

"The bad thing is, she does have people that corroborate her relationship with Beau. She says he sponged off of her until he got what he wanted and then moved on. Also, the CEO of Royal Mahogany is going through a divorce. His wife is claiming infidelity, but the other person wasn't named."

"Madison Archeneaux is sixty years old. I mean, seriously? Renee tied together a bunch of unrelated speculative half-truths and called it fact," I complained.

"Of course it is, but when you put it all together, there's enough smoke that it looks pretty flammable."

"That vindictive bitch," Belle ground out.

I punched on my speakerphone and hit speed-dial eight. Before he could say anything I told him, "You're on speaker."

"Hey Kitty," Carter answered.

"C—it's bad," I warned.

"Okay." He reacted calmly.

I ran down the latest for him. He was silent for a minute.

"Okay. Is there anything else?" He waited.

"Well, Belle might be pregnant," I volunteered to lighten the mood.

"I have no idea what to do with that right now," Carter said in confusion.

"Neither do I, bro. Neither do I," Beau spoke up.

Exhaling heavily, Carter announced, "Here's what we're going to do. We've played nice and we've tried to do this politely, but it's time to shut all of this down and pull out the big guns."

"We have big guns?" I asked curiously.

"We do. Beau, call Roman and meet me at Granddad's spot. Ladies, we got this." Beau got up, pulled his cell out of his pocket, and headed for the door without a backward glance. Belle, Danila, and I exchanged astounded glances. What the hell?

"I beg your pardon?" My voice went up incredulously.

"Yeah, um—what just happened here?" Belle queried with a lift of her brow.

"Ladies," Carter explained, "I'm not being a chauvinist. I promise I'm not. This just makes sense. BellaRich is your company. Your names are on the masthead. You need plausible deniability. The less you know about how we're about to fix this, the better."

"It's legal though, right? You all aren't going to go all wannabe GI Joe–black ops, right?" Belle asked nervously.

Carter laughed. "You shouldn't need bail money."

I didn't know about this. I was the target here and there was no way I was good with sitting on my hands daintily while the big, strong men rode in to save the day. "I don't think I'm okay with this. I'm used to fixing my own messes. If something needs doing, just tell me what you think I should do and I'll handle it for myself," I argued.

"Not this time, Kit-Kat."

"Carter . . ." I was deciding how much of a protest I wanted to make when he cut me off.

"Audelia Katrina," he said sternly in a voice he generally reserved for our private time. "I said I got this. *I. Got. This.*"

Belle and Danila froze and waited for my reaction. Everything I'd worked for—my family name, my future in this business—it was all on the line. I was supposed to put the fate of everything I was into Carter's hands? I rocked back in my chair and thought about it. This was it. Make or break. Trust or not trust. Cut or run. Forward or back. Concede or fight.

"K," he snapped, waiting for my response.

I looked over at Belle and a smile spread across

her face. She leaned back and put her feet up on the coffee table, crossing her fingers together and resting them on her stomach. Her whole expression asked, *What are you going to do about this?* I glanced at Danila, who cleared her throat, covered her growing grin with her hand, and tipped on out the office door.

Like it or not, he could handle it. He had a point: I didn't have to be in. It was probably best if I wasn't. I closed my eyes with a sigh. "Fine."

"Fine?" he repeated.

"Fine. You can handle it," I conceded grudgingly.

"That's so kind of you to allow me to do so," he bit out. "We'll discuss this at home later. You can bet on that." The call dropped abruptly.

He was pissed. "Oh, damn."

"Girlie, you in trouble," Belle said.

"Don't I know it." I kept putting the wrong foot forward where this man was concerned.

"Sugar, when a man like Carter Parks says he got you? Let him have you, okay?"

"C'mon, Belle." I tried to get her to see my point of view. "You know how it is. Before you had Beau, weren't you used to handling things for yourself? Would you be okay with some random guy stepping in and taking over?"

"I don't miss my days before Beau." She looked at me in confusion. "And what are you doing calling Carter Parks some random guy? Even if you haven't all but moved in with him, he's Beau's best friend and he's been a good friend to you for years."

I sighed again. "I know. I'm just . . . stuff is moving too fast, too many things going on."

She continued to glower at me and I felt about two feet tall.

"I was so happy this morning. I thought we'd turned the corner on all of this scandalous crap. I was feeling optimistic and just generally . . . good. I felt good. Carter and I had this incredible morning," I reminisced.

"Do tell?" She leaned forward.

I flushed. "Oh my God, he took these scarves and . . ." I paused. "You know what? Never mind. I'm going to have to keep some things private."

"Out of respect for Carter?" She quirked a brow.

I nodded. "Out of respect for Carter and our relationship." It didn't feel right sharing every intimate detail. What Carter and I did together was our business and no one else's.

"See what you did right there?"

She lost me. "What did I do?"

"Just then, you put the sanctity of your relationship with Carter over some hot gossip between girls. You and I have shared plenty of girl talk over the years."

"Yeah, until you started doing my brother. Took all the fun out of it."

She smirked. "For you, maybe. My point is, what you and Carter have is special. Now before I continue lecturing you on the error of your ways, I'm going to say one more inappropriate thing."

"Go ahead." She was going to say it anyway.

"That voice Carter used when he said your full name? Sugar! Panty-melting." Belle fanned her face with her hands.

"I know, right? He's so damn easygoing most of the time, but when he uses that voice and gets all strong . . . Woo. It just sends me." I absolutely loved it when Carter went all alpha male, though I never would've known what a turn-on that was if he hadn't done it so well. Both in and out of bed, the fact that he was so strong gave me the freedom to just be. It was nice not to have to take the wheel and steer. In thinking that, I just realized why I gave them such a hard time about fixing this for me. I guess I was a little conflicted.

When you are used to driving, sometimes it's hard to sit in the passenger seat. And doubly hard not to navigate while sitting there. But for a man the likes of Carter, I'd figure it out. He was not a man who liked to be doubted.

"Um. Um. Um. Carter Parks, who woulda thunk it?"

My cell phone beeped and I looked down at the display. I waved Belle over to the desk and answered. "Hey, Jewel."

"Hey. What's this macho bullshit the boys are pulling?"

"I don't know. Something about shutting it down and big guns," I told her.

"Well, Roman rode outta here like he was the sheriff rounding up a posse. Please tell me Carter's the one with the plan, not Beau."

"Hey!" Belle exclaimed.

"Oh, sorry, Belle. I love Beau like a brother,

but you know your husband. He can be big on ideas and a little lax on execution." Beau had stayed with Jewel and Roman for a few months back in his oat-sowing days, so Jewel had firsthand knowledge of some of his less stellar behavior.

"An-y-way . . ." I interjected. "The fellas are having some sort of testosterone tribunal."

"And we're supposed to sit by the hearth knitting booties or something while they do whatever damn fool thing they are going to do?"

"You gotta better idea?" Belle asked.

"Why does everyone keep forgetting that Renee was my friend first? I've known her since she had good sense. All of this mess with Kevin? I guarantee this was all Renee from the beginning. This was her plot from jump to watch us squirm. I'm over it. I got other things to do with my life than wonder when Renee will rear her head again. Veronica and I will be there in thirty minutes. Let the guys do what they do, we'll handle a few things for ourselves."

"Now that's what I'm talking about." I high-fived Belle.

"One other thing?" Jewel added.

"Yeah?" Belle asked.

"Can you order me in a veggie omelet with a side of bacon. And some hash browns. And toast? Oooh, and grits with cheese."

I laughed. "What are you, eating for two?"

"Well, actually . . ." Jewel hinted.

"Oh my God, congratulations!" Belle squealed.

I narrowed my eyes at her. "If you two heffas

end up pregnant at the same time, I swear to God . . ."

"Wait, *what?*" Jewel shrieked.

"I'm not pregnant. At least not that I know of. I could be, but it was only once and no matter what Beau says, he's not that damned potent," Belle answered. "But I am starving, so if we're trying to make brunch happen, I'm all in."

"We'll see you soon," I told Jewel and disconnected. "Tara, got a minute?" I called out to my intern.

She hustled in. "Yes, ma'am?"

Both Belle and I winced. "No more *ma'am*s, okay? I can be Katrina. Anyway, have you eaten?"

"I had a granola bar," she admitted sheepishly.

I shook my head. "Sweetie, that's not breakfast. See if the chef will come early and do a brunch for the office. If she can't, order in. Omelets, waffles, breakfast tacos, a variety of stuff."

"This place rocks," Tara said as she walked out.

"You know what?" I told Belle, "This place *does* rock. All those years prancing around in other people's clothes on other people's runways, taking midnight classes online and hopping planes and eating two sticks of celery for dinner? We did that so we could run our own house. This house. *Our* house. No one gets to ruin that for us. We built this. And it does rock."

"And once we take care of Ms. Renee? It's going to continue to rock, sugar." Belle and I exchanged determined nods and the fist bump for good measure.

"She musta forgot who we are," I said.

Belle sat on the edge of my desk, crossed her legs, and swung her foot back and forth. "She let the pretty fool her. People do that. They see all the pretty and think we'll put up with shit."

"She gonna have to learn the hard way," I muttered.

"Damn right."

17

I've been three steps ahead of you since you were knee-high to a curb

Carter—Tuesday, June 22—9:38 a.m.

Gramps's townhouse was in North Dallas in an area called North Park. The house was small enough for him to take care of, but big enough for him to have a small yard with a vegetable garden out back that he tended to like it was a favored child. In addition to helping out with the foundations, Gramps attended church, played bid whist, and got together with a group of retired vets at least once a week.

When I called and told him what we needed, he snapped to attention like he was back in uniform. I climbed out of my car just as Roman pulled up.

"Parks," He greeted me.

"Montgomery." I nodded and we headed up the sidewalk.

"This woman has been a thorn in my side from day one," Roman said.

"Renee has?"

"Man, listen, I get less drama from my ex-wife than this chick."

Roman had a son from his ex-wife, Jacquenetta. I heard she was some piece of work, so if he thought Renee was a bigger pain in the ass? Well, that was really saying something. "How is the little man?"

"Chase is almost ten now. He's gonna be a big brother before too long." Roman grinned proudly.

"Congratulations. Did you and Beau plan this?" I knocked twice and walked in the front door.

"Plan what?" Beau asked, reaching out a hand to fist bump first Roman and then me.

I looked from one brother to the other. "Are both of your wives pregnant at the same time?"

They exchanged amused glances. "Jewel is."

Beau clasped his younger in a hug that lifted him off the ground. "*Mon frère, impressionnant!* Belle might be." Roman slapped him on the back and they grinned at each other. I had to admit I felt a little twinge of envy. Katrina and I weren't there yet. Hell, we were barely at the point where she let me take a meeting on her behalf.

Gramps clapped me on the shoulder. "You're falling behind, son, you need to catch up."

"Whoa!" Roman put his hands up with a grimace.

"Since any catching up he would do would be

with my sister, I'm going to request that we change the subject." Beau looked pained.

"All right, then." Gramps waved an older man into the room. "Come on out, Calvin. This is retired Captain Jonas Calvin. After we served together, he went to work for an agency that shall not be named. I had him look into a few things on our behalf."

Jonas Calvin looked every inch the serviceman-turned-not-allowed-to-say guy. He was tall, lean, and fit, with short-cropped hair. He wore gray pants and a white polo shirt with a navy jacket over it. He was light-skinned, with dark brown eyes that missed nothing. He took a moment to look each of us up and down. None of us flinched under his regard. Apparently satisfied by what he'd seen, he nodded and stepped further into the room. He had a manila folder in his hand. "Gentlemen, angry people who bear grudges are sloppy and sloppy people get caught."

He had our immediate and undivided attention from that moment on. "If you add in the fact that most people are not as smart by half as they think they are, that opens up a lot of doors for us." He opened up his folder. "Kevin Eriq Delancey, thirty-five years of age, from South Carolina. Managed a B-plus average in high school, tanked his SATs, so his daddy bought his way into Morehouse. Though it's been kept mostly secret, he did not graduate from there. He left midway through his junior year under a cloud of suspicion involving him possibly paying a young woman to take tests for him in exchange for his unfulfilled promise to marry her. There is additional controversy that Mr. Delancey did not come up with the idea for

Serengeti, but stole the concept from his room-mate, a Lawrence Payne, who kicked up some dust when the Web site first gained prominence and then was never heard from again. Deeper digging reveals that around that time, a Mrs. Laurencia Payne received an 'inheritance' from an unknown relative allowing her and her family to relocate permanently to Costa Rica, where they currently run a beachfront bed-and-breakfast."

Beau whistled and rubbed his hands together while Roman and I sat down on the sofa. This guy was good. He was better than good. We'd had people digging into Kevin's past and hadn't gotten this deep.

The captain continued. "While all of that is interesting, we're just getting close to what you really need. The cameras that were wired up in Ms. Montgomery's domicile were transmitted to a cloud. The cloud is really just data that jumps from remote server to remote server so that it doesn't sit in one place. That's hard to track unless we could tie this to terrorism, which would justify a higher-level trace. However, someone on the other end had to pull that data, in this case the video feed, down out of the cloud. The minute that happens, there is an IP address. As you know, an IP address is tied to an actual computer, router, server, or Wi-Fi system. At some point, the video file piggy-backed on Katrina's home Wi-Fi to transmit. Once we figured that out, it was like having a GPS record of every virtual location where that file landed. Who touched it, who changed it, and who it got sent to. The last thing we have yet to do is to definitively tie your friend Delancey to this file. All we have to do is show that one of these files ever interacted with an IP address he has access to and we've got something."

"There's no way you got all of this in the half hour since Gramps called you," I said in awe.

"Son, I've been three steps ahead of you since you were knee-high to a curb and I don't aim to slow down anytime soon," my grandfather said.

"Collin has had me working on this since the day you called from Barbados, Carter." Jonas nodded.

"Well, when you say *big guns* . . . you mean big guns," Roman said.

"So what's next?" Beau asked.

"We've got someone who can tie one of Delancey's guys to the fake sex tape. So I'm going to reach out and see if we can incentivize that guy to flip. That's the rundown of what we have on the Katrina side of things. We went ahead and took the information your investigator provided and went a little deeper into Serengeti's business practices and books. I'm going to have to bring in a forensic accountant because it got real messy, real quick, in there. My goal is to get as many criminal charges thrown at this guy as we can. He's not a good guy."

"What about this Renee chick? Anything on her?" I asked.

"Not too much. I mean, she's a scandal; I wouldn't want my sons to date her, but I can't find anything other than routine messiness so far," Captain Calvin shared.

"She needs to go down. She's upgraded from

nuisance to pain in the ass to an actual problem," Beau said.

Gramps looked at us and nodded seriously. "Well, we can disappear the girl, but that's gonna cost you some. We don't wipe people off the planet for free anymore."

Roman's eyes went wide, my jaw dropped, and Beau froze, scared to take a breath.

Jonas and Gramps stood stone-faced until they exchanged glances and cut up laughing. "Woo, you should see your faces!" Gramps slapped his thigh.

Captain Calvin shook his head. "Boys, we're joking."

"Mostly," Gramps said.

The three of us chuckled nervously. "All right, then. You got us," I said warily. "What else do you need from us to keep going?"

"Not a thing, I'm all set. Let's get together again next week and I'll give you an update. Only in person, nothing online," Jonas declared.

"Sir, we can't allow you to do this for free," Roman said.

"You boys will all be getting an envelope so you can pledge a little something to the Foundation, don't you even worry about that," Gramps announced before shooting me a look. "And you, son? You get to work on my great-grandchild."

I exchanged uncomfortable glances with Beau and Roman and we rose as one to depart.

18

And why we gotta be nefarious heffas?

Katrina—Saturday, June 26—2:15 p.m.

"Oh my God, will you please hurry up! The smell of this potpourri she has everywhere is making me nauseous," Jewel whined while I typed fast and furiously onto the laptop.

"Everything makes you nauseous! I thought it was supposed to be morning sickness; it's well after noon." I snapped back at my sister-in-law as I entered in the information as quickly and accurately as I could.

"Like my body gives a damn." Jewel breathed slowly and deeply, speaking between the inhalations. "Just wait until you get pregnant. I'm going to torture you every second of every day."

"Don't hold your breath. Wait, the way you

were heaving earlier? Do hold your breath and don't stand directly behind me. But I have to agree, she went way too heavily on the scent infusers in here. Smells like a place where all the floral life in the hemisphere came to die. Like a botanical garden threw up in here." Jewel gagged and I chuckled evilly.

She smacked the side of my head. "Your day will come."

"Look here *Bijou*, it's your fault we've had to resort to this foolishness, so suck it up another few minutes."

"How do you figure?"

"Renee was your friend to begin with. You foisted her on the rest of us."

"Well, if you're going to be all technical about it . . ." Her cell beeped. "Oh shit, they finished early. Veronica is going to try and stall, but we can assume we don't have a lot of time left."

"I'm almost done. Text Belle and tell her keep her eyes peeled." I keyed in the last command and hit enter.

"Yeah, yeah. You do know what you're doing, don't you?" she asked for the hundredth time.

"I can follow simple directions. If you quit talking I can finish up and we can go," I scolded.

"My God, you Montgomerys are high maintenance!"

"You're married to one, raising another, and carrying a third—you are stuck with us for life!" I cackled and waited for confirmation that the program had finished running. Letters and numbers flashed by on the monitor and finally a double beep sounded. A message flashed up on the screen. "It says *program complete.* We are out of here." I erased the history, powered down the computer, closed the lid, and got up from the chair.

Jewel and I tipped around Renee's loft, making sure everything was as we found it. Yes, I said *Renee's loft.* After doing some investigative work of our own, we discovered that Renee lived in a building managed by Parks Properties. One covert call to Shawn and we not only had the code to get in downstairs, but the key to open the front door. When he discovered what we were breaking and entering for, he also provided us the software and some instructions. The software he gave us allowed us to clone Renee's computer and access it from a remote location without her knowing. I was just going to go in and look around, but having the time and leisure to search without worrying about getting caught was even better.

Veronica took one for the team and invited Renee out to lunch. Seeing as they hadn't really spoken since Veronica ended up married to Renee's ex-fiancé, it was a calculated risk, but we assumed that Renee wouldn't pass up the chance for some drama. We were right. So while Veronica had Renee occupied, Belle was downstairs in the parking garage acting as lookout and Jewel and I were in the loft loading the software.

Okay, so we may have gone overboard. We all dressed in black jeans and black T-shirts with black sneakers. Hair pulled back into ponytails, no makeup. What can I say? We'd watched too many crime dramas growing up. We got caught up in the moment. How many times in our life were we going to attempt something like this? Never again, we hoped.

But Renee had gone too far and we decided if she was going to just out-and-out lie, there was really no reason for us to play fair and square. The guys said they came up with a way to expose Kevin for the deceitful fraud that he was, but they weren't sure what to do about Renee. Well, we knew what to do about Renee. Girl power, baby. All we had to do was think like she thought, wait for her to overplay her hand, and then we would have her.

"We're clear," Jewel whispered over her shoulder and we exited the unit. I sent a quick text to Belle telling her we were coming out. The elevator *dinged* as we neared it and instead of chancing anyone seeing us, we dove for the stairs. Four flights down later, Jewel looked a little green around the gills.

"Uh-oh. Vertigo? Your pregnant mind playing tricks on you?" I asked as she swayed for a second on the landing. We had one more floor to go.

"Shut it before I spew that lovely chicken salad we had for lunch on your two-hundred-dollar jeans, supermodel."

"You know," I observed drolly, "pregnancy has made you snarky."

She whirled toward me and started laughing. "It really has. I about took your brother's head off this morning for eating the last croissant."

"Well, that's slap-worthy. He knows better," I commiserated.

"Right?" She giggled and took a deep breath. "I swear I can still smell those crushed flowers. Let's get out of here."

We reached the garage level and I stuck my head out to make sure we were good. We'd borrowed Carter's black four-door Benz and before I could even step out fully, it backed to the door. I snorted in amusement and waved Jewel out with me. We climbed into the car and Belle drove out of the lot sedately, turned the corner, and then floored it.

"Hold up, killa—it's not like five-o is hot on our tail," I teased Belle.

She looked left and then right before getting on the highway and accelerating again. "I didn't know, sugar. You two might have been coming out hot."

"Coming out hot?" Jewel cackled. "What is this? *Set It Off*?"

"Don't start with me, Jewellen! I'm an accessory. You two nefarious heffas may be easy tiptoeing along a life of crime, but I ain't tryna do no jail."

I crowed with laughter. "Did your bougie behind just say you *ain't tryna do no jail*?" I turned my head to see Jewel rolling around on the backseat in her amusement. "Was there a *Law and Order* marathon on last night?"

Belle sniffed. "*Criminal Minds*, if you must know."

"Umm . . . They hunt serial killers," I informed her. "We ran a software program. Is my brother not occupying enough of your time at night?"

"Crime is crime," she responded.

"Slow down, Jesse James. Speeding is a crime too," Jewel reminded her.

"And why we gotta be nefarious heffas?" I asked.

Belle finally slowed down to under seventy-five miles an hour. "Y'all took to that creepin' and sneakin' like ducks to water, that's all I'm saying."

I tittered. "Look here, debutante. It's not like we're going to take up bank robbery. We didn't even jack anything."

Jewel howled. "Ha! Jack anything! Stop, you're going to make me pee!"

My cell phone rang. I paired it with the in-car system so we could all hear. "Hey Roni."

"Hey ladies, how'd it go?" Veronica's melodious voice filled the car.

"Well, Belle thinks we're on a slippery slope to knocking over liquor stores on Friday nights. Beyond that, we were in and out no problem," I told her.

"Good, 'cuz that bitch is up to something."

"Whoa—why she gotta be bitchy?" Roni was the most mild-mannered of all of us, so her name-calling came as a surprise.

"Listen, after the lunch I just lived through—we need to be happy y'all aren't posting my bail for first-degree murder."

Belle slid me a look. "See? Nefarious."

"That bad?" Jewel asked, sitting up and wiping the tears of mirth from her eyes.

"She stood up in the middle of the restaurant and called me a treacherous Jezebel backstabber. Dramatic much?"

"Wait, what?" Jewel asked. "She cheated on Greg by sleeping with Beau."

"Hey!" Belle interjected.

"Sorry, Belle. Ancient history." Jewel shrugged. "Anyway, she cheats, gets caught, Greg bails, and you're the Jezebel?"

"She said that I was 'lying in wait' for 'her man' and the minute she slipped up, I 'swooped in' and stole him," Roni said.

"Oh no, she didn't. She is some piece of work." I shook my head. "Can I ask y'all: Was she ever a nice person?"

"The funny thing is," Jewel explained, "she actually was. She had a rough childhood that left her with some insecurities, but overall she was cool. At one point, she was my best friend in the world. And then one day she started getting very concerned about status and status symbols and having the right man, right ring, right car, right house, and right job. She got wrapped up in these plans, but then when she had what she thought she wanted, she wanted an upgrade."

"Oh, one of those never-satisfied types," Belle drawled knowingly.

"Exactly!" Veronica exclaimed.

"But really, and again—no shade to Beau, but it was about the time he entered the picture that she rode off the rails. She wanted him and Greg and after she lost them both, she became a different person. Now the older she gets and she's no closer to having what she thinks she should have accumulated by now, it just gets worse," Jewel continued.

"And somehow this is our fault?" I wondered.

Jewel answered. "She's never going to point

the finger at herself; she doesn't have that kind of mirror. But this is a new level of low, even for her."

"Yeah, she was acting kinda shifty underneath all the mud-slinging. Like she had some secret she couldn't wait to share," Veronica said.

"Now, see, Belle—that's nefarious," Jewel pointed out.

Belle agreed. "Point taken."

"Just tell me we're going to wipe the smirk off Renee's face," Veronica pleaded.

"And mop the floor with it if all my prayers and dreams come true," I added. The display indicated a call coming in from Carter. "Uh-oh. Everyone quiet! Veronica, we'll talk to you later."

I clicked over. "Hey Carter."

"Kit-Kat—I appear to be missing one car and one girlfriend."

"You have another car," I informed him needlessly.

"But only one girlfriend. Whatcha up to?"

"Just running some errands," I hedged.

"Errands, huh?"

"Uh . . . yes?"

"Errands that require you and your homegirls to dress all in black and run around Dallas in my Benz?" We exchanged looks. He was surprisingly well-informed.

"Do you need the car back?" I evaded.

"You and I both know this is not about the car," he snapped.

"I don't have to tell you where I am every moment of the day, Carter Parks. And since when do you care what I wear?" I lobbed that out there to see if that would stick.

"That's what you're coming with?" Carter responded. "Okay, then. Hold on a sec."

I heard some rustling and muted voices.

"Jew-Ro." Roman called Jewellen Rose by her nickname when she was in trouble. "What you out there getting into while carrying my child?"

"Busted," she whispered to us before speaking up. "Nothing, babe. We just had lunch. We're going to drop by Madere's and then head home."

Belle changed lanes to head toward Madere's house.

"Delaney Mirabella Montgomery," Beau's voice rang out. "I know you're in on this, *chère*. Probably driving the getaway car."

"Getaway car?" Belle chuckled. "That's some imagination, darling. A girl slithers into a black outfit and all of sudden she's some sort of—"

"Nefarious criminal?" I supplied, sending her a look. She raised one hand off the steering wheel and sent me a 'talk to the hand' gesture.

Jewel giggled from the backseat.

"*Une momente, 'tite chou*—you had to slither to get into the jeans? How tight are they?" Beau asked.

"How did you know we're in jeans?" I asked.

"Chase saw you all making your escape. He spilled all the tea. You all needed to get in and out of somewhere quickly and hoped you knew how to work the program. What program is that, ladies?" Carter asked.

Belle shook her head at us. I rolled my eyes at her. We had no intention of telling the guys anything until we knew what we had. "To a ten-year-old everything seems cloak-and-dagger. Wasn't

that big of a thing, babe. We're gonna feed Jewellen for the sixteenth time today and then I'll be
home. Your girlfriend and your car will be home
before you know it."

"Um-hmm," Carter murmured. "I'll look forward to that."

"Jewellen, I'll be waiting," Roman said.

"*Moi aussi*, Belle," Beau tacked on.

I clicked the phone off. "Men."

We pulled up in front of Madere and Pops's
place. Madere opened the door and stood there
with her hands on her hips. We climbed out of the
car and she shook her head. "There better be a
good reason why my boys are calling looking for you
and the three of you show up looking like the broke-
down Supremes on a stakeout."

Jewellen and Belle kissed her cheek. I linked
my arm through hers and stepped into the house.
"We're plotting and scheming, Mama. Wanna hear
about it?"

Her eyes lit up. "I thought it might be something like that so I sent your father to Home Depot.
He'll be there for hours. Spill it!"

"I'll tell you how your daughter and Jewel almost made me catch a case."

"*Catch a case?*" I whispered as Belle stuck out
her tongue at me behind my mother's back.

"Madere, did you cook today?" Jewel asked,
heading for the kitchen.

Madere smiled. "First trimester, I already have
the bowls by the stove. Red beans and rice and
shrimp Bienville."

"Now that's what I'm talking about," Belle said.
"I've been starvin' lately."

"Girl, will you take the test already?" Jewel said with a fork hovering over the pot.

Madere slapped her hand. "Belle will take the test when she's good and ready. Jewel, I put out bowls for a reason. Kit-Kat, get the bread out of the oven."

When we were gathered around the table, she said, "Now *mes enfants*, tell me everything!"

19

You could have Parks 2.0 right here

Carter—Friday, July 2—7:03 p.m.

It had been a long week. No new drama, thankfully. We were making progress with our investigations. I still wasn't 100 percent sure what Katrina and the girls had cooked up, but I was letting it go for now. Tonight, we were heading to the foundation headquarters for a talk with the kids and to serve a meal. We were late. It was my fault. When I walked past the closet, she was perched on the bench rubbing some sort of scented cream all over her naked body. She looked and smelled like dessert. Whatever good intentions I had were gone in an instant. I am a man. I had to taste. She was so open to me, it was addictive. All I did was walk over, lay her down, and kneel between those vanilla-scented thighs. Having her come apart against my mouth while calling out my name? It was so damned satisfying; I had to take her up and over once more. In my mind, that was just worth the twenty-minute delay. I left her to get cleaned up and headed downstairs. I stood at the kitchen counter, ignoring my insistent erection begging me to go back upstairs and be an extra thirty minutes late. The flat-front khakis didn't seem like such a good idea with the obvious tent I was pitching. Untucking the T-shirt was not an option and it was way too hot for a jacket.

Katrina swirled downstairs in a bright pink short cotton dress with strappy sandals on her feet and a glow on her face. Her hair was up in a curly ponytail and her lipstick matched the dress. She kissed my check. "You're so much awesome. Let's go, Sexy. We're late and Gramps will give us hell."

"Ain't that the truth?" I readjusted myself and snatched up the keys to the Range Rover. I followed her out to the garage, locked the back door behind us, and pressed the unlock button on the key fob. When I went to move past her to open her door, I felt my belt loosening.

Before I could figure out what she was up to, my pants were unbuttoned, my shirt was pushed up, and my briefs were yanked down. "Katrina, for Christ's sa—" I ground out as she wrapped both hands around my shaft and squeezed. Good lord, that felt good. My penis twitched happily in her hands. "You know we do not have time for this!" I reminded her. She responded by dropping down to her knees, mindless of the garage floor, and peered up at me through her lashes.

"You want me to stop?" she purred, reached out with her tongue, and licked the tip delicately. Short, pointy laps. Again and again, like a cat with a bowl of milk it was determined to get to the bottom of.

"Hell no." I placed one hand against the car door and the other in her hair while I braced my knees. Carefully, I pulled the band out of her hair that was holding it up so it spilled down around her face in curls. "Woman, you are going to be the death of me."

"So you keep saying, C. So you keep saying." With that, she swirled her tongue along the length before nipping me with her teeth from root to tip, up one side and down the other, while pumping slowly with her hand.

I looked down at her beautiful face with those shiny pink lips and the delight she derived from giving me pleasure and groaned out her name: "Katrina." I dug my fingers into her scalp as she took me deeper and deeper. Her hands and her mouth worked in tandem to pull every sensation out of me. I wanted Audelia Katrina Montgomery with a greed that stunned me on a regular day, but right now in this darkened garage with those gold eyes glittering up at me? I was gone. She sped up the tempo and moaned her enjoyment. Jesus, I was not going to last. Discarding all my usual stamina and finesse, I flung my head back and pumped my hips. The climax ripped through me as

I jetted into her mouth. "Oh, heavenly father," I whispered, running my hand through her silky hair.

Carefully, she leaned back and grinned up at me. She licked her lips. "Good to the last drop, C."

A shudder racked my entire body and I concentrated on staying upright. What this woman did to me . . . "Give me two minutes and I'll thank you properly," I rasped, still trying to catch my breath.

She tucked me back into my boxers and pulled up my pants. "I was thanking you for earlier. As much as I'd love to hop aboard and ride that delicious beast, we don't have time for that. Once you get to thanking me and I thank you in return . . ."

"All right, all right." I pulled her to her feet and checked both of us for dust and wrinkles. "But I need a rain check on that beast-riding thing."

"Any time, Mr. Carter. Any damn time." She pressed a soft kiss to my lips and I returned the pressure. We both groaned and pressed closer to each other, her hands snaking around my waist and mine dropping down to her hips. "We are already late," she muttered against my lips and twisted her hips against mine.

"Swear to God, Katrina! Don't move like that right now," I said and then contradicted my own statement by sliding my hands under her thighs and lifting her up against me. Those long, silky legs wrapped around my waist and I backed her up against the car.

"This is ridiculous!" She exhaled. "I can't keep feeling like this about you."

"Oh, yeah? Like what exactly?"

"Hungry, needy, humid."

I snorted. "Humid?"

"Carter, you make me wet just looking at you sometimes."

I rested my forehead against hers. "If you figure out how to stop feeling hungry, needy, humid, tell me. So I can stop feeling hungry, needy, hard."

"It's not just the sex, is it?" She stared into my eyes, looking a little overwhelmed.

"It's not just the sex," I answered truthfully.

"Dammit, we're a fine pair."

"I like to think so." My phone buzzed in my jacket pocket. "You know that's Gramps." I set her on her feet and held open her door. This conversation would have to wait.

"Tell him we hit a traffic jam," she suggested, sliding in and fastening the seat belt.

I walked around the car, climbed in, and started it up. "Last time I did that, he pulled up the traffic cam on his iPad and we were busted." The phone stopped ringing for a second before buzzing urgently again. "I'll tell him we had a problem in the garage. Some wildlife got loose and we had to take care of it."

She clapped a hand over her mouth to stifle the giggles. "What's the wildlife? Me or that beast between your legs?"

I opened the garage door and put the car in reverse. "Woman, call it a beast one more time and we'll never make it out of here."

"I'm sorry, Big Daddy; do I need to be punished for my naughty mouth?" she singsonged in the sexiest voice I'd ever heard as she slicked more pink gloss on her lips.

I slammed on the brakes and swiveled my head to look at her. "You are really asking for it."

"Yeah. I am. But later," she teased and pushed the button on the console to answer the phone. "Hey Gramps, we're on the way."

As luck would have it, there really was some traffic drama on the expressway. The Parks Foundation offices were housed out of a converted community center that the city abandoned over near the Hamilton Park area of North Dallas. The facilities were split down the middle with the kids' facilities on one side and the veterans on the other. Kitchen, gym, and assembly hall in the middle. We weren't two feet in the door when a voice called us out.

"Hey, look who decided to show up!" My brother Chris stepped down the hallway. He had on white linens pants and a navy blue T-shirt that I recognized as one he had "borrowed" from my closet. I had to admit my brother was a taller, more muscular, better-looking version of me. He knew it too. If I wasn't so damn proud of him, I'd have to really dislike his young ass. Moving me out of the way, he swept Katrina up before placing a smacking kiss on her cheek. "Hiya gorgeous! I keep telling you that you're wasting time with last year's version when you could have Parks two-point-oh right here." I raised a brow at the both of them.

"Tempting." Katrina kissed him back and then stepped over and took my hand. "I'm going to work with this one for a little while longer."

"Is that right?" Chris smiled and called out over his shoulder. "Gramps! I owe you a hundred bucks. Looks like she's gonna keep him awhile."

"Boy! Leave your brother alone, quit drooling over his woman, and get out here to round up your teammates before they eat up all the food."

"Gramps, I warned you about showing them where the kitchen was!" He hustled toward the back rooms.

Gramps looked from Katrina's face to mine and then dropped to our clasped hands. He pulled her into a hug of his own. "You two looking mighty happy with yourselves. I can only imagine why you are late. What's done is done. Let's get going."

"Who made it?" I asked him.

"Chris brought two guys with him. And your boys Kendrick and Spaulding made it."

I nodded. "Let's get started then." I walked over. Katrina and I were introduced to Paul Staley and Marcus Goings, two of Chris's teammates. I thanked them for coming and motioned for them to follow me. I headed into the main area of the assembly room with Katrina by my side.

There was a group of about forty boys ranging from age twelve to eighteen, seated around the tables. We had younger kids that came to the center, but the nighttime events were for the older boys. They were already excited to have professional football players in their midst, but the appearance of Katrina in all her short-skirted glory set the place on its ear. Jaws dropped, eyes widened, and murmurs started. They looked like those cartoons where the person's tongue fell out of their mouths and their eyes popped out of their heads. I was used to her being the best thing to look at in any room she entered, but seeing her through the eyes of teenagers was amusing. They'd never seen anything quite like her close up.

"Damn, homie, Mr. Parks got *all* the luck. She is da bomb!" one of the boys said.

Katrina walked over to him with some extra sway to her hips and kissed his cheek. "Thanks, handsome, but you should know—it's not luck. He works hard to hold onto this." She looked over her shoulder and winked at me.

"*Whoa!*" The boys shouted, high-fiving me as I walked past.

I got to the front of the room, where we had a podium and a microphone set up. I stopped to greet Kendrick Morris and Spaulding Hall. Kendrick and I were drafted in the same year and Spaulding had been a first-round draft pick two years later. We'd been friends ever since.

"I see life is still good for Big Sexy." Kendrick jostled me and tilted his head in Katrina's direction.

"I have no complaints," I said honestly. Life was good.

Spaulding shook his head. "Only took you a decade to close the deal."

"Don't hate the player . . . ." I said, smirking, before turning serious. "Ready to drop some knowledge on these kids?"

"Most definitely. Which two are the knuckleheads?"

Two of the older kids had been slacking off on their schoolwork because they were being courted by colleges and assumed that meant they were destined for a life of fame, fortune, and glory. I pointed the two of them out and then stepped to the podium.

"Men, I promise we are going to feed you shortly. Tonight, I brought some special guests to speak to you. You all were chosen for this program because you show extraordinary talent both in academics and athletics. There are one hundred thousand high school seniors playing football this year. Only nine thousand of them will make it to the college level. Out of that nine thousand, only three hundred and ten will be invited to the NFL scouting combine. That is point-two percent, gentlemen."

I could see the impact those numbers had as the boys began to understand their odds and the long road ahead of them.

Chris's teammate Paul stepped up to the mic. "If you are blessed and gifted and hardworking enough to be among that point-two percent, the average shelf life of a professional football player is a little over three years."

More eyes widened as reality started to sink in.

Marcus joined him. "The minimum salary for rookies last year was three hundred and ninety thousand dollars." The boys hooted and whistled. He put his hands up to quiet them down. "That sounds like a lot, right? But now assume that ten percent is going straight to your agent. You need somewhere to live, something to drive, you are required to wear a suit on game day and for travel on most teams, and you haven't even talked about the ladies."

Kendrick stepped up. "CP here got a woman

who has her own bank. She's a rare woman. Ladies will be coming at you with their hands out and their legs open."

Spaulding added, "And you haven't even kicked a little something back to Mama, Pop-Pop, your cousin Ray-Ney, and 'nem. Money evaporates faster than you can make it if you're not careful.

"You haven't played one down of football and most of your first check is gone. Now you are playing catch-up all year. If all you got is this salary for three years and then you're done? You are retired by age twenty-five and then what are you going to do? What's your mama gonna do? Ray-Ney and 'nem got used to eating good on your dime."

The room was silent as the young boys absorbed the harsh truths.

Paul spoke. "My best friend from high school was a better athlete than me. I was a better student, but he was naturally gifted. I worked hard and still was not as good as him. We played college ball together. After junior year, he declared for the draft. Agents were coming out of nowhere offering him advances and houses and jewelry. He took a lot of it because he was supposed to go high in the first round. Two nights before the draft, we were running to catch plane. It was raining and the sidewalk was slick. He fell down a flight of stairs and in a freak accident, shattered his hip. Nobody wanted to take a chance on him. He had six surgeries, but couldn't get the strength back. He's back in school now, trying to finish up his degree, but at twenty-three years of age his football career is over and he's had to declare bankruptcy to get rid of

the debts from all the stuff he bought and borrowed, waiting on that payday."

Spaulding nodded. "You all are way too young
to even remember my professional football career.
It lasted six months. I got knocked out in a play-off
game and suffered permanent nerve damage to
my spine. I was lucky. I can walk, I can talk, and I
am fully functional. I stayed in college my full four
years and got my degree so I had something to fall
back on. I have a computer animation company
that creates sports-simulation games and CGI for
movie special effects. But again, I'm one of the
lucky ones."

Chris came forward. "I've probably been the
luckiest one here. I had both a grandfather who
demanded the best from me and an older brother
to clear the path for me. My road has been easy. All
I've ever had to do is show up and put in the work.
But even with that being said, I understand that in
the long run it's my brain and not all this brawn
you see me working with that's going to take me
the farthest." The boys laughed as Chris flexed his
muscles.

I nudged him out of the way and motioned to
Gramps to start setting out the food. "Education is
absolutely critical for whatever you want to do in
life. But in case you're wondering what it has to do
with football, here are some more statistics for
you: Players with a degree earn between twenty to
thirty percent more than those without one and
their careers last about fifty percent longer. No
one is sure why—probably a combination of fac-
tors like intelligence, determination, concentra-

tion, and discipline. But for whatever reasons, facts are facts. Mo' school equals mo' money."

"Put it on a T-shirt, Sexy!" Kendrick joked. "Mo' school equals mo' money."

Katrina came up from behind me. "Mo' brains is mo' sexy. And mo' money means mo' ladies. I'm just saying." Everybody laughed.

"I hope you all listened tonight." I cautioned. "If you have questions, these guys are here for the rest of the evening. They'll play it straight and tell you what's real. Now, I don't know about you boys, but I smell some fried catfish and there's dirty rice calling my name. Let's eat!"

Gramps nodded in approval as he started dishing up plates. I overheard one of the kids asking Spaulding what kind of classes he took to learn computer animation. This is why I did this. If I had one young man more interested in books than balls, the evening was a win. Not that I was against athletics. Hell, it got me to where I was today, but I wanted the world to be a wide-open place for these kids, where they had choices and options and still saw the sky as the limit.

"You know, seeing you here with these kids and watching your face as you spoke . . ." Katrina murmured in my ear as we headed toward the food . . . "makes me even hotter than in the garage. You've built something here. You're changing lives."

"Thanks, Kit-Kat." I kissed her forehead.

"Makes me wonder if Belle, Beau, and I shouldn't do some sort of program for the models that wash out at age nineteen and twenty. Those that don't make it." Her head tilted as she thought about it and then she smiled on me. "Look at you being both a bad and good influence on me all in the same night."

I chuckled. "Well, pile your plate high, Kitty. I plan to be all sorts of bad influence later on tonight." We exchanged a look and took our places in line.

20

Isn't it only a crime if you get caught?

Katrina—Sunday, July 4—2:00 p.m.

I stirred the Cajun chicken salad one last time before sprinkling paprika on the top, closing the lid, and sliding the container into the fridge for later. Turning back to the large island, I took a quick inventory. Green salad, baked beans, potato salad, corn, and biscuits . . . all done. I turned down the temperature on the pot of barbecue sauce simmering on the back burner. The patio door slid open and Carter stuck his head in. "Can you hand me a platter, Kitty? The burgers and ribs are ready to come off."

Holding back the desire to ask why he hadn't taken one with him when he went out as I suggested, I picked two up and walked them over. Beau was standing by the grill flipping pieces of chicken. "Here you go."

"Thanks, babe." He brushed his lips across my brow and headed back outside.

The doorbell rang before I could get back to the kitchen. No one was expected until three o'clock. I glanced out at my sauce-splattered T-shirt and baggy cotton shorts and shrugged. Whoever it was would have to take me as I was. I swung open the front door and beamed at the tall woman wearing skinny capris in mint green and a sequined tank top in teal.

"Yaz! You're early." I greeted my friend. Yazlyn stood six feet tall in flats with a curly Afro that added another three or four inches to her stature. She was dark-skinned with a flawless complexion and slim, willowy body. Raised in Arkansas by Kenyan parents, she was about the realest person you'd ever want to know. Known as much for her rapier wit as her distinctive prowl on the catwalk, she was one of the most business-savvy people I knew and a natural pick when Belle and I needed someone to run our office in New York.

She flashed a wide grin. "I got in last night and was just sitting around your empty condo so I decided to come on over." She handed me a huge bottle of rum and hugged me before stepping in and looking around. "This is how you're living, huh? Not bad. Not bad at all. This is not what I expected from Carter Parks."

"I know, right?"

"I would have pegged him as more of a glass,

steel, leather kind of guy, all sleek and contemporary. Muted grays and black."

"Me too, but Mr. Parks is quite a traditionalist," I explained.

She walked to the sliding glass doors and looked out at Carter and Beau. "Hmmm . . . he's a man who cooks, is smart, interesting, and hot, and has you lit up like the noonday sun. What are you going to do about that?"

I smirked. "Oh, I'm doing plenty, believe that."

"Quit bragging. I mean, long-term and serious-like. If he's as traditional as you say, he's going to want to wife you up and get started on some kids."

Every time someone talked along those lines, I got more than a little bit nervous. "I don't know, we're just enjoying each other's company right now. He hasn't mentioned anything more than that right now."

"And what are you all of a sudden, a shrinking violet? Ask him what he's thinking."

"Not sure I'm ready to hear it," I admitted.

"Girl, I'm gonna have to request that you put your big-girl drawers on."

I was saved by having to respond by the ringing of the doorbell. I found Tara, my assistant, standing on the front porch with Shawn. They'd been reviewing the information on Renee's laptop. From the looks on their faces, it looked like they'd found something. "Tell me you've got something." I waved them inside.

"We've got something!" they announced together.

"Awesome. Let's see it," Yazlyn said.

Shawn connected his iPad to the big-screen TV in the living area and pressed a few buttons. An image of Renee's loft came up on the screen.

"Whoa! How did we get this? I did not plant any cameras." The patio door slid open and Beau and Carter walked in carrying platters of meat.

"What's up?" Carter asked.

Shawn looked at me uncertainly and I nodded at him reassuringly. "We'll explain all in a second. Shawn?"

"After you put the tracking and cloning software on Renee's laptop—"

"You did *what*?" Carter asked, smacking the ribs down on the countertop.

"Babe, seriously. One second." I motioned for Shawn to continue.

"When Tara and I started looking at it, we realized that Renee has a smart house."

"A what?" Yaz asked.

"A smart house," Tara explained. "Everything can be controlled by a computer or cell phone."

Beau started smiling. "How much of her life is connected through that?"

"Damn near all of it," Shawn offered, "Her phone numbers, both home and cell, are digital numbers so every call and text both in and out are tracked through her e-mail. She has cameras set up outside her door and in her living room to guard against intruders, but either she doesn't want to or she forgets to turn them off, so we can see and hear everything that goes on near that area. She gets her work e-mail on her cell phone, which backs up onto her laptop. As do her calendar and her contact lists."

"We got access to this how exactly?" Carter questioned, sliding me a look.

The doorbell rang and I motioned for Beau to answer. Belle and Jewel walked in.

"*Ou est mon frère?*" Beau asked where Roman was.

"Roman went over to pick up Chase and Madere and Pops," Jewel answered, looking at the food first and the TV second. "Uh-oh, I recognize that living room." She looked at me with wide eyes.

Carter folded his arms across his broad chest and quirked a brow.

"Fine!" I caved. "We did a little breaking-and-entering. I got some software from Shawn to clone Renee's laptop so we could go in and look at what she was up to. We were just trying to see her e-mails. Who knew she was such a control freak that her whole life is on there for just anyone to see?"

"Anyone who broke into her place and hacked her computer, you mean," Carter snorted.

"We had good intentions," Belle mumbled.

"You were driving the damn getaway car, weren't you?" Beau said, glowering at Belle.

"My car. Driven for felonious purposes," Carter groused.

"More like a misdemeanor. We didn't really *break* and enter. We had the key, so we just entered," I hedged.

Carter's head tilted. "How exactly did you get a key?"

Shawn shuffled his feet and looked off into the distance.

I cleared my throat. "We're off topic. I felt and still feel that the ends justify the means."

"The criminal means?" Beau argued.

"Isn't it only a crime if you get caught?" Jewel wondered as she plunked down on a bar stool and gnawed on a rib.

Yazlyn clapped her hands together. "People, people! Focus. However this was obtained; let's see what it is before we decide if it was worth catching a case."

Beau sat down in one of the armchairs and tugged Belle down next to him. Carter and I perched on the other two bar stools.

Tara glanced around the room nervously, waiting to see if any more fireworks were forthcoming. When they weren't, she continued. "Anyway, check this out." She slid her finger across the iPad's touchscreen and the video started to play. We watched an older man standing outside of Renee's apartment for a minute before she let him in. Renee had kept herself in shape. She was a size eight chocolate-skinned cute girl with a shoulder-length bob and a tendency to wear clothes that were stylish but a little too tight, particularly across her generous hind parts. I'd never seen her when her face was not flawlessly made up, her hair not perfectly coiffed, and nails not perfectly done. Even answering her door, she was in a tight red sweat suit that was studded with crystals with matching five-inch cherry-red pumps. It was one of my pet peeves: Women who wore sweats with heels. It looked like they were either trying too hard or couldn't make up their minds. Are you casual or dressed up? Your outfit said one thing and your feet another. But maybe it was just me.

"Why is that woman wearing evening pumps with a velour sweat suit?" Belle said, frowning. Okay, it wasn't just me.

"Because she belongs to the 'Doing the Most and I Don't Care Who Knows It' club," Jewel said with her fork hovering over the potato salad.

The view switched to Renee's living room and still the man had his profile to the camera. Something about him was familiar, but I couldn't put my finger on it. In the next frame, Renee took two steps and pointed a remote. A slow, sultry Brian McKnight song started playing. My eyebrows skyrocketed. That was "it's about to go down" music.

"Wait a minute, is this about to get freaky?" Jewel asked. "Because you know, I'm not trying to see that and my stomach is delicate."

Shawn nodded and looked embarrassed. "You might want to push the plate away for a second, ma'am."

Jewel set her fork down with a snap. "Did he just call me *ma'am?*"

"Shh!" I scolded as Renee did an impromptu, but surprisingly skilled, striptease to the completely appropriate strains of "What We Do Here." "Whoa. She's got some moves."

"This bringing back any fond memories for you?" Belle slid Beau a sardonic glance.

"Ah *chère*, you know I forgot every other woman once I had you." He patted her arm.

"Um-hmm. Good answer, sugar," she drawled.

When Renee stood in see-through lingerie and pumps, the man reached for her and drew her close. He slid his hands down to her rear and squeezed.

"I'm so not trying to see this." Jewel grimaced.

The couple spun around, groping each other, and I was able to get a clear look at the man's face. "Pause it right there!" Belle, Beau, and Yazlyn all gasped.

Shawn nodded. "See that?"

"What are we looking at?" Carter asked.

"We are looking at Madison Archeneaux, the CEO of Royal Mahogany, getting his swerve on with Renee Nightingale, his former PR director," Yaz announced.

Jewel's jaw dropped. "I guess we should have seen that coming, but this is kind of a skank move, even for Renee."

"It's actually kind of smart in a smarmy, adulterous, ambition-at-all-costs way." I shrugged. "How better to entangle him? If you want influence over a man, if you want to really control him? You have to know his weakness and make him need you. Either for money, love, sex, or survival. Once a man feels that he needs a woman, that woman owns him. He'll do or say anything for her."

"Is that right?" Carter said silkily, in a quiet and dangerous voice.

Oops. Yaz, Jewel, Belle, and Tara looked at me in disbelief. I was over-sharing. There were certain things that women knew that men didn't need to hear about. Sometimes when I was thinking out loud, I forgot to filter. I spun toward him. "You don't count. I've already learned not to try and manipulate my way around you. You're your own man and fairly immovable once you have your mind made up."

"Uh-huh. Nice save, Kitty." He patted my hand.

Whew. "Anyway, anything else we need to know?" I looked toward Shawn and Tara.

"We've found a lot in her e-mail. She really has no love for all things Montgomery. We're going to summarize and get it to you next week. As far as video goes, there is quite a bit of activity, mostly of Renee with this guy and some other guy we haven't identified yet," Shawn shared.

"Send it over to Captain Calvin and let him take a look," Beau said.

"Who is Captain Calvin?" Belle asked.

"A former military friend of Gramps who is looking into Delancey for us," Beau answered.

"He's the big gun?" I asked Carter.

"He's the big gun." Carter nodded.

Beau nodded too. "Let's see what the big gun has and compare notes before we decide when and how to use this. What do you think, C?"

"I agree. If we have opportunity to take them both down and can do it in the grandest, most public way possible, we should go for it."

The doorbell rang and I glanced at the clock on the microwave. "I've still got to change. Can you get that?" I headed for the staircase.

"I got it," Beau said. "Carter needs to get some water up next to his musty parts too."

"This is the thanks I get for slaving over a hot grill for you?" Carter smacked Beau on the back of the head as he walked by.

"I'll set the rest of the food out," Belle offered.

"I'll start mixing drinks," Yaz added.

"Make yourselves at home!" I called out and hit the stairs at a run.

I ran into the closet and started tossing my dirty clothes toward the hamper. Carter strode in and paused at the sight of me naked.

"Don't even think it, C. Pops will come up here and check on us. Like, walk right in."

"Yeah, so would Gramps. Chris too for that matter." With a sigh, he stripped and stepped into the large walk-in shower.

I used a washcloth to freshen up before slipping on lingerie, pulling my hair up with a clip, and dragging a simple sundress over my head. Carter was stepping out of the shower as I buckled woven metallic sandals onto my feet. I eyed him in the mirror as I threaded dangly silver earrings through my lobes. For some reason, the strangest thought popped into my head.

"Would you ever make a sex tape?" I asked.

"Haven't you had enough of being a film star?" he teased.

"Not for public consumption. Just . . . you know . . . to see what we'd look like."

"That's what mirrors are for," he said drolly. "And they can't be hacked."

"Good point."

"What made you ask?" he wondered.

I gestured to him. "You looking like you look. Us doing what we do. I wondered if it looks as hot as it feels." Then right after I said it, I wanted to take it back.

"Hmm. You're a deep pool of a woman, Audelia Katrina."

"Sometimes."

"Katrina, I'm coming up there in two minutes if you're not down here!" Pops called out. "You're not grown to me, l'il girl!"

I rolled my eyes. "He's got zero chill. What did I tell you?"

"Go, I'll be down in a second."

I hurried back down and greeted Madere, Pops, Gramps, Chris, and Chase, who snuck his arms around my waist. "Auntie Kit?"

"Yes, baby?" Chase was the spitting image of his father, with the charming personality of his uncle and the shrewd mind of his grandmother. He was going to be deadly when he got older.

"Why does Pops call you l'il girl? You're big now."

"Not to him I'm not. To him I'm still his little girl."

"What about me?"

"Well, you're on your way to being a man, so we'll just have to remind Pops of that."

"Okay, where is Uncle Carter?"

"He'll be down in a second," I answered.

"Is he your boyfriend now?"

"Yes, yes he is."

"Does that mean you kiss and stuff?"

"Yes, yes it does." I smiled down at him.

"Are you going to have a baby too?"

The room fell silent and all eyes swung to me.

"Uh, why do you ask?"

"Daddy said sometimes when two people are like that and they kiss and stuff, they make a baby."

"Yes, but only sometimes." I shot Roman a look. He threw up his hands and turned away. Coward. Troublemaking coward, at that.

"It's better if you marry him before you have a baby so people know you're a family," Chase said seriously.

"That's very smart advice."

"Are you going to marry him?"

I cast my eyes about, looking for some help, and got none. Carter stood in the middle of the staircase, enjoying my discomfort. I decided to give as good as I got. "We haven't talked about it. But look, there he is now. Why don't you ask him?" I gave my nephew a kiss on the cheek and walked into the kitchen.

Carter picked up Chase and whispered something in his ear before adding, "That's our secret, though, okay? Bro code?" He put out his fist and Chase bumped it.

"Bro code." Ready to move on to the next subject, Chase asked, "Can we play football now?"

Roman spoke. "Son, it's a little hot for football today."

"Water football? In the pool?" He gave his best I'm-so-cute-you-can't-say-no-to-me face.

"Fine. One hour. Water football. Pick your team," Roman relented.

"I want Chris and Uncle Carter."

"Son, you don't want me and Uncle Beau on your team?"

"No, I can play with you anytime. I want professionals," Chase announced.

"Dat chile is gettin' more like his Uncle Beau ev'day." Madere shook her head.

"Heaven help us all," Belle declared.

Beau stood up. "More of me is always a good thing, ladies. So that leaves me, Roman, and Shawn on the opposing team. Pops, Gramps—if we could have you as our official referees and scorekeepers, please. Into the water, gents." The men filed outside and started stripping down to their swim trunks.

Yazlyn set down the spoon she was using to stir the beans and hurried toward her purse. She pulled out a camera and hotfooted toward the back door.

"Where do you think you're going, Miss Missy?" I asked.

"You all may be related to them or whatever, but this is prime man candy and I plans to get me an eye-gaze full." She waved her camera. "And a few choice pics for my screensaver. Good God almighty, Kat. Have you seen your man's abs lately?"

"Actually, I have." But I set down the aluminum foil and stepped closer to take another look. Yep. Still drool-worthy.

"And whew, Roman's buns! Fresh out the oven and just as tasty-looking," Yaz drooled.

"Okay, watch it now," Jewel scolded and walked over. "He is looking mighty right in those trunks, though. Buns of steel. Bless him. Bless every bit of him."

"Pregnancy hormones much?" Belle teased.

"Perhaps, what's your excuse?" Jewel returned.

"Anyway . . ." Belle turned away.

"And no disrespect, Mrs. Montgomery." Yaz continued her unabashed swooning. "But your husband is quite well preserved and holding his own against these youngsters."

"I keep him young, sweetie. He's a prime piece of man meat." Madere giggled and poured herself a daiquiri.

"Mom, did you just call my daddy *man meat*?" I asked in dismay.

"You want me to lie? When I met dat man, my first thought? Dat dere is the tastiest damn morsel I'd laid eyes on. All da rest? The love, the conversation, the sweet stuff? Came later."

"Well, Madere, you made some beautiful children," Belle said, eyeing up her husband like he was sizzling steak on a platter.

"Had a hell of a time making them too," she chortled mischievously.

"I can't un-hear that," I groaned.

"Hey, uh—does Chris have a girlfriend?" Tara asked breathlessly, watching him descend into the water.

"Not that I'm aware of," I said, smirking.

"You think he's out of my league?"

"No such thing," Madere said. "If a woman wants a man, all she has to do is figure out what he wants in a woman and be that to get his attention. After dat, if it's meant to be, it will be. *C'est vrai*."

I watched as Carter threw his head back and laughed at something Chris said. They jostled each other until Gramps spoke up and then they waited until his back was turned to elbow each other in the ribs. The brothers Parks were not bad to look at either. Not at all. "You know, we're not on a schedule. The food is done and the cobbler has at least another thirty minutes. We could sit on the covered patio and have a frosty beverage or two."

"Dat would be far more dignified then standin' here with our faces pressed to the door," Madere snickered.

I grabbed the pitchers of juices and cocktails while Belle grabbed the drinkware. We trooped outside and settled in to enjoy the show.

21

You woke up this morning feeling some kinda way

Carter—Wednesday, July 7—6:18 a.m.

As was my habit, I woke up before my alarm could ring. I needed to get up and get a workout in before facing the day ahead. I blinked twice and wondered what felt off. Looking to my left, I noticed Katrina sitting cross-legged in the middle of the bed, staring at me. "Problem, diva?"

"Do you ever wish I was less trouble?"

I glanced at the clock. It wasn't even 6:30 in the morning yet for all this deep conversation. "Less trouble than what?"

"Less trouble than the way I am. I know I'm a handful."

"You're two handfuls, but I have big hands, so it's not a problem." I held my palms up and grinned.

She frowned and fiddled with the hem of her nightgown. "I'm serious, C."

I pushed up and rested my back against the headboard. "What brought this on?"

She shrugged, looked down, and fiddled some more. Katrina was not one who displayed nervousness. Ever. I reached out and grasped her hands. I just held on and let her work through whatever she was struggling with until she was ready to talk about it. After a few moments, she raised her eyes and I was both surprised and dismayed to see tears in them.

"Hey . . ." I pulled her to me and tucked her into my side. "C'mon now. If you don't tell me what's broken, I can't fix it."

She sniffled and curled into me, resting one hand on my chest. "I'm what's broken. I did this."

"You did what?"

"It's my fault that Kevin went nuclear and because of him, Renee took her shot and now we're all having to fight for our reputations. Because of me. I saw an article online last night saying you could do better than a two-bit washed-up model who was more soiled dove than solid designer. They said I was like an anchor around your neck dragging you down."

"I take it that was a direct quote?"

"Yeah." She sighed.

"That's total bullshit and you know it," I said angrily.

"You could do better than me."

Katrina had a healthy ego and sense of self-esteem, so it thoroughly angered me to hear her getting down at herself. In that moment, I realized how much of a toll Kevin and Renee's mudslinging had done. I'd been by her side almost every day since this whole thing started and I'd never seen her falter or doubt herself. She'd taken everything in stride, moving forward and staying focused on the end game. Every new accusation or embarrassment that was lobbed at her, she appeared to deflect the hit. I should've known that it would catch up to her sooner or later. No one could continue to hear themselves disparaged day after day and not internalize some of that. I mentally kicked myself for not supporting her better and making sure she knew she didn't have to shoulder it all alone. I decided to correct that now.

"There is nobody better than you. Not for me. So I don't want to hear what some bitter journalist who never had a shot with you has to say. You know better and I know better and that's all that matters. You're not in this alone. I'm here for you to lean on. If you need me to prop you up, hold you together, whatever. I got you."

"For how long?" she asked in a small voice.

Without a pause, I answered, "As long as you want." I waited to see if she wanted some formality attached to that statement. I knew the minute I saw her set her suitcase down in my home and start redecorating that I was ready for her to be Mrs. Parks. I also knew I was all in, waiting for her to catch up.

"What about what you want?" she queried.

"I want you for as long as you'll have me."

"Why?" She looked genuinely confused.

"You fishing for compliments?"

"No, just thinking. You see me like no one else does and it doesn't seem to bother you."

"What's to be bothered about? You're smart, funny, sweet when you feel like it, fun, you like football, you make amazing chicken wings, you can be a girly-girl and a girl who hangs out with the guys, you have the same values as I do, you get me, and you're hot. Even in that ratty LSU T-shirt you've hung onto for all these years."

"You gave me that shirt," she reminded me.

"I can get you another. Even one that doesn't have holes in it," I teased.

"I like that one."

"Have it your way, diva." I was not going to argue about a T-shirt.

"Hmm. Bringing me back to my first question: Do you ever wish I was less trouble?"

"I never wish you are anything but what you are. Except maybe when you run off and commit crimes without telling me."

She peered up at me through her lashes and ran her hand down my chest. "Not ready to let that one go, huh?"

"Katrina, when other people put you at risk, I know how to handle that. When you put yourself at risk, it undercuts me. I can't take care of you. And yes, before you say it . . . I know you can take care of yourself. But I like being the one to make sure you're safe and sound and happy."

She huffed. "You make me sound like a pampered princess."

I cleared my throat and looked up at the ceiling. Katrina has been protected and pampered from the day she was born. On some people, that manifested itself in a spoiled attitude and deluded self-importance. With Katrina, it showed through as self-confidence, a belief that she was right (even when she wasn't) and a determination to get her own way.

I, on the other hand, grew up with a bit of struggle and had made it through on the other side. That had given me self-confidence, a belief that I was right (which I usually was), and a determination to get my own way.

"Carter Parks, are you calling me spoiled?" Katrina asked incredulously.

Sensing this conversation could go bad and I didn't have time for it today, I patted her arm and slid out of bed. "No babe, I'm saying you haven't had to struggle. Which is fine; I don't want you to struggle."

"I'm not some pretty little helpless kitten that sits on a cushion to be kept from harm." She swung off the bed and slammed her hand onto her hips.

Oh, here we go. "I didn't say you were. No one recognizes and admires your independence more than me," I said, though I sensed there was nothing I could say that would defuse the ticking time bomb that was her temper this morning.

"But you think I can't stand on my own feet. Just like my father and my brothers, you're underestimating me. At the first sign of trouble, you swoop in to save the day. You show up in Barbados, announce we're going to be together, and whisk me away. You and the men go off to meet with some super-spy while the little women are supposed to sit by the phone and wring our hands?"

I knew there was no good response and thankfully, I didn't have to come up with one. Katrina was on a roll and I couldn't get a word in edgewise even if I wanted to.

"You know what, Carter? I don't need you to handle me, take care of me, or fix me. I'm a grown woman."

"Okay." I didn't think it was prudent to point out that she wasn't really acting like one at this moment.

"*Okay?*" she shrieked.

"Okay," I repeated.

"Don't placate me. Or patronize me," she hissed.

"I'm not," I answered simply

"Is that what this whole thing is about?" She gestured with her hands back and forth between the two of us.

"What whole thing?" I repeated the gesture.

"This relationship? You and me hooking up after all these years."

Now I was getting riled up. "Hooking up? You call what we're doing *hooking up?*" That seemed to be an understatement.

"Whatever. Is this about you taking care of me?"

"I thought we were taking care of each other." I spoke carefully and deliberately.

"I'm not talking about the sex!" she shouted.

"Neither am I!" I raised my voice as well.

She stared at me, chest heaving in agitation, and I stared back. Either she was genuinely upset or she was still in a spin over the article she read or she was picking a fight. Whichever it was, I didn't have time or patience for it. I thought we were building something here. For her to refer to it as a *hookup* stung. A lot. Stung to the point that I had to take a mental step back. I was all in; I wasn't sure where she was. I wondered if I had put too much of myself on the line with her. I didn't like the feeling. It was foreign to me, not knowing where I stood and feeling uncertain. Instead of leaving myself open to taking any more hits, I felt my guard going up and I shut down.

She continued. "I need to believe this is more than you having some sort of hero complex with me playing the damsel in distress. I don't want to be some sort of project for you. I need to believe that *you* believe we stand on equal ground."

I was over it. I'd never treated her as anything less than an equal. If I had a tendency to be protective, I wasn't going to apologize for that. Maybe that was her issue, maybe she'd dated one asshole too many. "I've been straight with you from the beginning. I am what you see. Believe what you want." I stepped in the closet and started pulling on shorts and a T-shirt.

She followed me. "You're walking out?"

"I'm going to the gym and then I'm going to work." Entering the bathroom, I splashed water on my face, rolled on some deodorant, and reached for the toothpaste.

"We're in the middle of something here," she argued.

I swished mouthwash and rinsed. "I thought we were. Come to find out we're just hooking up." I sent her a look.

She threw up her hands. "I don't need this. I've got enough going on that I don't need a pouty boyfriend on top of it all."

"Okay," I said. I wasn't going to argue with her anymore. I didn't even know what we were arguing about at this point.

"Okay what?"

I shrugged. "Okay, whatever."

She stormed into the closet and started jamming clothes into a suitcase. She looked up at me. "I'm moving back home."

I shook my head. "Of course." I refused to show her how much this hurt.

"Of course?"

"Of course, princess. A little bump in the road and you're out. Heaven forbid you stick it out and figure out what's worth saving. The minute it gets a little too real, you run." That's fine. I was used to it.

"I do not!"

I wordlessly pointed to her suitcase. I pulled on socks and Nikes and walked out of the room and downstairs. Striding to the refrigerator, I took out the ingredients for an energy smoothie and starting prepping them. I heard Katrina slamming around upstairs and reached forward to switch on the television. If she was going to go, I didn't need to see it or hear it. Tossing the ingredients into the blender, I punched the button and tried to reign in my anger. I was really pissed off. This was how it was going to end? After all these years of waiting, we had a few good months and that was that? I felt blindsided and cheated. It never occurred to me that Katrina and I wouldn't go all the way. I did everything right. We were friends first. I sowed all my wild oats. I gave her time to figure out who she was. We had our own lives that meshed well together. Dammit, I had done everything right. Why was it never enough?

Pouring the smoothie into a travel cup, I drank half of it down and slammed the lid on with an angry twist. I shouldn't have done this. I shouldn't have left myself open for this kind of painful rejection. It was like dealing with my parents all over again. You let them in, they take what they need and then they walk away. I was done being that guy. Done.

I plucked my keys off the counter just as Katrina hit the bottom step in jeans and a T-shirt. A rolling suitcase and duffel bag rested beside her. She stood there with a stubborn tilt to her jaw and an angry glint in her eye. I felt the exact same way. So be it. Done.

"I'll come back for the rest later. I'm leaving," she announced, sliding her purse onto her arm.

"Me too." I jingled my keys. Stopping to turn off the TV, I kept moving toward the back door.

"This is it? Aren't you going to ask me to stay?"

I paused without looking at her. "I never asked you to leave."

"You want me to go?"

"*I. Never. Asked. You. To. Leave,*" I ground out.

"You're not going to fight for me?"

At this, I set down the travel cup and turned toward her. "Why don't *you* fight for *me*? For us? Grow the hell up, little girl. I'm too old to play whatever game this is. You woke up this morning feeling some kinda way and I don't know how to deal with it. I want you, I want us. I've told you that and I've shown you that. I am who I am. If that's too restrictive for you or whatever, go ahead and go. Because whatever this is right here, right now? Not working for me."

She dropped her purse and prowled toward me like a hunter stalking its prey. When she stood toe to toe with me, she looked up. "Carter. Ask me to stay."

"Tell me you don't want to go," I countered, not giving an inch. We stared each other down, waiting for the other to break. I waited for one moment and then two before making a point of checking the time on my watch. With one last look at her, I began to retreat, giving her every opportunity to say something. Finally, frustrated with both of us, I threw up my hands and headed for the door. I was reaching for the doorknob when she launched herself at me. I had to take a step back to catch her since I didn't see that one coming. She wrapped her arms and legs around me and whimpered into my neck.

"I don't wanna go. I like it here. I like you here. I like you and me here," she gasped out while bawling.

This woman . . . I exhaled in relief. I tightened my arms around her and nuzzled the side of her neck. "I like you and me here too."

"You can't make me go," she mumbled, gripping me tighter.

I walked over to the sofa and sat down with her still wrapped around me like a python. Quietly, I repeated, "I never wanted you to go, baby." I rubbed her back while she calmed down. Finally she loosened her grip and swiped at her wet cheeks. I took my thumbs and wiped the last of the tears away. "What is all of this about, Kitty?"

"I got scared."

"Of what?"

"That you're going to figure out I'm not worth all of this drama and walk away."

I peered at her in confusion. "So you decided to pick a fight and bail?"

"When it ends, I'd rather be the one to end it," she explained.

"Nice. Why does it have to end?"

"Doesn't it always?" She shrugged.

"What if we have another five good months, five good years, or five good decades first? You wanna miss out on all that in-between time?" I didn't understand her logic.

"I didn't think it through. I just got scared. Are you mad?"

"Yeah. I am," I answered honestly.

"So we're over?" Her breath hitched.

"No, Audelia Katrina. I can be in a relationship with you and not adore you every second of every day," I explained with far more patience than I felt.

"You're not adoring me right now?"

"No. I'm not," I answered honestly.

"You're thinking I'm a spoiled, pampered princess who's not worth the trouble."

"I'm thinking you've twisted yourself into a million knots and decided to tie me up in the middle. You put us—me—through something this morning unnecessarily."

"I'm sorry," she whispered.

I kissed her forehead and lifted her off of me. "I know you are. I'll see you later on tonight, okay? I need to go to the gym and work some of this mad off." I stood up and jammed my hands in my pockets.

"I could help you out with that . . . some angry makeup sex?" She gave a wry smile.

One side of my mouth lifted in a half smile. "Maybe later."

She nodded slowly. "I'll just unpack. I think I'll work from home today. So . . . I'll be here if you want to call or talk or anything."

"Okay."

"I'll be right here. Not going anywhere," she reiterated.

I leaned over and kissed her softly. Her hands came up to grip my face and she deepened the kiss. Our lips and tongues spoke desperately, saying things we weren't ready to speak aloud. With one last clinging kiss, I lifted away. "I hear you, baby. I hear you." I scooped up my smoothie and walked out without a backwards glance.

22

I might have messed up

I swung the door open and exhaled in relief. "Oh, thank God. Get in here." I grabbed Chris and Beau by the arms and dragged them inside. I led them to the kitchen island and directed each of them to sit. I slid plates with shrimp and crawfish po' boys in front of them and poured glasses of iced tea for both of them. I plunked a basket of waffle fries in between the plates.

They both looked at the plates, up at me, and then at each other. Beau leaned back and crossed his arms across his chest and Chris pursed his lips. They gave me accusatory and suspicious looks.

I 'fessed up. "Okay . . . so, I may have messed up."

"*Vraiment?* I thought you called me up all hysterical and whatnot because you were dying to feed me. The meal is a dead giveaway; an obvious bribe," Beau drawled.

Chris sighed. "What did you do?" He looked around. "You didn't kill anyone, did you? Because I'm not about felony accessory after the fact."

I glowered at the both of them and scooted their plates forward. "You eat. I'll talk."

Beau picked up the sandwich and sniffed it. "Is it poisoned?"

"Shut up, Beauregard!" I nervously picked up a dishcloth and started wiping down the spotless counters I'd cleaned twice already. "I saw an article online last night."

"The one from the sports blogger about how Carter could do better?" Chris asked around a huge bite of sandwich.

"Yeah. That one. I guess you saw it?"

"The guys in the locker room saw it. We all thought it was crap." He finished one half of the sandwich and started on the other.

"I didn't see it." Beau said swirling a waffle fry around the rémoulade sauce. "But anyway, you saw it and what? You freaked out?"

"A little bit. I woke Carter up this morning and asked him if I was more trouble than I was worth—"

"You are," Beau answered at the same time as Chris said, "No way!"

"Anyway, somehow we got into this fight about him trying to protect me and thinking I'm spoiled," I continued.

"You are spoiled," Beau said matter-of-factly.

"I am not!" I adamantly denied

"Really?" Beau challenged me. "Have you ever

worried about your next meal, your next job, your light bill, whether there are people in the world who love and will take care of you? Ever?"

"No, have you?" I asked my eldest brother.

"*Mais non*, because I *am* spoiled. But I embrace that about myself." He smirked.

I looked at Chris, who gave a shrug. "I can't help you. I'm spoiled too. Carter and Gramps always made sure I never wanted for anything."

"Anyway, the fight got all twisted up and the next thing I knew I told him this was just a hookup that wouldn't last. I accused him of some stuff, packed a bag, made a few more nasty declarations, and told him I was leaving him."

Both of their mouths fell open. Uh-oh. So it was as bad as I thought.

"Then I told him to fight for me and ask me to stay and instead he got me to say I didn't really want to go and we hugged it out. But he was still mad. He went to the gym. But worse than that, he looked really hurt. Like, really hurt. I think I broke something I can't fix."

Beau's voice was deadly quiet. "You threatened to walk out on *Big Sexy*? On Carter Evan Parks? Are you freakin' kiddin' me?"

"What?" I looked from him to Chris and back again.

"Do you not understand my brother at all?" Chris looked at me in equal parts dismay and confusion. "After the way my parents played him? Pretending to love him and getting close to him until he gave them what they really wanted—which wasn't him, by the way—and left him over and over again?"

Beau added, "After he spent his childhood being shuttled from one relation to the other, then to strangers and teachers feeling like no one wanted him? The man who has worked his entire adult life to feel a sense of security, you wake up and flip out on him? This is the man you threatened to walk out on?"

"Wait . . . what? I didn't know!" I protested and put my hand to my stomach. I felt sick.

Chris shook his head and looked at Beau. "Even I didn't know about that. How old was he when Gramps came for him?"

"He was twelve. Your grandfather had been in the service overseas and thought he was still with your mother. When he got discharged he went to find him," Beau explained.

"And then he came and got me," Chris said in wonder.

"Family, relationships, people who believe in him and stick by him? Knowing that the people around him trust him to do the right thing. He's that guy. The one who is there. No matter what. Whenever you call. All he asks is that the people he cares about accept him for who he is. No more, no less. That means everything to Carter. Everything." Beau looked at me with reproach. His voice was pained when he spoke again. "Katrina. I spent so much time warning him about hurting you, I never thought you'd hurt him. I never thought in a million years that you would do that to him." He looked at me like he didn't even know who I was at that moment.

"Why didn't he tell me?" I whispered, tears springing to my eyes.

"Why didn't you ask?" Chris wondered. "I mean, he's your man, right? Don't you want to know what made him the person he is today?"

"I've known him for so long, I just assumed I knew all the important stuff."

"Don't you want to know what he needs to be happy or is it all about you?" Chris asked.

"I want to know. I want him to be happy. I want him to be happy with me. But you're right. Really. It's all about him now," I clarified.

"Wow." Beau pushed the rest of his sandwich away. "You have to fix this."

"I offered him makeup sex. He said maybe later."

"Oh, Jesus," Chris exclaimed, finishing his food. "He turned down the cookies? You broke him."

"And I never need to hear about your sex life ever again. I mean like *ever*, Audelia." Beau gave me his sternest big-brother voice. "He is my best friend. He would walk through fire for any one of us. I don't give a shit what you have to do; you better make him feel like Superman tonight."

"I thought you said—"

"Not with the goody bag, Katrina, for Christ's sake. You can't really think that's all he wants from you?"

I hesitated. I knew it was more than just the sex, but a lot of it *was* the sex. "That's what keeps guys coming back."

"Wooo! *Mon Dieu!* Okay. You have dated some hella-losers in your day. I'm sorry that as your older brother, I wasn't around to stomp dey asses and teach you better, but believe me, Carter is not putting up with you for the swerve of it all."

"You're sure?" True, Carter was a great guy, but underneath it all, he was still a guy.

"Seriously?" Chris said. "I mean, you're hot and all, but do you know how many hot women throw it at my brother regularly? Like supernova hot women?"

"No. Do tell." I quirked a brow.

Beau elbowed Chris in the stomach. "It doesn't matter because he's not catching. He's yours. Now do you want him or not?"

"I want him." And I knew in that moment it was absolutely true.

"For real and for keeps?" Chris asked.

"Maybe."

They both glared at me.

"I'm being truthful. If I am cut out for that 'real and keeps' stuff, then I definitely want it to be him."

"Find a way to make him believe it," Beau said. "Or else."

"Or else what?"

"I will sic Madere on you."

"And I'll sic Gramps." Chris and Beau exchanged a fist bump.

"Fine. I'll fix it. I know what I have to do."

"Fabulous. Just don't let it end up on YouTube." Beau stood and wrapped up the rest of his lunch to go. "Can you get your spoiled ass into the office tomorrow? We have a summer line to work out."

I glared at him. "Just because you sleep with the boss doesn't mean you can tell me what to do."

"Actually, yeah—it kinda does. Get your shit together, Kit-Kat. You're not a kid anymore." He kissed me on the cheek and headed to the front door.

"But I'm still a growing boy; can I have seconds?" Chris asked, putting his folded hands under his chin and blinking.

"Aren't you supposed to be at camp?" I remembered belatedly.

"I told them it was a family emergency. Hey, it's camp, not game day."

"Training camp. Like I should have given you a salad instead of that sandwich?"

"I hit people all day, I need the carbs. If you give me seconds, I'll give you some insider tips," he bargained

"Like what?" I leaned forward.

"His favorite mood music, his favorite movie, his favorite poem."

"I know those—huh, no I don't." I realized I had to do better.

"His favorite drink."

"It's not single-malt scotch?"

"No."

"Spiced *añejo* rum and Coke?" I guessed.

Chris snorted. "Rookie."

I took the sandwich I was saving for myself, cut it in half, and handed it over. "Spill."

"Deal."

By the time Carter arrived home, the house was completely transformed. And so was I. After picking Chris's brain for close to an hour and listening to him tell stories about Carter when they were growing up, I felt I knew my man better. I was ashamed that I hadn't taken the time to find out before. Turned out that Carter Parks was not only a traditionalist, but a romantic at heart. Underneath the finely tailored suit and warrior's body was a sweetheart of a man.

I'd spent the day adding my own touches to the living room. I swapped out some of his traditional lamps for a few more contemporary styles with turquoise and berry shades. I'd added a plush mint green throw to the chaise and three lavender pillows with sequins to the couch. The large, heavy square marble slab that took Chris and three of his buddies to move was gone, replaced with two tufted suede rectangles that could be used as ottomans, tables, or storage.

The area rug under the dining room table was a Middle Eastern–inspired swirl of greens and blues with a little bit of peach. I brought over two bright floral paintings from my house to replace two of his sedate landscapes. Because I had bad memories of the way I'd acted on the bed that morning and just because I felt like it, I bought a new bed with a new mattress set. Also, upstairs I'd exchanged all the bedding and towels and bathroom accessories. I'd rearranged my side of the closet and brought in a vanity stool for my side of the bathroom. The entire house was infused with the scent of vanilla and passionflower.

The minute I heard the garage door go up, I sprang into action. Though it was starting to get dark, there was plenty of moonlight already, so I lit a few lanterns outside on the covered patio. I turned on the sound system so the soundtrack to *Love Jones* played softly indoors and out.

I was dressed in a simple LSU tank top over white capri leggings with sandals. Carter liked me no matter what I was wearing, but he liked it best when I was just myself. No artifice, no props, just Katrina. I did spend an hour on my hair, though. He liked it curly and curls took time. The result was a flowing mane of curls that framed my face and hung down my back. A little mascara and lip gloss was all the decoration I bothered with.

Checking the table settings one last time, I went inside to fix his drink. He walked in the back door slowly, as if not sure what to expect. A little twinge gripped my heart. I did that to him, made him wary walking into his own house. I vowed to make it up to him. He paused and looked around, as if making sure he was in the right place.

I started toward him. "Hi honey, how was your day?" I purred, taking his laptop case off of his shoulder and setting it on the side before sliding off his jacket and loosening his tie. I lifted up on tiptoe and kissed his cheek. He slid his arm around my waist.

"My day? Well, it started off a little rough, but it's looking up right about now. How was yours?"

"Busy. Can I offer you a drink?"

"I don't see why not." I stepped away and he caught my hand and twirled me in a circle. "You look nice, Kitty."

I curtsied and threw back my head and laughed. "Only you, CP." The man had seen me in ball gowns and bikinis and business suits, but was wowed by an outfit I would go to the grocery in.

He grinned. "I like what I like."

I handed him a tall glass. "Bourbon, sparkling water, and two slices of orange."

His brows jumped up and he took a sip. "Someone has been busy today. This is perfect, thank you."

I took his free hand and turned toward the living room. "You like?"

He took it all in and the smile on his face spread. "I do like. It looks like you."

"No," I corrected. "It looks like us."

His eyes met mine in consideration. "You're right. It looks like us now."

"Are you hungry?" I led him outside.

"Always." His eyes lit up as he took in the covered dishes, the set table, the lighting. He looked like a kid on Christmas morning as I led him to a chair and handed him a napkin. It made me wonder how often anyone had taken the time to do something special for him, just because. I was ashamed that I hadn't made more of an effort before to do more for him than just show up, look cute, and bounce on him whenever the mood hit. Moving a few things in, getting settled, making an effort for dinner; these were little things to do that brought him so much joy. After talking with Chris and Beau this morning, I realized that it really wasn't all about me. Or at least, it shouldn't have been. Not all the time.

I uncovered the dishes. Spicy fried chicken, buttery mashed potatoes, greens, and biscuits. I started loading his plate.

"Oh my God," Carter moaned. "You cooked. You cooked carbs for me."

"Yeah, I did, baby." I grinned as he snatched my hand and kissed the back of it.

"Goddess. You're a goddess."

I shook my head, poured myself a glass of wine, and sat down next to him. "Nah, I'm just a woman who realizes she has a good man who could stand to be appreciated."

"Yeah? You've got me, huh?"

"Hope like hell I do." I handed him butter, Tabasco, and maple syrup.

He looked down at the items and back at me. "All right, Katrina, who'd you grill?"

I blinked innocently. "Beg pardon?"

"My favorite food with all the right condiments, my favorite drink prepared perfectly, my favorite album?"

"Your favorite girl?"

"My favorite girl," he agreed. "Apparently, you've got some sleuthing skills."

"I've got all kinds of skills. Eat up; I have praline cheesecake for dessert."

He bit into the chicken and made a sound I'd only heard him make while naked. "Girl, when you apologize you do it up right."

"This?" I gestured toward the table and living room. "This isn't an apology. This is me playing catch-up, doing what I should have been doing from the beginning. Upstairs later, on the new bed? That will be an apology."

"New bed, huh?" He scooped up some mashed potatoes.

"Indeed. Eat up, Sexy. We're just getting started."

He set his fork down. "Kit-Kat?"

"C?"

"If I forget to say it, this is excellent and thank you." He started slathering butter on his biscuit. I envied that kind of guiltless eating.

I kissed him on the neck. "Thank you for being you, babe."

"Who else would I be?" He looked confused.

"Exactly. That's why I love you. Now stop blocking the butter."

He passed the butter and then went still with the biscuit halfway to his mouth. "What did you just say?"

"I said you were kinda bogarting the spreadable butter a little bit. You were."

"Before that."

"The *I love you* part?" I bit into a drumstick and mentally patted myself on the back. This was good.

He cleared his throat. "Yeah. That part."

"I do," I confirmed and forked up some greens.

Taking a sip of his drink, he nodded as the smile spread across his face again. "Good." He picked up his fork and we ate in companionable silence while the song switched over to Maxwell's "Sumthin' Sumthin'." "I love you too and not just because you put your foot all up in this food."

"Good, then." I stayed calm even though I wanted to get up and dance around the pool. The neighbors wouldn't appreciate me screaming *Carter loves me, ME* over and over again.

"If I weren't determined to clean my plate and have seconds, I'd do you right here in the middle of these mashed potatoes. To commemorate the moment and all."

"You sentimental sweet-talker, you. Hold the thought. I'm not going anywhere any time soon."

"You're not, huh?"

"No Carter Evan Parks, I am not. You're stuck with me."

"That's a hell of a day you must have had."

"You don't know the half. Got scared, got some sense knocked into me, got my mind right."

"That's a good day."

I raised my glass. "Getting better every minute." We clinked glasses and I gave him a smile full of promise. He would go to sleep tonight much happier than he woke up.

23

Because neither of us has enough to do

Carter—Saturday, July 10—1:11 a.m.

"Why don't they make movies like this anymore?" Katrina groused as we watched the last scenes of *Love & Basketball* fade to credits. When I found out that Katrina had missed a lot of the neo-soul neoclassic films of the late 1990s, early 2000s, I decided we'd have a little marathon. We watched *Boomerang, Hav Plenty,* and then *Love & Basketball.*

"They do," I argued, though I tended to agree with her.

"We get maybe five or six African-American romantic comedies or relationship stories a year and two of those either suck or have some guy dressing up as a woman in the lead role."

"Somebody should do something about it," I

told her and moved the empty popcorn bowl to the ottoman.

"We're somebody," she said, shifting the empty drinkware to the tray on the side table.

I stood up and started putting the dozens of pillows she seemed to think we needed back on the sofa. "We are two somebodies, neither of which knows a damn thing about making movies."

"We know people, we should look into it. Maybe do something small. Think about putting together an independent production house and start looking around for interesting stories to tell." She sat up and stretched.

"A joint venture between you and me in an industry that is notoriously fickle. I see you, diva. Because neither of us has enough to do." I looked down at her as she tossed aside the lightweight blanket-thing she had been curled up under. I picked it up and folded it into a rectangle and tossed it over the back of the couch. It wasn't that Katrina was messy. It was that she felt there was a time and a place to pick up and clean things. That was usually Saturday mornings. The rest of the week, she tended to let things go. I had a housekeeper who came in on Tuesdays and Thursdays to do a few hours of light cleaning and straightening. Once every six weeks Katrina's housekeeper came with a team and did things that we weren't going to do, like windows, drapes, and something to do with bleach and grout in the bathrooms that I didn't care to know too much about. My point was, between our jobs, families, friends, household stuff, and time together, I didn't see how we were going to launch some sort of independent film company.

But one of Katrina's charms was that she was also a dreamer who frequently found ways to make dreams come true.

Katrina smiled up at me. "I know you're thinking this is another of my pie-in-the-sky dreams."

"A l'il bit."

"It doesn't have to be today, just something to start thinking about."

"Montgomery-Parks Productions. I'll keep it in mind."

"That's sweet of you to put me first, but I'm thinking Big Kat Productions. And the logo would be this lean lion with a grin on its face and its paw on a football."

I smiled down at her. "Did you just come up with that on the spot?"

Her lids drooped and a sultry smile crossed her face. She reached down and whipped her T-shirt off and tossed it away. Then she took two fingers and pulled the drawstring on my pants. They fell to the ground, leaving me bare-assed naked in the middle of my living room. She stretched across the length of the sofa and leaned back with her hands above her head. "I'm inventive."

"So I see."

She spread her legs so one foot rested on the floor. "And rather wet. Can you help me out with that?"

I pulled down the next-to-nothing shorts she had on and laid down on top of her. I slid a hand behind the nape of her neck and brought her mouth to mine. Slowly, I parted her lips and relished her unique flavor. Her mouth was warm, sweet, and uniquely Katrina. Her tongue flicked against mine eagerly and I delved deeper. Her arms came up and wrapped tightly around my neck as we dueled with more and more urgency.

Her hips instinctively matched the rhythm of our kisses, circling hungrily against me. Tempting as it was to give her what we both wanted right now, I was determined to savor the experience. The passion between Katrina and me ran so hot that often we just dove in, drove each other to distraction, and lay gasping in the aftermath. Don't get me wrong. It was hot and amazing, but this time, I wanted to take our time.

I pulled away from her mouth and nipped down her neck, pausing to run my tongue along a particularly sensitive spot. She shivered. I peppered kisses across her shoulders and chest, running my hands up and down her upper arms.

"Carter," she implored, shifting restlessly underneath me.

"I know baby; wait for it."

Her lashes rose and she pinned me with her gaze. Her eyes were more whiskey than gold with heated intensity. "I don't wanna wait."

"But you will."

"You make me crazy."

"I make you hot."

"That too."

I shifted her up and traced patterns around the perfect globes that were her breasts. Lazily, I circled and watched as the dusky nipples pebbled to hardness. I drifted my tongue from one puckered tip to the other and blew streams of air before taking them into my mouth and sucking. She arched her back and groaned in the back of her throat.

"More," she breathed.

While my tongue lathed one tip, I brought my fingers up to tweak the other and then alternated. She was grinding up against my thigh and I felt her heated wetness spreading. I drew the nubbin deeper into my mouth and flicked faster. Her movements became frantic and I increased the pace and pressure. With a low cry, she climaxed under me in trembling pleasure.

I dropped my hand to her hips and kept the pressure of my thigh against her so she could ride the wave fully. Her breath hitched and she shuddered once more before sinking with a satisfied smile back to the sofa cushions.

"You good?" I asked, sliding down her body. Glancing, I took a moment to be awed by the erotic vision laid out beneath me. Katrina's hair was a tousled crown around her head, her eyes were heavy-lidded and heated, her lips swollen and parted. Her skin had a delicate sheen of sweat and her chest rose and fell quickly as she dragged in air. She was everything I wanted and ever dreamed of.

"It gets better every damn time," she whispered.

"Um-hmm." I lifted one of her legs and rested it over the back of the couch to spread her wide for my attentions. I slid my thumb through her folds before settling down to delight in her honey-eyed center. Parting her outer lips, I sampled the very heart of her before nibbling on the hardened nubbin peeking out. I coaxed and teased with my fingers, lips, and tongue with varying pressure deliberately designed to drive her wild. I enjoyed the rush of wetness spilling into my mouth, the sound of her quickened breathing, the scent of her increased arousal scenting the air.

She began to buck against my mouth, her nails digging into my shoulders as she chanted my name over and over again. I slid two fingers inside of her and stretched them while suckling that sensitive button. Her inner walls quaked as she hit her peak again. She pulled at me frantically. "I need you. Inside me. Now. Now!"

I licked my lips, rose up and shifted so that I was nestled between her thighs and then paused. "Protection."

She reached between the cushion and the arm of the sofa and pulled out a foil packet.

"Is that where we're keeping these now?" I asked playfully.

"I hid them all over the house. Like you said, I'm spoiled. I want what I want when I want it."

"Well, let me give it to you then." I sheathed myself quickly and tilted her hips upwards.

She wrapped her legs around my waist and I penetrated her core slowly. The swollen folds of her sex rippled around me and I gritted my teeth as she undulated against me. Her hips lifted and fell in a frantic rhythm and I stilled her movements. She was so freaking hot, it threatened my control.

"Carter?"

"Yeah, babe?"

"Just let go."

"I want it to last."

"We have forever."

My control broke and I plunged into her with hard strokes. She met me thrust for thrust as I allowed myself to mindlessly seek nirvana in the joining. I opened my eyes to find her staring back at me. Instinct took over from technique as the physical and emotional combined to take us to a height we'd never visited before. I felt the ecstasy building up deep within and watched the bliss of it mirrored in her eyes. We reached the summit together and clasped each other tightly as we plummeted over the edge.

It could have been five or fifty minutes later when we finally roused ourselves to separate, clean up, and head to bed. Climbing in, we rolled towards each other and I slung my arm around her waist and nestled closer.

"I should warn you that it's getting harder for me to imagine being without you," I murmured into her neck.

"Then I should warn you that I have no intention of letting you go," she answered with a yawn.

"Good to know," was all I could say before falling into a dreamless sleep.

24

Let's not do this dance
Especially not here

Katrina—Saturday, July 17—8:43 p.m.

"Miss Montgomery, can we talk to you for a minute?" a reporter called out.

"It's not my night," I said with a gracious smile and a wave and kept moving up. This past week we had started leaking some of Kevin's past misdeeds to the media and all the hype had kicked back up again. Even at the height of my fame, I'd always been able to dress down and escape detection. And lately, I'd worked especially hard to stay low-profile in public.

But it was too much to expect that tonight. We were on the second level of the Saint Ann restaurant, which had open-event space as well as a Samurai museum. This evening was the book launch party of Carter's mentor, Stavros Carmichael. He owned twelve of the best-known casinos worldwide (among many other things) and was currently on the cover of *Fortune* magazine. The event was an invitation only who's who of movers and shakers. I counted two actors, three politicians, one doctor who had a daytime talk show, a Pulitzer Prize–winner, two celebrity chefs, and more than a few Wall Street bigwigs. In addition, Chris had come with some teammates. Low profile was not going to happen this evening. Flashbulbs were popping off at regular intervals. Carter tucked my hand into his arm as we mingled around the room.

Bless Carter's heart . . . all he'd said about the evening was that it was a little get-together for the guy who gave him his start in business. Thank goodness I'd erred on the side of caution and pulled on a little black dress and blingy shoes. Left up to his instructions, I would have shown up to this high-profile event in jeans and ballet flats. Carter had on a white sport coat over a navy T-shirt and matching tailored navy pants. Yum.

We finally circled back around to Stavros's side. Stavros Carmichael was a sixty-year-old tycoon who immigrated to the United States from Greece with his family when he was four years old. He was a self-made man who managed to stay pleasant even with all his success and well over a billion dollars in the bank. He was a good-looking man who was short in stature, but huge in personality and charisma. Stavros took my hand from Carter and took it in-between his. "You know, Kevin Delancey asked to come to this party this evening."

The smile fell from my face at the mention of Kevin's name.

Stavros patted my hand. "I don't say this to hurt you, my dear. You are far too lovely a spirit to have one such as him in your sphere. I declined his request to attend."

"Why, thank you." I knew that tweaked Kevin's ego something fierce.

"And, if I may speak frankly?"

"Of course."

"He's an asshole. Made a few dollars and doesn't handle himself well. It reflects poorly. I must ask why his ass hasn't been thoroughly kicked?" Stavros asked in the politest of tones.

Carter tipped his head in agreement. "I voted for the ass-kicking."

"It's never too late, that could still get handled. If you so choose."

I kissed Stavros on the cheek. "I appreciate the thought, gentlemen. Truthfully, I may or may not have entertained the fantasy of seeing Mr. Delancey dragged down the street by his sensitive parts. However, I think it's best to handle these things at a more cerebral level."

Stavros nodded in deference. "Well, then."

"Katrina, is this your new boyfriend?" A reporter rolled up and snapped a picture of me and Stavros. Stavros laughed in delight.

"I'm a lucky man, but not that lucky. Unless Miss Montgomery is interested in becoming Mrs. Carmichael number four?"

"Tempting. Let me consult with the first, second, and third Mrs. Carmichaels while I consider it," I teased.

Stavros beamed and handed me off to Carter. "Here's the man you're looking for. Ah, to be young again. I believe in this area, Parks, the student has become the teacher."

Carter flashed a smile, curved his arm around my waist, and pulled me closer. "Definitely feeling blessed." He looked so damn proud to have me on his arm that I just melted against him. God, I loved this man. Okay, fine. My mother was right: When you find the One, you start to think that anything is possible. The honor and cherish, til-death-do-us-part and happily-ever-after—it could actually happen for me.

"Katrina, we heard you liked older men," the reporter said snarkily. Carter's eyes narrowed and I spoke up before he could go all protective alpha male.

"I do—Carter's ancient." Everyone laughed, breaking the tension, and the reporter wandered off.

Stavros spoke up. "I was telling Carter earlier that I'd be interested to watch and see what you do next. You seem the kind of woman to have her finger in a lot of pies. I keep telling this one that the key is to diversify your interests and income streams. You never want all your eggs in one basket and you want each and every egg to be golden."

"Funny you should say that. CP and I were kicking around an idea of launching a production company for independent films."

Stavros's brow rose. "That is an area I've had a passing interest in. We should set up a time to talk."

Chris had come up behind us. "I'm in. I'll personally be in charge of auditioning all the female leads."

Stavros clapped him on the back. "This one we keep our eye on."

A young, nervous staffer in a white shirt and black pants hustled over to us. "Um . . . Mr. Parks?"

Both Chris and Carter turned. "Yes?"

"Oh." She got flustered as if not sure what to do next. "Either one of you, I guess. There are some people at the entrance who say they are your parents." Both Chris and Carter's head swiveled to where an older black couple stood, overdressed for the occasion and looking irritated that they were not being let in. The woman was tall, thin, and would have been beautiful if not for the angry, bitter expression on her face. The man was a lighter-skinned, older version of Carter and Chris and wore the same aggressive expression as the woman.

Carter looked grim, Chris looked dismayed, Stavros looked angry. I was confused. I realized that there was bad blood and worse history between Carter and his parents, but these reactions seemed severe.

"How did they find us tonight?" Chris asked.

Carter pointed at all the media in attendance.

"What do they want?" Chris said in a strained voice.

Carter shook his head ruefully. "It's July. They've run through this year's money already."

I kept my mouth from dropping open. Carter gave them some sort of an annual allowance? Chris pulled out his phone and fired off a quick text.

Stavros lowered his voice. "Let's take this to the back office." He motioned to two of the staff members. They went to the elevator bay and spoke to the couple. Carter steered me toward the room that Stavros pointed out. Chris hurried over to keep his parents from getting loud and making a scene, which they appeared to be on the verge of doing. I didn't know what to say, think, or do, so I followed in silence.

We entered the small office and turned toward the door. Stavros put his hand on Carter's shoulder and I threaded my fingers through his. He tightened his grip and hung on. Carter was not a man who clung, so I knew right then that this situation was worse than I'd thought.

The door swung open and the couple walked in with Chris following. Chris had a tight, pinched look on his face. The woman walked over to me with arms outstretched. "You must be Katrina. I've heard so much about you."

I froze for a second. Usually I was socially adept, but I didn't even know this woman's name and I could feel the waves of pain radiating off of Carter and Chris. I extended my hand. "Glad to meet you, ma'am."

She pulled up short and looked at the hand I'd extended. "So this is the kind of woman you like, Carter Evan? And why does he have to be here?" She gestured toward Stavros.

"He's a friend. He's been here for me. Katrina Montgomery, Clara and Caleb Parks," Carter said blandly.

I extended my hand again. "Pleased to meet you."

Clara curled her lip and turned away. Caleb at

least stepped forward and accepted the hand-shake. "Pleasure, girlie. A pleasure."

"So what brings you here?" Carter asked in a controlled voice.

"Can't a mother come—" Clara whined and was interrupted.

"Stop," Chris said. "Let's not do this dance. Especially not here. Let's just cut to the chase. Is the money gone again?"

"Let me explain what happened, son," Caleb said.

"I know what happened. You spent a year's worth of money in half a year's time," Carter snapped.

"Unbelievable!" Chris said. "Carter bought the two of you a building in Baton Rouge and another in Shreveport. You can live in either one rent-free. The proceeds of the buildings' lease income go directly into your bank accounts. You also each have one hundred thousand dollars a year at your disposal. This year I kicked in an extra twenty-five thousand dollars apiece. It is completely unacceptable that you can't live off of that. Completely."

"Don't you smart-mouth us. We brought you into this world," Carla curled her lip and snarled.

"Thank you. I like it here. When do we stop paying for the gift of life?" Chris said shortly. He was the happy-go-lucky one of the two brothers, so his sharpness was telling.

"What's the damage?" Carter asked, wearily obviously, having heard it all before.

"Well, son, we ran into some problems with the Baton Rouge building," Caleb explained.

"There is a property management company that handles that," Carter answered calmly.

Clara spoke up. "We let them go."

His voice went deadly. "I beg your pardon?"

Caleb shrugged unashamedly. "We had to fire them, they weren't working out. Most of the repairs we could do ourselves."

Carter exhaled. "So where is the money that I was paying the property management company?"

Neither of them said anything. Carter pinched the bridge of his nose. Stavros whispered something in his ear and he shook his head forcefully. I didn't know what to do. I wanted to help, but I didn't know what to do. I had no point of reference for parents like this. It would never occur to Alanna and Avery Montgomery to take an allowance from their children and then to run through it and ask for more. Thinking back, I thought of just how many Christmases and Thanksgivings that the three Parks men had spent with us. I'd never seen Caleb or Clara before. Never heard them call to check up on their boys, nothing. It seems like Caleb and Clara thought of their offspring more like a bank and less like family. That was inexcusable.

"What's the bottom line here?" Carter asked wearily.

"Just . . . you know, whatever you two can spare," Clara asked.

"And if the answer is no?" Chris asked.

"How would it be *no*? You just signed a thirty-eight-million-dollar contract and Carter just sold an eighteen-million-dollar complex. Giving us two buildings and a couple hundred thousand is like a slap in our faces," Clara snapped.

"All we want is what we're due," Caleb tacked on.

My eyes narrowed. "What you're due? Chris and Carter work hard for every penny they earn. You have got to be kidding me. You want to get paid for bringing your own damn children into the world? Do you even know their worth beyond what they earn? These boys—"

Carter squeezed my hand, cutting me off before I could explode into the rant I was dying to unleash. "It's no use. You're trying to appeal to their kinder, gentler side and they don't have one. At least, not where we're concerned. We're not their sons, we're just their meal tickets. Let me see where I can stash them for tonight so I can get a cashier's check to them in the morning." He looked defeated. It broke my heart.

"No." Carter's grandfather stood in the doorway. "This ends today."

"Gramps, what are you doing here?" Carter asked.

"Chris texted me." He nodded at Stavros. "Thanks for standing in; you should get back to your party." Stavros bowed his head and left. "As for you two?" He pointed at Caleb and Clara in warning. "It's over."

"Now, Dad," Caleb said, trying to appeal to his father.

"Nope. We're done. I shouldn't have let it go on this long. Carter—sell both those buildings. The proceeds go into an account for these two. When the money is gone they can suck it up and get jobs like everybody else. No more yearly pay-outs, no more rent-free living, no more middle-of-the-year begging."

"We can make life uncomfortable for Chris and Carter if we have to. We don't want to go that route," Carla threatened.

I stared at her in confusion. What in the hell kind of mother was she? If I hadn't seen it with my own eyes I don't think I would've understood it. Unfortunate as the scene was, it gave me better insight into the mind and heart of Carter Parks.

"No, you don't," Gramps said. "Recently, I've gotten back in touch with my friend in intelligence, Jonas. You remember him, don't you Caleb?"

Caleb nodded and shuffled uneasily.

"Well, he was doing a little bit of work for me on another issue and I had him dig into some of y'all's shenanigans for the past few years. Let's say this: You take the settlement and walk away and we don't file fraud and forgery charges."

"You can't keep me from seeing my boys!" Clara wailed.

I rolled my eyes.

Gramps folded his arms across his chest. "They will know where to find you if they want to see you. One last thing? If you roll up again without an invitation, we'll get a restraining order and shut the accounts down. Are we clear?"

Clara's eyes welled up with tears. "Is that what you both want?"

Chris looked at his watch. "I have curfew. I'll talk to you later, bro. Thanks, Gramps." He moved toward the door and I stopped him. He looked down at me and I enveloped him in a big hug.

"Thanks for sending the text. I'll see you at Madere's tomorrow," I whispered in his ear. He hugged me back.

"Sorry you had to see this. Take care of my brother tonight?"

"No worries. Every night if he'll let me," I'll promised.

Without a look back, Chris escaped.

Caleb turned to Carter. "Son?"

Carter hugged his grandfather and reached out a hand to me. "Thanks, Gramps. Bye, Caleb, Clara. Let's go, Kitty."

We left the room and flashbulbs went off again. I took a step back. "I'm ready to get outta here."

"Let's head home." We signaled to Stavros that we were leaving. The valet brought the car around and we slid gratefully into it. As we drove off, he said, "I'm sorry you had to see that."

"I'm kind of glad I did. It explains a lot. I wish I'd asked you about them sooner. I had no idea that they were so . . ."

"Mercenary?" he said sardonically.

"Disengaged," I amended diplomatically.

"That's a polite way to say it."

I turned in my seat to look at him. "Anyway, I think you're amazing."

"How do you figure?" He flashed me a look.

"To have those parents and those experiences and still be the man you are? That's pretty awesome, Mr. Parks." Carter could've chosen to play the victim. With the parental example he had, it would have been so easy for him to wallow and take shortcuts to get where he was today. He could've allowed his upbringing and circumstances to define him, but that was not who he was. Carter was the kind of man who rose above; who went above and beyond to be the best that he could be with no excuses. It was one of the many things that I admired about him. I wasn't sure that faced with the same set of circumstances I would've turned out as well. I was blessed. Not only in my family, but also the man who had chosen to love me.

I also understood why he waited so long to take our relationship beyond casual. The Montgomerys, myself included, were the only traditional family unit he had ever known. I knew in that moment that no matter what happened between us, I would never take that away from him. But I planned to work like hell to make sure it would never be an issue. Carter Parks was a keeper.

"Thank you, Katrina. That means a lot, coming from you. Now you see why I love your parents so damned much. As if I need any more reason than the fact that they gave me my best friend and the love of my life."

I smiled at him. "You're sweet. I'd show you how sweet, but I'm exhausted."

"My parents have that effect on people."

"Why didn't you tell me how bad it was?"

"I don't like talking about it."

"To me?"

"To anyone," he said tersely.

"You're gonna have to change that behavior, CP. From here on out, we're a team. If it bothers you, it bothers me and I want to hear about it. Got it?" I said sternly.

"Yes, ma'am."

"All right, then. I like Stavros, by the way."

"Yeah, he's been great to me."

"You may not have had the best parents in the world, but you managed to align yourself with really great people along the way."

"I've been lucky," he said modestly.

"Blessed."

"That too," he agreed. "You know one blessing I am thankful for?"

"I can think of several. Which one did you have in mind?"

"Specifically that big, new bed my hot new girl-friend purchased."

"Ha! Your hot new girlfriend is useful."

"I have to agree with you. The spirit is willing . . . but I'm exhausted too. All the sexy is gonna have to wait; sleep is about to happen."

"You get no argument from me. I can't think of the last time we got eight straight hours."

He grinned at me. "How about we go for six and see what the morning brings?"

I grinned back. "You've got yourself a deal, mister." We drove the rest of the short distance home in comfortable, contented silence.

25

What's all the hugging and happy dancing about?

Carter—Sunday, July 18—2:39 p.m.

Chris and Chase were playing video games, Madere was in the kitchen, Pops and Gramps were dueling over a chessboard in the sunroom. Belle, Beau, Roman, Jewel, Katrina, and I had finished eating brunch after church; we were reviewing the files left for us by Captain Calvin.

"I say we expose all of this the night of Katrina's party," Belle said as we sat around one of the tables in Madere and Pops's family room.

Nodding, Roman flipped back through the information we had been given. Looked like Kevin Delancey and Renee Nightingale had quite a bit to answer for. "Did they really think we wouldn't figure it out?"

"The last straw was the anonymous offer to buy BellaRich," Beau said.

Katrina smirked. "If they had covered their tracks a little better, maybe not pulled together financial backing that had ties to Greg's bank. Once we found that, it wasn't so hard to look at the proposed business plan they attached to the financial documents and see not only who was behind the offer, but also who they planned to put in charge once the sale went through." She rolled her eyes.

"I'm actually a little insulted that Renee underestimated us like this," Jewel said, grimacing.

Captain Calvin had put together a pretty clear trail of documents showing that Kevin had decided to buy BellaRich well over a year ago. He'd had a third party make an offer and it was rejected. The offer was rejected for the simple reason that BellaRich, much like Parks Properties, was a privately owned company. They were both family companies. It was my intention that Parks Properties stay in my family for at least the next generation. It was Belle's plan that either a Richards (her family) or a Montgomery would own and run BellaRich.

For some reason, Kevin took his offer being turned down as a challenge, so he decided he needed a way in with the Montgomerys. His first plan was to meet and marry Katrina. His backup plan was to disparage the company, hoping to drive the price down, maybe thinking they would want to get rid of it because of the bad publicity. He failed at both.

Somewhere along the way in his research on Katrina, Belle, and Beau, he must have come across the connection to Renee. Apparently, he reached out to her and together they planned the hidden cameras, the leaking of the photos, the release of the fake sex tape, and all the rest of the rumors and innuendos.

When we paired what the captain found with the video, e-mails, and phone calls from Renee's own laptop, we had all the evidence we needed to not only file civil and criminal charges, but also to turn all the negative publicity right back around on them.

It felt good to be able to tie this up in a bow. The sooner we got past this, the sooner we could get on with our future. I was ready to live the rest of my life with Katrina, no looking back. I spoke up. "Belle, you should let a few people know that you are interested in entertaining offers for the company. Get Danila to leak that we are planning on making a big announcement at Katrina's birthday party. That's just enough to get Kevin and Renee to relax their guard, start thinking things are going their way. Really, this party is perfect timing. We should make this event a big deal. I have a building downtown in what they're calling SoCo now, South of Colorado Street. We're converting it into life-work-play units that would be perfect. Let's invite all of Roman's customers, Jewel's customers, mine, BellaRich's, and the media. All of the press we can get there. We make a point of inviting Kevin. We invite that Royal Mahogany CEO, the other accusers. We definitely invite Renee."

"You think she'll show?" Belle asked.

Jewel nodded emphatically. "She won't be able to pass up the opportunity."

Beau rubbed his hands together. "Yes. I like

this plan. We do cocktails, sit everybody down for dinner, act like we're going to roll a montage tape on Kit-Kat and—"

"Yep, we shut all the shit down in one fell swoop." I nodded.

"Boom. Busted." Roman grinned.

"Sounds great," Jewel said. "I am beyond ready for this to be over. Now who is going to pull together this extravaganza in less than a week's time?"

Katrina was typing on her Galaxy tablet. "I'm e-mailing the admins, Shawn and Tara. Jewel, Suzanne is still with you?"

"Yep, and she knows a great event planner too."

"Excellent," Belle said, stifling a yawn.

"Someone keeping you up nights, Delaney Mirabella?" Katrina teased.

She smiled wearily. "Actually, I didn't sleep well and Pastor Moss got all long-winded this morning about the wages of sin. It was all I could do not to nap in the pew."

"Denial is more than a river in Egypt," Beau muttered.

"Girl, you still haven't taken that pregnancy test?" Jewel smothered a laugh. "Are you gonna wait until you're in the delivery room?"

"I'm not pregnant," Belle responded with a sniff.

Beau, Roman, and I exchanged looks. We knew enough to keep our mouths shut.

Madere came out of the kitchen. "Enough business. I have lemon bars and strawberry short-cake. Anyone have a sweet tooth today?"

Every hand at the table went up. I pushed back my chair and stood up. "I'll come help you, Madere."

"Suck up," Beau whispered as I walked past. I smacked him on the side of the head and kept moving.

Pops looked up as I followed Madere and I tilted my head toward the kitchen to ask him to follow. He raised a brow, said a few words to Gramps, and joined me.

Opening the freezer, I handed Madere the whipped cream. I started slicing dessert as I decided how to say what I needed to say. This needed to be done right the first time. I only wanted to do this once.

"Son, we ain't gettin' no younger." Pops crossed his arms and leaned back against the counter with a sly grin.

Madere rapped him on the hand with a wooden spoon. "Let the boy get his thoughts together."

There was nothing to it, but to do it. "You both know I think of you as parents."

They smiled and nodded. "And you're a son to us. Always have been, always will be." Pops said gruffly, "You're a fine man. We couldn't be prouder."

Clearing my throat, I pushed past the emotion and continued. "I want you to know that I love your daughter, Katrina, very much."

"We know that, *mon fils*. We know. You really don't have a good poker face around her," Alanna tittered.

"Then I would very much appreciate your blessing to marry your daughter."

Alanna and Avery looked at each other and after a high five and a fist bump, they began laugh-

ing joyously. It might have been more of a delighted chortle. Madere raised her hands to the
heavens dramatically and started shaking her hips
and snapping her fingers. "Praise God."

"All praises," Pops said, bumping his booty with
Madere. They did some sort of dip and a skip and a
step-together-step dance around the kitchen.

"Hallelu! Last one down and we thought it
would never happen." Madere giggled.

I pursed my lips to keep from laughing at the
two of them. "So I take it that's a yes?"

"That's a *hell yes*, boy." Pops grinned from ear
to ear. "Time's a-wastin'. How soon are you think-
in' you want to do this? Any chance you can do a
twofer birthday party-slash- wedding?"

"Ease up a minute," I scolded them. "All in
good time. I've got to ask her first."

Madere stopped dancing long enough to
come over and kiss me on both cheeks. "No child
of mine would be foolish enough to turn you
down. We've always been so gratified to have you
in our lives. This makes us so very, very happy."

"Thanks Madere." It meant a lot.

"Good job, boy. Damned good job." Pops
pulled me into a hug.

"All I did was fall in love with the woman you
raised. So good job to both of you and thank you
so much for everything you've done and been to
me all these years." I got a little choked up and
Pops patted me comfortingly on the shoulder.

Madere teared up and ran out to the sunroom.
She flung herself into Gramps's lap and kissed him
on both cheeks. "You raised a good boy."

"He raised two good boys!" Chris called out

from in front of the TV. No one paid him any attention.

"What's all the hugging and happy dancing about?" Katrina asked.

"Just talking about the gift your man got you for your birthday," Pops answered with a wink at me.

"Ooo!" She clapped. "I love gifts. Gimme a hint, it's got to be good if you two are reliving your disco days. Someone tell me!"

I pretended not to hear her and leaned down to Madere and Gramps. "You all wanna run an errand with me?"

"Right now?' Gramps asked, looking wistfully at the lemon bars that were disappearing from the platter.

Madere laughed at him. "Collin, you know I put some on the side for you."

Gramps stood up with Madere in his arms. "Avery, you better watch yourself. I'm going to steal this filly from you yet."

"Take your best shot, old-timer," Avery responded with the confidence of a man who was happily married for four decades and counting.

"Madere, Gramps, and I are stepping out for a second," I announced to the room. Heads swiveled in our direction.

"What's that about?" Beau asked.

Madere stared them all down. "Everybody just mind your business and try not to tear the house up while we're gone. Chase?"

Chase dropped his video controller and stood up. "Yes, ma'am?"

"You're in charge."

"Don't worry 'bout nuttin', Madere," he announced.

"There goes the neighborhood." Pops sat, settling into his La-Z-Boy with his dessert and a spoon

The next generation of Montgomerys didn't fall far from the tree.

We sat in the back room of a discreet office tucked in an innocuous building in Uptown. In front of us sat an open briefcase with row upon row of diamond rings. I considered myself a connoisseur of fine things, but all of the rings looked exactly the same. Nothing stood out. "None of these look like Kit-Kat to me," I groused before turning to Gramps and Madere. "What do you think?"

Madere shook her head. Gramps frowned. "She can buy her own regular diamonds. You need to get her something she wouldn't think to get herself."

"*Exactement.*" Madere bobbed her head affirmatively.

I looked at Alton, the wholesale jeweler, and raised my hands. "We're gonna need to see something exotic." *Exotic* probably meant expensive, but how often did one get engaged? My hope was just this once.

"Yup." Gramps nodded. "That's the word I'm looking for: exotic."

Alton closed the case and slid it to the floor before pulling out a different one. "Okay, then. How about these?" He opened a case where a lot of colored stones perched in a mixture of settings.

"Ooo. Now were talkin'. *Que c'est beau!*" Madere exclaimed and reached for the same ring that I was reaching for. It was a large pear-shaped pink stone set in a band of small, round stones in shades of green and blue. "What is this?" she asked, her eyes wide.

Alton grinned and I stifled a groan. A grin like that was guaranteed to cost me a mint. "You have a wonderful eye, Mrs. Montgomery. That is a flawless four-karat pink diamond. The band has sapphire, emerald, green amethyst, aquamarine, and tanzanite. That gives you a total of eight-and-a-half-carats' worth of stones set into a platinum band."

Gramps laughed. "I don't even know what half of that is, but I can hear the *ca-ching* from here."

Madere looked at the ring and then back at me. "Perhaps we could pick out something less ostentatious. A little more sedate, no?"

"Because your daughter is so toned down?" I teased. "Alton, how much is that?"

He named a figure that had my grandfather cackling while slapping his thigh. Madere gasped audibly and I just shook my head. Fancy woman, fancy ring.

I sighed dramatically. "No worries, we can dip into Chris's trust fund, Gramps can move in with me, and I'll sell the Benz."

"Wait a minute!" Gramps protested worriedly.

"*Mais non!*" Madere looked appalled and set the ring down on the table quickly.

A bead of sweat popped out on Alton's brow as he sensed the sale slipping away. "I could take fifteen percent off since it's you, Carter." Right. Like he was doing me a favor? Time to play hardball.

"Or you could cut twenty-five percent off, knowing I'll need the matching necklace and earrings. That way, you'll toss in the bracelet for old times' sake." I stared him down.

He winced. "For old times' sake."

With a wide smile, I handed him my credit card. "Have the ring sized down to a six. I'll be back for it later in the week. Wrap the rest up for me."

Madere's mouth fell open and then closed again as Alton jumped up with a smile of his own. Madere leaned over to hug me and one more item caught my eye. I pointed at them and signaled to Alton that I would take those as well. He scurried to go run my card and get the packages together before I change my mind.

"So much money!" Madere exclaimed with a hand over her heart.

"I had to do it; that ring is Katrina all day."

"It's one of a kind, just like Katrina," Gramps agreed. "When I married your grandmother, I took out a three-hundred-and-fifty-dollar loan that I paid off in twenty-four months. I got her a bigger ring for our ten-year anniversary, but she never took off the first one. Wore it until the day cancer took her, God rest her soul." I nodded sympathetically. I had never met my grandmother, but no one ever had a bad thing to say about her.

Madere held up her hand. "I've worn this beat-up gold band every day of my married life. Avery got me a big old diamond for our twenty-fifth anniversary, but I only wear that for special occasions."

"You think I should go simple?" I wondered if I was going too over-the-top.

"Katrina doesn't even wear simple T-shirts." Madere smiled fondly. "She's been a bigger-than-life girly-girl from day one. Always with the glitter and the sparkles and the colors. *Mon ange* is a peacock, not a pigeon."

"Um-hmm, that's true. And this one"—my grandfather pointed his thumb at me—"has always liked fine things. Expensive taste, even when we could only look at them through the window. Worked his fingers to the bone to be able to do more than look. Check my boy out now; settling down, making commitments, buying pink diamonds." He eyed me in speculation. "Listen son, just how rich are you exactly?"

"Gramps!" I shook my head. "Don't worry about it. You don't have to move in with me and Christmas isn't canceled."

Madere assessed me. "I'm wondering myself. How many buildings you own exactly, handsome?" She plopped a hand on one hip.

I was saved from answering by Alton stepping back in the room. He discreetly handed me a leather folder. I opened it and looked at the total before signing and returning it to him. He passed me a medium-sized bag and a small square box. I took them both and smiled at Madere. "Alanna Montgomery, a token of my esteem." I handed her the black velvet box.

"What did you do?" She opened the lid and gasped at the pink diamond solitaire earrings nestled inside. When she looked up at me, I had an image of the beautiful woman Katrina would be when she got older. And I couldn't wait. "You can't—it's too much," she protested, fingering the small gems as they winked up at her.

"Woman, put those rocks in your ears so I can go get my lemon square and my nap. When my boy gives, he gives from the heart," Gramps harrumphed and gave me an approving glance.

"Oh, Collin," she scolded, quickly taking off her hoop earrings and replacing them with the studs. She checked herself out in the mirror, moving her head from one angle to another, catching the light. "I shouldn't accept, I really shouldn't . . . but I'm going to." She kissed me again. "You're such a blessing."

"See that, Gramps—I'm a blessing." I nudged him as we headed out of the offices.

"Equal part curse, if you ask me," he grumbled, but dropped a hand on my shoulder and squeezed.

"Nobody asked you, Collin," Madere told him, stopping to admire her earrings once more in the car window. She tucked her long hair behind her ears and grinned like a child on Christmas morning.

"Get in the car, Alanna, and maybe they'll name my first great-granddaughter after you."

"You're just grumpy he didn't get you anything."

"What you mean? He's getting me a fancy new granddaughter. She's going to be Katrina Parks."

"How do you know she'll go by Parks?" Alanna challenged.

"And why wouldn't she? Parks is a fine name and much shorter than Montgomery," Gramps argued.

"I'm just saying that my daughter goes by a professional name. She can call herself Montgomery or Parks or purple flying squirrel—I don't care as long as she marries the boy and soon," Alanna sassed.

"She marries my boy she's going to be a Parks." Gramps nodded as if the subject was closed.

I stayed out of it. When the two of them got to bickering like this there was nothing to do but stay out of the way and let them fight it out. Though I had to admit, the sound of "Katrina Parks" had a nice ring to it. But I did not want to encourage them. We had just bought the ring and they had me married with children already. I wouldn't have it any other way.

26

Big Sexy is dead: Long live Mr. Parks

Katrina—Friday, July 23—10:57 a.m.

I was thirty years old today. Thirty. Years. Old. The big 3-0. Officially past the age where you got to do stupid things and chalk it up to youth. Time to put away childish things and all that. Time flies when you're having fun or working so hard that it seems like fun. Whatever. Time flies. Six months ago, I would have been all up in my feelings about turning thirty. But looking around my office, looking and feeling good in a striped pink-and-white pantsuit I had designed, knowing that I had friends, family, and a man who loved me? I had nothing to complain about—not one thing.

Kevin Delancey and Renee Nightingale had taken their best shot and I was still here. Still standing. Better than ever before, actually. I wouldn't say they did me a favor, but . . . I couldn't complain about the way it all turned out. For me, anyway.

"Delivery for Katrina Montgomery," a young guy carrying a huge bouquet of roses announced.

"I'm Katrina Montgomery." I waved.

He looked around the bouquet and his jaw dropped. "Cajun Kat. You are hotter in person than on the Internet," he whispered in awe.

"Oh well . . . thank you." I flashed my professional smile and came forward to get the flowers. I set them on the corner of my desk and since he looked so damned happy to meet me, I reached in a drawer and pulled out an 8 x 10 glossy of me in a bikini top and jeans. Signing it with a flourish, I kissed the picture below my signature and handed it to him.

"Hey! That's awesome. I'm going to put this up in my bedroom!" I tried not to wince at the thought of that. God only knew what that picture would bear witness to. He motioned toward my table. "You might want to make more room on that desk and that table. There are a lot more flowers coming, Miss Kat." A stream of delivery people with roses filed in. Belle sauntered in behind them and looked around.

"Somebody loves you," she singsonged.

"The man is crazy!" I exclaimed as the last set of roses appeared in my office. Flowers covered every available surface and overflowed into the hallway.

"How many is that?" Belle asked with wide eyes.

I twirled around the room, counting. "Thirty dozen. One dozen for every year. All in different colors. Did you know there were this many different shades of roses?"

Belle shook her head in amazement. "I did not. That Big Sexy is something else."

"You know what?" I said. "I don't think he should be Big Sexy anymore. He's Carter Evan Parks." I didn't want Carter marginalized. This was a grown man, my man. He was big and sexy to me, not the rest of the world.

"Well all right, then." She looked over my shoulder. "Here he comes now. Mr. Parks, I presume."

Carter was in a light gray summer-weight suit with a pale pink shirt and striped tie. He looked good enough to eat. He strolled in, a man completely as ease with himself; greeting everyone he passed. And the best part? He was all mine. He stopped and raised Belle's hands to his lips. "Mrs. Montgomery, looking lovely as ever. Why so formal?"

"Princess here says you are forevermore and henceforth to be known by your Christian and given name. No more Big Sexy for you."

He glanced over at me. "Oh, yeah? Problem, diva?"

"You can be Big Sexy to me," I declared and settled my hands on my hips in challenge.

"And you only, huh?" he asked, sliding up next to me.

"Exactly. Me only. Really, who else do you need?" I smiled into his eyes.

He wrapped an arm around my waist and dropped a kiss on my lips. "Fine by me. Happy birthday, Kit-Kat."

"Thanks, babe. These flowers are gorgeous." I kissed him back.

"Not as gorgeous as you." He wrapped his second arm around me and leaned in. I snuggled in with a contented smile. He was so damned charming. And did I mention mine, mine, mine?

I asked Belle, "Isn't he charming?"

"For sure, sugar. If y'all gonna be all smooch-smoochy, I'll just excuse myself." She stepped out of the office. "Has anyone seen my charming husband?"

"Eh, *ma femme*, I'm right here trying to work my way through the enchanted forest. What level of besotted, over-the-top, setting-a-bad-precedent-for-men-everywhere foolishness is this?" He strode to the door and viewed my office. "I should've known you were behind this, Se—"

Belle put her hand over his mouth. "His name is Carter."

"I know that," Beau muttered behind her fingers, giving his wife a strange look.

"Only Carter. Or CP. Or Mr. Parks," I reiterated.

"*Mr. Parks?*" he said, snickering.

"You gotta problem with that?" I squinted at him.

Beau put his hands up in surrender. "Big Sexy is dead. Long live Mr. Parks." He reached out a hand to Carter. Carter took it and pulled him in for one of those man hugs where they pat each other on the back or whatever. "It's been a long time since we were the Pontchartrain poonhounds, eh *mon ami?*"

"Oooo, you had to bring it up, sugar?" Belle shook her head.

"For real," I scolded, "we could just let those sleeping dogs lie."

Carter asked, "Sleeping dogs, though, Kitty?"

"They didn't call you the Pontchartrain priests, now, did they?" I quirked a brow in his direction.

Beau waved that away. "Aw, sis, the past is the past."

Carter smirked and nodded without saying another word. Maybe one day I'd get him to share one of his tales from his wild days. Then again, did I really want to know? I actually didn't care who he used to be. The person who he was now was absolutely perfect for me. He caught me staring at him and with a final slap on Beau's shoulder, he reached out and grabbed my hand.

"You ready to get out of here for the rest of the day, lovely?" he inquired.

I was more than ready to go. I wasn't even sure why I hadn't taken the day off. "What about all the flowers? I don't want to leave them here."

He shrugged. "These are for your office; you've got the same at home."

"You are spoiling me." I beamed.

"Don't act like you don't love it," he teased.

"I do love it. I love you," I cooed and leaned in for a kiss.

Beau grimaced. "Ugh. No. Please get out of here, the both of you. Happy Birthday, *ma petite souer*. We'll see you later."

"Not tonight," Carter stated firmly.

"Mr. Parks has spoken," I announced. I grabbed my purse and laptop case. We headed out, calling out to everyone that I would see them tomorrow night at the party. Amid birthday salutations, I sailed out with my man.

We made great time getting back to the house. The flowers were everywhere. Even though people teased me and called me a princess—honestly, with the exception of my father, I'd never had a man treat me this well. Never, not a one of them. I wanted Carter to know that as much as I appreciated every grand gesture, I didn't have to have it to love him.

We set down our cases and phones and keys. He threaded his fingers with mine and tugged me toward the stairs. "Come up with me."

"In a sec," I told him and instead tugged him toward the couch. He sat in the corner and I curled up next to him. "Carter, I want to tell you something," I said in a grave tone.

"Am I in trouble?" He met my eyes.

"No, why—did you do something to get in trouble?"

He snorted. "You wanted to tell me something?"

"Yeah. I love the things you do for me. The grand gestures. I love your life. Our life. The house, the cars, the villa in Punta Cana, the earrings for my mom—I love all of that."

"Good." He nodded.

"But I don't need it," I stated firmly.

He looked confused. "You don't want it?"

"Listen to me, C—I said I don't *need* it. I just want you. If we go broke tomorrow and have to move in with Beau and Belle—"

"Woman, bite your tongue," he interrupted. "Have you lived with Beau? He's a slob!"

"That he is, but on the good side, he's an amazing cook," I rationalized.

"You're an amazing cook. I grill things. We'd survive."

"I'm just saying. For me, it's not about what you can do for me that way. I don't want you to think that I need furs and shoes and pearls to be happy. I like those things, true—"

He coughed discreetly.

"Okay, fine," I raised my foot, clad in a pink patent stiletto with a red bottom. They were lovely, I had to admit. "I love expensive shoes, I cannot lie. But if I had to choose between giving up all my shoes and giving up you? I'm keeping you."

"Whoa. That is serious talk from a shoe addict. I'm flattered."

"Right?" I snickered. "The deepest declaration I can make."

"Kinda sexy. But here's the thing." His tone went serious. "I can easily afford it. If I couldn't, I wouldn't do these things. You'd get a single rose and a handwritten poem."

"You write poetry?" It seemed I learn something new about him every day. Life with Carter Parks was never boring. When was the last time I could say that?

"I've been known to put pen to paper a time or two," he admitted.

"What's a girl gotta do to earn a poem from Carter Parks?" I wondered.

"Keep living right and you'll find out," he teased.

"Is that a challenge?" I gazed at him through my lashes.

"Baby, that's a guarantee."

"Poetry by Parks. Now, that's sexy."

"Oh, I keeps it sexy. No matter what you call me."

"Are you going to miss being called Big Sexy?"

"Not really." He smirked. "As long as I still hear it from you, that's all that matters."

"You can count on that."

He turned serious for a moment. "I like how we live and I worked hard to get here, so I'm not going to apologize for it. If I do too much, just reign me in."

The few times I had tried to put Carter in check had not worked out well for me. "When has anyone ever reigned you in?"

He shrugged. "You could if you wanted to, but you like me this way."

"Bold, audacious, arrogant, and over-the-top?" On any other man I would find these traits irritating, but for some reason they worked with Carter.

"I see that and raise you. You can be fancy, fickle, funny, and forceful."

"I am fancy."

"Speaking of fancy . . ." Carter pulled a small, wrapped box out of his jacket pocket and handed it to me. "Tell me if these tickle yours."

I ripped the paper open and found a long, skinny jeweler's box. Squealing with delight, I opened the box and found the black velvet box inside. Popping up the hinges, I saw the most beautiful bracelet I'd ever seen. It was a tennis bracelet with pink diamonds and blue and green stones interspersed, set in sparkling platinum. "Oh my God, this is gorgeous! This is what you picked out with Madere and Gramps! I can now admit I was so jealous of Madere's earrings, but this more than makes up for them." I snapped the bracelet on my wrist and held it up to the light. Gorgeous!

Carter handed me a second box. "No, that was a gift of your own. *This* makes up for them."

"You didn't!" I ripped open the packaging to find the matching dangly earrings.

"Oh, but I did." He grinned.

"So apparently you like me fancy." He helped me put on the new earrings.

"Indeed I do." He traced his hand down my calf to my ankle. "Furthermore, I like those fancy shoes."

"Before you get all birthday sexy on me, I just want to be clear. For the record, Carter Parks. You are sufficient. Just being with you is the cake; all the rest of this is frosting and sprinkles and sparklers."

His grin widened. "Ni-ice. So, uh . . . there are two masseurs upstairs in the guest room waiting to give us a couples' massage. Is that too grand of a gesture?"

"It's a beautiful gesture and normally I'd say let's do this. But right now I'd rather you sent them away and we gave each other a couples' massage for the rest of the afternoon. You are about to get so damn lucky."

"I like how you think. I also had a chef coming at seven to cook for us."

I nodded. "Nice touch. Instead, tell him to cook it where he is and have someone drop it off around eight."

"And then I was taking you dancing," he continued.

"You can spin me around the pool deck before midnight and we'll call it a perfect birthday all the way around."

"You're easily satisfied," he murmured, grazing his lips against my forehead.

"No, I'm not, but all I need today is you," I answered simply.

"I do love you," he sighed.

"That's handy, cause I love you right back."

"Happy birthday, Kitty."

"Best one yet."

"Many more to come." He squeezed my hands.

"I'll send the masseurs packing, you call the chef." I hopped up off the couch.

He smacked my rear as I went by. "And then meet me in the bedroom wearing nothing but those shoes."

"Ooo." I shivered just thinking about it. "This is going to be a *very* happy birthday."

"Bet your fine ass it is."

27

That beat-down idea was sounding better and better

Carter—Saturday, July 24—7:14 p.m.

"**M**r. Parks, Ms. Montgomery—over here!" Katrina adjusted the lapel on my jacket of the simple black linen suit I was wearing and ran her hand down my tie.

"Did I mention I like you in black and white?" She tilted her head and tossed her long mane of artfully tangled curls over her shoulder. She clasped my hand and gave the photographers a pose they would love.

"I hope so, since this is a black-and-white party. I'm just trying to keep up with you, diva. That dress is a miracle of modern science," I murmured under my breath as Katrina and I made our way up the red carpet outside of her party. As guest of honor, she could wear whatever she damn well pleased. My girl was in a skintight dress of bright red that was held together by tiny straps that crisscrossed up her back. The hem stopped an eyebrow-raising length up her thighs. A creamy expanse of leg drew the eye down to sky-high silver and red sandals with skinny heels. Not that she didn't always look great, but tonight she looked amazing.

"You like?" Her ruby-glossed lips curved upwards as we turned away from the last group of photographers and headed inside. The venue was a three-story industrial conversion I was working on. With no tenants in the building it was a blank canvas. The party-planning team had turned one half of the first floor into a party space with dinner seating, dance floor, lounge areas, and several stations for drinks and hors d'oeuvres. The walls of the space were wrapped in a white fabric and tiny white lights twinkled from above. Simply but elegantly decorated in silver, white, and black; Katrina stood out like a vibrant flame in her red dress. We made our way around the room meeting and greeting friends, family, and clients as we went. Interspersed around the room were giant pictures of Katrina throughout the years.

There was a gap-toothed six-year-old Katrina jumping off the diving board. A preteen Katrina falling down on the ski slopes. A picture of Katrina prowling the catwalk in Milan was mounted next to one of her swimming in the ocean as a teenager. Another picture showed Katrina talking to me on the sidelines of one of my football games. I paused in front of it; I think she had just turned twenty-one.

"I don't even remember this, do you?" I asked her.

She shook her head. "Only vaguely. But look at us." In the picture we were standing in the middle of a flurry of activity. Amid all the hustle around us, we only had eyes for each other. I was staring down at her intently as she spoke animatedly.

"Well, that's a revealing photo," I said. Here I thought I'd been so discreet all these years. Like Madere said, I had no poker face around her.

"Quite." Katrina nodded. "So we've been into each other for years."

"Apparently." I grinned, not all that surprised.

Katrina looked back at me with equal delight. "Good thing we ended up together."

"Damned good thing." Over her shoulder, I saw Kevin Delancey striding into the party. "Last chance to ditch this whole 'let's beat them at their own game' plan and let me and the fellas commence a beat-down."

She pivoted on one heel and let out a deep breath. "Let's see how the night goes. We might do both." She took a step closer to me and I tightened my hand at her waist.

"I got you. Now let's get this asshole."

Katrina wove her arm through mine and pasted her brightest smile on her face. "Let's do this."

Kevin paused, looking around. He also took the opportunity to let the two photographers we'd hired for inside the event click his better side. His glance landed on Katrina and his smile went tight around the edges. I watched as his eyes fell to our entwined arms. His face tightened even more. When he met my eyes, I allowed the satisfaction to show through. *Yeah, you messed up a good thing. I stepped in and I'm not letting go.* I could tell by the tightening of his lips and the hardening of his jaw that my message was broadcast loud and clear.

Katrina giggled and I glanced down at her. "What's amusing?"

"You need to behave," she scolded under her breath.

"What did I do?" I asked innocently, knowing full well what I had done.

"You totally just sent him the eye-gaze equivalent of marking your territory."

With an unapologetic shrug, I added, "So what if I did? Might as well let him and everyone else eyeing you up this evening know, you're off the market." I wanted everyone to know she was mine.

"Oh yeah?" She stood up on tiptoe to look me in the eye. "You making declarations up in here, in front of all these folks?"

I touched my forehead to hers. "Most definitely."

"Well, don't you two make a lovely couple." Kevin Delancey stood in front of us, doing a really poor job of hiding the sneer on his face.

We stared into each other's eyes for another second before turning our heads toward Kevin. I noticed Beau and Roman standing nearby.

"Hi, Kevin," Katrina said.

"Hey, Delancey. No date?" I asked silkily.

"I thought it best to ride solo tonight. I was so surprised you went through with a party. What with all the troubles you've been having?" Dude had zero chill. He just couldn't pass up the opportunity to stir the pot and see who took the bait.

"What troubles? There's no such thing as bad publicity. Sales at BellaRich are through the roof. I finally found a mutually satisfying relationship and fell in love with a man who . . . gets me. Plus, I look amazing. What troubles?" Katrina purred with a devil-may-care tilt of her chin.

Kevin's eyes narrowed. "Good for you, then. I was surprised to receive an invitation."

Katrina shrugged. "Just because we didn't work out personally is no reason to cut all ties. This is business. No matter our differences, we're business people at the end of the day. Are we not?"

He nodded in acknowledgment. "Well, thank you for the invite. This is quite the turnout. I'll just mingle about. Happy birthday, Katrina."

"Thank you so much for coming," she cooed and smiled even brighter.

Kevin pivoted and strode away without another word. And suddenly, I knew that no matter how the night played out, I was going to have my say. "Katrina, excuse me for a moment, won't you?"

She tightened her grip on my arm. "CP, what are you about to do?"

I raised a brow and reassured her. "Nothing that requires bail." With that, I disentangled myself and walked after Kevin. Beau sent me a look asking if he needed to come with me. I shook my head. Catching up to Kevin as he crossed the dance floor, I clapped my hand on his shoulder. "Step over here with me for a minute, Delancey."

He shrugged my hand off. "That doesn't sound like a request, Parks."

"Funny you should notice that. It isn't. Either

step politely over here away from everyone else or we can discuss it right here out in the open. For everyone to see and hear. Either way, things will get said." I crossed my arms over my chest and waited. That beat-down idea was sounding better and better.

Kevin decided to test whether I was serious or not by eyeballing me in the middle of the dance floor. I was done playing with this fool. I growled and took a step forward. He took a quick step back before pivoting toward the back of the room near the bathrooms. Katrina was surrounded by people, but took a second to send me a "what-the-hell-are-you-doing" look as I walked past. I winked, sent her a "don't-worry-about-it-I-got-this" look back and kept moving. This little talk was long overdue.

When we reached a quiet area behind two tall decorative trees, Kevin turned to face me. "What is it, Parks?"

"What do you think it is, Delancey?" I raised a brow.

"I don't know, some sort of dick-measuring contest?" he scoffed.

"It's not a contest when the outcome is so obvious. This is about your behavior. And how I expect it won't be repeated?"

"Is this some sort of reaction because I had Katrina first? Otherwise, I'm afraid I don't know what you're referring to." So he wanted to play dumb. He was trying my patience. And I didn't have a lot to spare.

I squinted hard at him. "Okay, we can play it this way for now. Let's start by admitting between just us, that it's not who comes first. Particularly when that person took only ten uninspired minutes to come, at that. We both know it's the man who gets to be last, who actually lasts, who wins. Moving on, let's just say you don't really know what I'm talking about. Let's pretend you're not a needle-dick scumbag who bad-mouthed a good woman because she had the good sense to cut you loose."

"Wait just a damn—" he interrupted angrily.

I held up my hand. "No, it's your turn to listen. I've been playing nice because that's the way Katrina wants it, but after tonight if you break bad with Katrina or any member of her family, you'll have to answer to me," I stated firmly.

Kevin smirked and I stepped into his space. We were not going to play that way this evening.

"Don't get it twisted. I'm not like you. I had no silver spoon growing up; I used to hit people for a living. I would prefer not to take it there, but try it again and see what happens."

"So you're a hood rat," he jeered.

I shrugged. "If it makes you feel better to think so, sure. Know this: I will reach back to my hood roots and make you suffer in a million different ways if I deem it necessary. Delancey, I would hate to deem it necessary. Are we clear?"

"Since I don't know what you're talking about, I don't know what to say." He sniffed and adjusted his tie. He took a step forward and I blocked his exit.

"I said . . . are we clear?" I reiterated.

"Crystal," he ground out. "You're a Neanderthal. The two of you deserve each other."

I took a step back and smiled widely. "Thank you. We think so too." With a sweep of my arm, I

motioned him back to the party. "After you, Delancey."

"Parks, you haven't won anything here."

"Actually, I've won everything, you just don't
know it yet."

"We'll see." He rolled his eyes and strode away
without a backwards glance. I noticed with no little
amusement that he put as much space and as
many people between us as possible.

The three tables closest to the front of the room
where the large screen was set up were reserved for
immediate family and close friends. One table held
Madere, Pops, Gramps, Stavros and his date, Greg
and Veronica. Another table held Shawn, Tara,
Yaz, Fredrika, Danila, and other members of our
staff. I walked over to the table where Kat stood
with Jewel, Belle, Roman, Beau, Chris and his
date.

Belle snickered as Kevin practically sprinted
past. "He ran out of there like the hounds of hell
were on his tail."

"Looked like you were about to swing on old
boy," Chris said.

"It was a near thing," I admitted.

"Well all right, we're off to quite a start," Katrina said, smirking.

"I hope you're ready for round two, because
something wicked this way comes," Jewel announced,
indicating the door. Renee walked in wearing a short
white sequined tank dress. She entered the room
not even a full ten steps behind Madison Archeneaux, the CEO of Royal Mahogany. Not subtle, if
you knew what to look for. She scanned the room
and then her steps faltered when her eyes met

Kevin's and then they looked away from each other. Then they spent the next few minutes sending surreptitious glances in each other's direction.

"They are the worst spies ever," Roman complained.

"No double-oh-seven about them at all." Beau sucked his teeth.

"Kind of pisses me off that it took us so long to put it together," I added in disgust.

"Well, now that we have and the gang's all here," Katrina said, "let the games continue."

28

Grab a seat and get comfortable, we've got a few surprises in store

Katrina—Saturday, July 24th—8:03 p.m.

No matter how the night turned out good or bad; it was one I would never forget. That I knew for sure. I glanced around, taking mental snapshots. Beau, elegantly clad in a white suit with black piping that only he could pull off. Belle, stunningly garbed in a color block black and white sheath dress. Roman, pulling off a charcoal-gray jacket over black shirt, tie, and pants. Jewel, glowing in a silver blouson-style dress that hid the beginning of a baby bulge.

Madere and Pops were resplendent in black, chatting with Gramps and Stavros. Chris was dapper as ever in a perfectly tailored ivory sport coat.

The decorated white lights descending from the rafters gave the room an elegant feel. Smiling waiters carrying platters of juicy shrimp and whatever other succulent appetizers the team had picked out.

And of course, Carter. He resembled a chocolate-dipped Greek god. I would never forget the look on his face when he had Kevin hemmed up in the corner. He looked ready to slay dragons for me. All of that "I don't need a man to ride to my rescue" attitude went out the window as I watched him taking Kevin to task on my behalf. I had to admit, I liked it. I liked it a lot.

Just as I liked the expression on Jewel's face as she moved toward Renee. Renee Nightingale was an attractive woman with a smart brain and all the potential in the world, so I never understood why she seemed determined to live constantly immersed in drama. When I was working with her at Royal Mahogany, I knew she had a flair for public relations and marketing. She was a natural and great at her job, but often seemed to let her attitude and personal demons spill over into her professional behavior.

Speaking of professional, Madison Archeneaux appeared in front of me with a chagrined smile on his face. He was nattily attired in a summer-weight black suit with a subtle light-blue pinstripe. "Katrina, you look lovely as ever." He leaned down to kiss my cheek.

"Thank you, Madison." I struggled not to flinch and to keep an expressionless face as my mind flashed back to one of his more adventurous moments on that tape with Renee. There were some things that absolutely should not be immortalized on film.

"Not to bring up any unpleasantness, but I wanted to tell you how sorry I am that your name ever got mixed up in my unfortunate divorce. I never encouraged that gossip," he imparted earnestly.

I blinked at him; did he think I was stupid? "You certainly never discouraged or negated it either. I wonder why that was?"

He looked affronted. "I think it's better to remain discreet in matters such as these."

"Oh, I completely understand. Completely. No worries, Madison. All's well that ends well," I said graciously.

He paused, as if not sure I was letting him off the hook, and then smiled again. Yes, he definitely thought I was stupid. "Well, thank you for inviting me, Katrina. It's a spectacular event."

"Oh, indeed. Grab a seat and get comfortable; we've got a few surprises in store." I flashed an extra wide and pretty smile, trying to appear as guileless as possible. As he hesitated again, I gave his shoulder a pat to send him on his way. With one last uncertain nod of his head, he wandered off to find a table.

I turned just in time to see Veronica and Jewel herding Renee to a table not far from ours. Greg stayed seated.

"Greg. Roni Mae," Renee greeted them, deliberately using a nickname Veronica no longer liked. "Still together, I see."

"Somehow, we're surviving," Veronica drawled with a sardonic roll of her eyes.

Greg raised a cocktail in Renee's direction. "Some might say *thriving*, but anyway. You know, Ray, they say if you don't have anything nice to say . . ." He turned back around and went back to ignoring her.

"I was just so shocked to get the invitation, knowing my history with the Montgomerys," Renee gushed loudly, ensuring that everyone in a five-table radius could hear her.

"Well, we certainly don't hold grudges. You and I go too far back to let these little disagreements come between us. Don't you think?" Jewel poured it on.

"Of course. But Beau and Belle are good with me being here?" Renee asked skeptically.

Belle glided over to reassure her. "Oh, honey!" Her voice dripped with Georgia charm: "If we cut ties with every woman Beau ever slept with, we would never leave the house."

I had to take a quick sip of water to keep from laughing out loud. Looking away, I caught Carter's attention. He too was struggling to keep a straight face.

Beau swooped in and dropped a kiss on Renee's cheek. "Belle exaggerates. You look lovely, Renee. *Absolument magnifique!*"

Renee preened under all the attention. To add a cherry to the top of the sundae, we'd invited Chris's teammates and Carter's former teammates who spoke at the foundation to sit at the table with Renee. One by one, the well-dressed athletes sat around her. As Kendrick, Spaulding, Paul, and Marcus chose seats at her table; Renee's eyes grew wide. You could tell from her expression that she thought her ship had come in. Invitation to an exclusive party, VIP seating, eye candy? She looked like the cat that ate the canary.

I couldn't wait to wipe that smug grin off her face. I leaned over and called out, "Hey, girl, I'll come over and chat after dinner. I love that dress!"

"Oh. It's an Arizona Wind. I'm sorry," she said silkily.

Our smiles stayed in place at the mention of Belle's rival. The creator of Arizona Wind had stolen designs from Belle a few years ago. Belle and I exchanged a look. "Certainly enough business to go around." I turned away before I gave in to the urge to slap her silly and slid into the chair Carter was holding out for me.

"You're thinking my ass-kicking, elbow-throwing is both justified and viable now, aren't you?" he whispered in my ear as he sat down beside me.

I had to clasp my hands together in my lap tightly and take a few deep breaths. "She's just so damn hateful for no damn good reason."

Belle slid into the chair on my right and squeezed my hand. "Patience, sis. We're almost there."

Yazlyn sent us both a look indicating that she knew exactly what we were thinking. She rose from her seat, wearing a stunning black bandage dress before striding toward the podium placed beside a large drop-down movie screen. She picked up the microphone. "If everyone will be seated, we'll begin dinner service. We'd like to thank everyone for coming out tonight to celebrate the anniversary of the birth of an extraordinary woman, Audelia Katrina Montgomery." Applause rang out and I nodded and smiled, too anxious to truly enjoy it. "We'll let you enjoy your meal and then we'll show a short video made especially for the birthday girl's enjoyment. *Bon appétit!*"

Yaz winked at me as she glided back to her seat. The waiters came out and made an impressive presentation of serving a mixed field greens salad with strawberries, hickory-smoked almonds, and sunburst tomatoes.

They offered everyone a choice of red wine, white wine, champagne, or a nonalcoholic beverage of their liking. I glanced down at the plate and wondered how I would take a single bite. A glass of champagne appeared in front of me. I hadn't ordered any.

Carter nodded and pushed the glass closer to my hand. "Sip, Kitty. Slowly, for your nerves. Then eat. We got you."

Suddenly, I knew it was all going to be okay. Carter, my friends, my family, people who genuinely cared about me, were all in this room. But, I still had to fight off the urge to swig the entire glass like a shot. I sipped and managed to make small talk as people dropped by the table to visit. I took several bites of the surf-and-turf dinner with asparagus tips and sipped a little bit more champagne. By the time Veronica and Beau got up to start the presentation, I was pleasantly mellow, but still had all my wits about me. Beau motioned for the press outside to be let in.

I reached for Carter's hand under the table. He grabbed it and squeezed. I turned to check on Madere and Pops. Madere had a mischievous grin on her face and Pops sent me a wink. I caught

Chris's eye and he mouthed, "It's about to go down!" I smothered a giggle and turned back to the screen. Here we go.

Veronica had spent years hosting a late-night radio call-in show. Her voice was ideal for this kind of presentation. She was wearing a black-and-white pantsuit with a nipped-in waist and palazzo pants from last year's spring line. I made a mental note to try a similar one in crepe for next summer.

"Good evening," she greeted the crowd of close to three hundred. The lights dimmed and a video started rolling on the screen. "Thirty years ago yesterday, an adorable baby girl was welcomed into the world by her parents, Alanna and Avery Montgomery, and looked upon with skeptical wariness by her older brothers Roman and Beau." Pictures from our childhood flashed with humorous commentary from Veronica. Even I was amused, knowing what was coming next. They moved through my teenage years and into my early twenties with the same light-hearted tone. When they transitioned to my work with BellaRich, Beau took over the microphone. He cracked a few jokes about how my design aspirations had netted him a job, a wife, and a life. Then his voice slipped from easygoing and light to serious.

"The thing about Katrina that we hope is coming through is that she's a person who has worked hard to get where she is. She's a strong, independent woman with an unflagging moral compass. None of this was in question until I had the poor taste to become involved with this woman." The next video on the screen was Renee dancing in her underwear with Madison Archeneaux.

Amid gasps, Chris's teammate Paul leaned over to Renee. "Yo shorty—is that you? You lookin' right!" His voice carried and snickers broke out. I had to cover my mouth with the napkin to keep from laughing out loud.

"What the hell is this?" Madison snapped. No one answered, as it was pretty obvious exactly what the hell that was we were looking at.

Beau continued. "Katrina's life was further complicated when these two people met." The next video showed Kevin and Renee in an equally intimate situation. My jaw dropped open. I knew the two of them had hatched up a plot against me; I didn't realize they had quite gotten that personal. "Apologies for the R-rated nature of this portion of the evening, folks. Since Kevin and Renee felt at ease making up and dispersing false information about my sister, I feel just as at ease sharing some truths with you. Here's a conversation between Ms. Nightingale and Mr. Delancey."

Kevin's voice came through the speakers loud and clear.

"We've got them on the ropes, Ray. I hear Belle is looking to sell," he said smugly.

"Kevin, I told you it would work," Renee cooed back. "I can't wait until we take over that company and kick them all out on their snooty asses."

"I think spreading the rumors about her and Archeneaux is what turned the tide," Kevin chuckled.

"Probably. Now that he's on the hook for additional financing, I'm going to quit sleeping with him. It's just not that satisfying."

"*Whatever you'd like. I appreciate you taking one for the team. I'll make it up to you, baby.*"

"*You bet your ass you will.*" Renee giggled. "*I like diamonds.*"

"*All women do,*" Kevin replied drolly. "*We'd better lay low until after the sale goes through. I don't want anything to blow this deal. The offer is going in next week.*"

"*I can't wait to be with you again, lover. So good between us.*"

"*Ummm, keep it warm for me, baby. Daddy's gotta go make a few million.*"

Beau cut the feed and signaled for the lights to come up. Kevin was making a break for the door. Renee was frozen to her seat and Madison Archeneaux stared glumly into his cocktail.

Captain Calvin stepped in front of Kevin. "Hold up there, partner." He escorted Kevin out of the building.

Beau signaled to Tara and Shawn, and they started handing out flash drives to all of the media. "We're giving you information on various infractions Kevin Delancey committed over the course of the past ten years. From just plain-brewed to all kinds of wrong to downright illegal—it's all on there. Over the past year he has participated, with the help of Renee Nightingale, in a conspiracy to defame my sister and devalue BellaRich, all in an effort to purchase it for a lower price. I don't know which of these actions are criminal, which are civilly liable, and which are just despicable actions. But we have people here from a number of different agencies who are going to figure it out. Some of you are going to be asked to leave. The rest of you are welcome to stay—we're about to cut a step up in here. And by the way, happy birthday, Kit-Kat!" He threw back his head and laughed.

The room broke out into nervous laughter as the Beyoncé song "Grown Woman" came on. Reporters rushed forward to ask questions. Renee pushed her chair back and I hopped up quickly to intercept her before she could go too far.

"What?" she said defiantly, eyes flashing with malice.

"Well, you tried it," I declared with a smirk.

"I've never liked you," she hissed and stalked away. Captain Calvin had someone waiting to take her away for further discussion as well.

"The feeling has always been entirely mutual," I called after her and spun away to sing along with Bey, "*I'm a grown woman, I can do whatever I want!*" I raised my hands over my head and spun around before landing in Carter's lap. I threaded my arms around his neck. "This is the best birthday ever."

He grinned down at me. "Glad you're enjoying it. You want to talk to reporters?"

I sighed. "Not really, but let's make it quick. I want to dance with my guy." I stood up, pulling him with me, and walked over to where the media were lined up.

"I'm just so pleased that the truth has come to light and I hope in the future, people will stop and consider what's real before they rush to judgment. As much as I appreciate your interest, you don't mind if I ask you to continue your reporting from the staging area . . . outside?" I smiled sweetly. "We've provided food, drinks, and free Wi-Fi." When they scattered, Madere, Pops, and Gramps were standing beside me and I hugged each of them happily.

"Well, that's that," Gramps said.

Chris spoke up. "Kitty, can we get the real party started now?"

"Indeed, sir." I smiled and called out to my brother. "Beau, cut the lights down and bring the music up." The old Commodores song "Brick House" rang out and I sent a flirty look over to Carter. "You got your dancing shoes on?"

He took my hand and twirled me three times in fast succession. "I think I can manage a l'il sumthin' sumthin', diva." We led the way onto the dance floor and soon most of the party was on their feet. With the pesky distractions out of the way, we could get down to the serious business of celebrating my birthday. Year thirty was looking all right by me.

29

I'm Carter freaking Parks, woman

Carter—Thursday, August 4—10:18 p.m.

It had been close to two weeks since Katrina's party and things had been moving at a crazy pace ever since. Chris was playing preseason games, Gramps had the foundations running smoothly, and business was busier than ever for both Katrina and me.

Instead of the publicity dying down, it had scaled back up. Once the media got hold of the initial threads of the story, they started uncovering all sorts of dirt on Renee and Kevin. Every new revelation triggered a fresh wave of calls to Katrina, to me, to everyone who had been touched by the mess. Eventually it would wind down, but in the meantime, it was wearing on all of us. Katrina included. This morning, I scooped her up with

Belle, Beau, Jewel, and Roman and we headed down to Stavros's vacation home in Dana Point, California.

There was financially comfortable, there was rich, and then there was this level of wealth. All of our homes combined could fit into this 12,000-square-foot property. The place was so huge that when the three couples retired for the night, we were on completely different wings of the house. We had to text each other to meet for dinner earlier. We had dined on grilled shrimp and vegetables. It was the first truly relaxing meal any of us had enjoyed in a few weeks.

A few hours later, Katrina and I sat out on the patio adjacent to our room overlooking the Pacific.

"This was a great idea, CP." She smiled and took a sip of her wine.

"Thank you. I thought we could use a little time away from it all. Monday is soon enough to get back to the grind. We deserve the time-out for dealing with the next phase of our real lives."

"Whatever that is." She smiled.

"We should talk about what that will look like." I took a deep breath and exhaled.

"What real life will look like?" She frowned in confusion.

"Yes, now that it's just you and me without all of the drama and impending doom. What's life going to be like for us? Let's get into it."

She nodded and then her face fell instantly. "Wait, now that everything is straightened out, are you trying to back out of this?"

"Out of what?" I asked in confusion.

"Out of this relationship. Like, it's been fun but see you later?"

"Why would I do that?" I repeated, still lost. I didn't know what she was talking about, but I did know it was pissing me off.

"Yes, Carter, this is what I'm asking. Was this whole thing just about saving me and now that I'm saved, you're done? Do you want out? Have you decided you had enough? Because I have to tell you, if you dragged me halfway across the country with my friends and family just to cut me loose, you have a hell of a fight on your hands. I don't shake easy. I'm not going down without a fight. You are stuck with me. Like it or not." She glared at me and swigged a generous portion of wine.

"What the hell are you talking about?" I still had no idea where she was coming from. This woman could take the most innocuous comment and turn it into a major thing. It was one of her less endearing traits.

She shrugged. "I assume that you've realized that it's not going to be all moonlight and roses and you're ready to go back to your old life. Well, that's just too damn bad."

I set my own wineglass down with a snap. "Who do you think you are talking to? When has this relationship ever been moonlight and roses? You and I are never going to be a walk in the park; we just don't work that way. But I know that. And what old life am I supposed to be going back to? I haven't been that guy I think you're referring to for years. Are you crazy?"

"Are you leaving me?"

"After all of this, do you not know who I am? Have you no clue what I'm really about? Like none?" My voice escalated at the end of the sentence.

She figured out that I was upset. "Ummm. Well . . ."

I cut her off. "I am Carter freaking Parks, woman. I am in love with you and I was trying to propose before you lost your fool-ass mind. For some damn reason, I thought spending the rest of my life with you would be a good idea." I slapped the velvet box down on the table and stomped inside the room, slamming the door behind me. If I'd said it before, I'd said it a thousand freaking times . . . that woman was going to be the death of me.

30

I'm slow, but I'm not stupid

Katrina—Thursday, August 4—10:21 p.m.

I squeezed my eyes shut and shook my head. I stayed messing up with Carter Evan Parks. Sorry, make that Carter Freaking Parks. He whisked me off to the ocean to this beautiful state with people I cared about for some much-needed decompression time. He waited for this special moment to propose and what did I do? I promptly accused him of wanting to be free and play the field. I slapped my hand to my forehead. What could I say? For all my life experience, this was still my first real relationship with an actual grown-up. I had some catching up to do. I was programmed to expect the worst. I still had trouble embracing the best.

Reaching over, I plucked up the jewelry box and twirled it around in my hands. There was nothing else to do but woman up and face the music. I rose and headed inside, determined to restore some special to this evening.

Carter stood beside the fireplace with his hands in his pockets. "You know, Katrina, I don't know what else to do. What else to say to prove that I'm in this."

I gave him a crooked smile. "You don't have to say or do anything else. But I do."

He relaxed his stance and kept listening.

"I promise I'll do better. I'm spoiled, more insecure that I thought I would be, and generally when I get scared, I suck. Seriously, I get a little irrational and then I say stupid, hurtful things that I don't mean. "

"This is an interesting tactic," he noted with a tilt of his head.

"Be that as it may, I'm slow, but I'm not stupid. I recognize a good thing when it's right in front of me." I stepped closer. "And you are right here. You, Carter Freaking Parks, are a very good thing."

"Oh yeah?" He nodded slowly. "It's about damn time you recognized, woman."

"People tell me I can have any man I want and maybe that's true. I don't know. All I know for sure is that the only man I want is you. If you're deluded enough to want to marry me, I'm selfish enough to hold you to it." I went down on one knee in front of him and held up the ring box. "Will you do me the great honor of asking me to marry you, please?"

He flung back his head and laughed before kneeling beside me. He took the ring box from me, flipped it open, and turned it toward me. My jaw dropped open. What was *that*? It was big and pink and sparkly. Gorgeous. I wanted. I grabbed for it. He held it out of my reach. "Not so fast. Audelia Katrina Montgomery, any interest in becoming Audelia Katrina Parks?"

I raised my eyes from that magnificent ring and met his. "Every interest in the world."

"Yeah?"

"Yeah. That's yes. A hell yes, in fact." I held my hand out and he slid the ring on. It was a perfect fit. A perfect color. Perfectly me. I smiled. "I'm going to be Mrs. Sexy."

"Yeah, you are. Katrina Sexy." Carter snickered. "So you're sure about this. You're not going to freak out or anything? Cause this is it. You and me. No more nonsense."

I flung myself at him and wrapped my arms around his neck. We rolled around laughing and tussling on the rug. I landed on top. "I'm a freak out. I may drive you crazy. But I'm in this. Sickness, health, all of that. Like I said earlier, you're stuck with me."

"Looks like we're stuck with each other," he murmured into my hair.

"How lucky are we?"

"Not lucky, blessed," I said with a smile.

"I agree. And Katrina?"

"Yes?" I responded.

"Let's remember this," Carter said seriously, "what this feels like, what it took for us to get here. Let's just do whatever it takes to feel a little bit of this every day for the rest of our lives. Can you do that?"

I stared into his eyes and saw all the reasons

why he was the only man for me. He kept me grounded; even when I felt I was floating above the air. He kept it real; even when we were living out a fantasy. He understood me; even when I didn't understand myself. "I can. I will. Because we are so totally worth it. Now shut up and kiss me, Sexy."

Epilogue

Luckiest day of my life

Jewel, Roman, Beau, Belle, Carter, Katrina—Saturday, August 6—12:42 p.m.

The three couples sat on the back patio of the house in Dana Point by the outdoor fireplace. They'd made pizza in the custom oven outside for lunch and were lounging around for the rest of the day before heading back to Dallas tomorrow.

"God, I'm happy," Katrina announced, holding her ring hand up toward the light for the umpteenth time that day.

"It's a damn fine day," Belle agreed. "You put that hand down before you blind all of us, Kit-Kat."

"Don't hate, diva," Katrina teased.

Belle rolled her eyes. "I'm not hating, I'm just saying."

"You know, as problematic as she was, when you think about it—we all have Renee to thank for this happy day," Jewel said, swirling the sparkling cider in her glass. Heads swiveled toward her in disbelief.

"How exactly do you figure that?" Carter asked with a glare.

Jewel explained. "It started when Renee dragged me to a basketball game where I met Roman."

"Luckiest day of my life." Roman smiled at her as she slid her hand into his.

Jewel continued. "And then after she and Beau broke up and he moved in with us—"

Beau interrupted. "Don't forget the part where you threw me out."

"Right," she said and nodded with no apologies. "But you landed at Katrina's."

"He broke into Katrina's," Katrina corrected, giving Beau a side-eye glance.

"Anyway, that was the day he walked in on me while I was in your shower," Belle added.

"Luckiest day of my life." Beau flashed his trademark grin.

"Wait," Katrina spoke up. "You walked into my bathroom while the shower was running? What if I had company?"

"Please spare us the visual," Roman complained. "But I suggest, Beau, that you and Belle clean up that 'how we met story' before the kids come along. Something PG-thirteen perhaps might be more appropriate."

"Anyway," Jewel went on. "Then when Renee went on her vengeful rampage with Kevin, that's what sparked Carter to own up to his feelings and finally get together with Kit-Kat."

"Oh, I owned my feelings a while back," Carter shared, "but Beau posted the *no trespassing* signs all around his baby sister and when I asked him if I could date her a few years ago, he told me he hoped I was joking and we dropped it."

"*What?*" Katrina whipped her head around to glare at Beau.

He shrugged. "Knowing what I knew about the two of you? It was better that you both waited. Trust me, you both needed the extra time. I gave my consent eventually."

"Luckiest day of my life." Carter nodded.

"See, there you go," Beau finished. "All's well that ends well. I don't know about thanking Renee, but as least something good came out of knowing her."

Belle nodded. "Y'all heard she took a plea?" The other five people stared at her and she raised her hands. "Don't shoot the messenger. I got the e-mail today that she's turning on everybody and saying they forced her to do everything."

"Figures," Jewel scoffed. "That woman has nine lives and she always lands on her feet."

"As long as she lands nowhere near us, I'm good," Katrina stated.

"I'm told she's moving to Los Angeles," Belle shared.

"She'll fit right in." Roman nodded.

"What I was trying to say . . ." Jewel raised her glass. "No matter how we got here, we made it. We're all here where I believe we are supposed to be. So, a toast to us and our continued happiness and success."

They all raised glasses. Katrina squinted at Belle's flute. "What's that you're sipping on, Mrs. Beau?"

Belle sighed. "Mineral water."

"Finally took the test, huh?" Jewel teased.

"Last night," Belle admitted. "I'm officially cooking another generation of Montgomery in the oven."

Varying forms of congratulations and we-told-you–so's rang out. Carter twined his fingers with Katrina's and pulled her to her feet.

"If you'll excuse us," he said, smirking.

"What's the hurry?" Beau asked.

"If Carter Junior is going to keep up with the Montgomerys, we've got some catching up to do."

"Oversharing," Roman muttered with a grin.

"Oh, awesome. Sure, go impregnate my single baby sister," Beau said, hiding a smile.

"Don't worry, we'll get married before the due date," Carter promised.

"Maybe Vegas again," Katrina said, smirking. "We had such a good time there."

"Well, all right, get it, girl," Jewel called out, raising her glass once again.

"We'll see y'all for dinner later?" Belle called out.

Carter and Katrina exchanged a glance. "We'll see you at breakfast." They turned the corner and hit the stairs running. A muffled shriek and chuckle were heard before the sound of a door slamming cut off any more sound.

"Life is good," Roman announced.

"And getting better," Beau agreed, rubbing his hand on Belle's stomach.

Contentedly, the foursome watched the waves lapping against the shore. It was a moment to reflect on the events that had brought them here and the promise of the future yet to come. Life was good.

Glossary

absolument magnifique—absolutely fabulous; magnificent
allons—let's go
bébé—baby
bel homme—handsome man
bon appétit—enjoy your meal
c'est vrai—indeed; okay
chère—term of endearment, like *dear*
cochon—pig
de rien—you're welcome
enchanté—pleased to meet you; enchanted
exactement—exactly
fillette—little girl, daughter
frère—brother
imbécile—idiot
impressionnant—impressive; excellent
Je suis bon—I'm good
ma femme—my wife
ma fille—my girl
ma petite souer—my little sister
mais non—of course not
mais oui—that's right; of course
mais oui?—is that right?
merci, mon frère—thank you, my brother
mes enfants—my children
moi aussi—me too
mon ami—my friend
mon ange—my angel
Mon Dieu—my God
mon enfant—my child

mon fils—my son
ou est mon frère?—where is my brother
que c'est beau—how beautiful
quelque chose—something
qu'est-ce que je fais—what did I do
'tite chou—little one
tu comprends?—you understand?
une momente—one moment
vraiment—really; truly

Meet the Montgomery family for the first time in

Heard It All Before

1

The Kleenex, the Prince, and the Rose?

Jewel—Friday, May 18, 8:00 p.m.

"Chivalry is dead and Prince Charming fell off his charger years ago, you hear me?"

I heard her.

"I know what you want, Jewel. You want some tall, fine, intelligent, sensitive, heterosexual, drug-free, financially stable, Christian, chocolate god over the age of thirty with a great sense of humor to come knock-knocking at your door!" Renee paused. "Don't you?"

When she put it that way, it *did* sound kinda pathetic.

"Well, *don't* you?"

"He doesn't have to knock on my door," I protested weakly.

Renee snorted in disgust. "And where, exactly, are you going to find him? You go to work; he's not there. You come home; he ain't here. You go to church twice a month, slide in the side door five minutes before service starts, and slip out the back before we've sung the last Amen. So if he's there, you'll never see him. You work out at an all-girls' gym. That leaves the grocery store and the cleaners." She snorted again. "You think Mr. Wonderful is hanging out at Martinizing or Safeway?"

I threw my hands up. "Okay, okay. You're obviously trying to tell me something. What is it?"

"Actually, I'm trying to tell you a *few* things, Miss Capwell. Number one, even Cinderella had to dress up and go to the ball to find *her* prince. Number two, life is like the last Kleenex in the box, so be careful how you blow it. And number three, you've got to gather your rosebuds while you still can!"

At this point, I was starting to get mildly annoyed with Renee. Only mildly because I was somewhat confused over all these mixed metaphors. The Kleenex, the Prince, and the rosebuds were throwing me off. What were we talking about?

Okay, see, I invited Renee over for *dinner.* How this turned into a "let's talk about what's wrong with Jewellen's life" thing, I'll never know. But that was Renee for you. Renee and I met freshman year in college. She took one look at me and decided I was an uptight princess; I took one look at her and decided she was ghetto fabulous without the fabulous. We kept running into each other on the campus of the University of Texas in a series of catty exchanges that culminated in an epic battle for the last chocolate pudding pop in the all-girls' cafeteria. On a campus that was only 2 percent African American, we decided it was better to be allies than enemies. When all the dust settled, we discovered we somehow clicked.

I had grown up a bit sheltered. My mom was a bank manager, my father an investment specialist, and prior to their divorce, we had been one unit. I have an older sister and a brother. My sister, Stefani, got married about three years ago before moving to Alaska with her husband. I never could understand moving way up there to the frozen tundra, but that was where Lamar got promoted, so Stefani went. She loved it. Of course, none of us have been as close as we used to be since Mom and Dad's divorce and subsequent remarriages. Mom moved to Denver. Dad moved to New Orleans. My eldest sibling, Ross, got his international law degree and had been globe-trotting ever since. At Christmas, we all get together in a neutral city. Last year it was Miami. This year we're going south of the border to Cancun. I talk to them once a month or so. Since college, Renee, my former roommate Stace, and the gang have been my immediate family.

Renee, on the other hand, had grown up way before she should have. Her mother had Renee at age fifteen, so they kind of grew up together. Her mother was that unfortunate woman who could not be without a man. Renee grew up with a large group of random "uncles." After watching her mom get dogged by player after player, she developed a kill-or-be-killed attitude toward dating. By the time I met her, she had decided that if no one else would love you, you'd better love yourself . . . a lot. She was determined to get the best of everything and the better of everyone. Somehow this translated into convincing herself that the world was as in love with her as she was with herself.

When we started this conversation, she was telling me about the latest love of her life. No exaggerating, Renee Nightingale was the most in love person I knew. She was in love with her job as promotions manager for Royal Mahogany Cosmetics. You know, one of those new spin-offs a white cosmetic company puts out now that they've finally realized that, yes, black people need makeup and hair and skin products of their own! God bless them and I bear no grudge, but I've yet to meet a white person who truly understands the terrifying concepts of ashy legs and nappy hair.

But back to Renee. She was in love with her lazy dog, a froufrou little white chow named, of all things, Peaches. I told her to get another and name him Herb; she didn't take my reference.

Renee was also in love with some new man she met about a month ago. Yes, I said one month. Renee fell in love like other people washed clothes, regularly and in cycles. This cycle, she was into the "Corporate Self-Made Black Man." You've seen him. That swaggering, overconfident, look-what-I've-made-of-myself buppie with the round tortoise-shell glasses, navy Armani suit, Polo paisley tie, Dior white shirt, and Cole Haan leather tassel loafers, don't you know? I think this one was named Gregory.

But most of all, God love her, Renee was in love with Renee. She loved the way she talked, which was rapid and often around the girls, slow and sultry around the boys, and a fascinating combination of both in mixed company. She loved the way she moved, which was exactly how she talked. She loved the way she looked, which I had to admit was pretty damn good. Skin the color of rich, dark chocolate, smooth as silk, and crystal clear. Your basic African American wide brown eyes, gently sloped nose, and a perfect bow mouth.

She had short jet-black hair, and it was *always* whipped up. I mean, I'd known her for ten years, and even first thing in the morning, the clever page-boy was *on*. Sometimes curly, sometimes wavy, sometimes straight but always on. And the makeup, which she actually does change for morning and evening even if she stays at home, was flawless. She kept her manicurist on speed dial.

Her clothes? The woman planned her outfits every Sunday evening for the entire coming week, down to exercise wear and undies. She was 5'6", a size 8, not real big but adequate on top, and was in possession of a true sister's ass and thighs. She had fretted and sweated since "the ass" really kicked in at about age twenty-two but to no avail. I kept telling her nothing short of liposuction was going to rid her of it. And in all truth and fairness, she looked good with it. Only occasionally did I raise my brows when she tried to stretch some Lycra or knit across there. If you asked me how she caught half these Mr. Could-a-Been-Mr.-Rights, I'd say with her smile and that ass. Okay, not my point. I was reflecting on Renee's narcissistic ways. So, back to my growing annoyance with her little diatribe. Nine times out of ten, Renee talked to hear herself talk. Unfortunately, she was talking about me.

Where did she leave off?

Oh, yeah. "Cinderella met her prince at the ball with one Kleenex and a rose?" I muttered. "Girl, what the hell are you talking about?"

"You, girlfriend." She pointed a finger with a red-lacquered nail at me. "You've gotta get out there. Mohammed ain't making his way up this mountain, okay? I've decided it's time to hook you up."

I didn't even try to hide the dismay on my face. "Hook me up?" I shook my head rapidly from side to side. "Ah, hell to the no. You remember the last time you tried to hook me up? I didn't get rid of him until I moved away! You hear me? I had to change *area codes* to get rid of that psycho!"

She had the good grace to look chagrined momentarily. "Oh yeah, him. Well, who knew he was obsessive-compulsive with an Oedipus complex. Is it my fault you reminded him of his mama? Hell, at least he was fine!"

That year she considered minoring in psych obviously didn't do a thing for her. She skipped right past that obsessive-compulsive thing. "At least he was FINE? That was his redeeming quality?" I asked.

She waved that away dismissively. "Anyway, that's history. This time, I don't have anybody specific in mind; I just want to get you out into the proper arenas so you can see the available players, that's all."

Ignoring the sports imagery, I sighed my deepest, weariest sigh. "Renee, let's not do this, really. I'm happy enough with my life. And if the Lord intends for me to have a good man and a good relationship, then I'm sure one will come my way."

Renee shot me a look of stunned disbelief. "What way is that? Safeway?" She leaned forward, warming to her topic. "Listen, sugar, the Lord helps those who help themselves; you hear me? Sitting in this house waiting for something to happen . . . I just can't see that as being the good Lord's plan. You're thirty years old, you own your own house, you run your own company, you're in possession of a decent bank account, you have good sense in your head, and when you give a damn, you look good! All we've got to do is enhance your market-able traits, camouflage your flaws, and present you to a wide and appreciative audience." She sat back with a flourish and a smile.

I raised a brow. "Oh, so I'm your latest market-ing project?" She started to speak, but I held my hand out to stop her. "No, no, a thousand times no. My life is fine. Or, here, in words you'll under-stand—if it ain't broke, don't fix it!"

She turned her nose up and tilted her head to the side. "How ya know it ain't broke? When was the last time anyone turned it on, took it for a test drive? Hell, even kicked a tire! And since you like things in plain English, I'm asking you flat out—when was the last time you had some? Okay, no . . . We don't even have to go all there. When was the last time you had a date?"

Uh-oh, she had me on that one. "A date?" I stalled, trying to think back that far. Could it have been that long ago? Maybe I was getting a little stale?

She smirked. "Yeah, honey, you know the thing . . . when a man asks you out, you go somewhere to-gether merely for the sake of being together, he brings you home, he makes a play, and knowing you, you send him home. A date."

"Well . . ." I squinted up at the ceiling, determined to recall one. Let's see, we're in May, and there was that one guy I went to that concert with. . . . Was that Thanksgiving? Couldn't have been too memorable since the whole experience was a distant blur in my mind.

"You can't remember, can you?" Her expression was irritatingly smug.

"Yeah, yeah, just gimme a minute." Surely I'd gone out over Christmas? No, went to visit my sister's family. New Year's? No, went to the candlelight service at church. Valentine's Day? No, watched the *Flava of Love* reunion show with a bottle of wine and a gourmet pizza. Ah, shit. This *was* just sad. I had some male friends; could I count lunch with them as dates? My brother and I were at the mall last week, and some guy came up and offered to buy me a smoothie—that's sort of datelike, isn't it?

Truthfully, since Patrick (the ex-fiancé) and I walked away from each other without a backward glance about two years ago, I can't say as I've felt motivated to dive back in the deep end of the dating pool. I was comfortable here in the shallows. A mocha here, a movie there . . . I was all good, right?

Renee was shaking her head. "You don't need a minute. I'll tell ya. Your last date was that jazz concert downtown over the Thanksgiving weekend with that tall boy with the bad haircut. What was his name?"

"It was Richard or Roland or something." What *was* his name?

"Umm-hmm." She said nothing else, just sat there with that know-it-all smirk on her face.

"Okay, okay! So I haven't exactly been the social

butterfly lately. I'll start dating again." I shrugged. How tough could it be?

Her eyes narrowed. "How, who, when? You don't go anywhere to meet anybody!"

I rolled my eyes. "Oh, I guess I'm supposed to break out the leather miniskirt and the pumps and start hitting the club scene? No way. I outgrew that six years ago and didn't like it much then. I don't mind going out to cut a step every now and again, but, uh-uh, I'm not getting back into the meat-market scene. No way." All that smiling and posturing and tell me your life story and I'll tell you mine—who wanted to go through all that? Standing around in killer stilettos pretending not to care if anyone looks at you or not . . . yeah, I sure miss that.

"Who said you had to, Miss Priss? I happen to know of a dozen places to go to roll up on some brothers, not one of them 'meat market' in the least!" She sounded sincere, but Renee always does.

I was suspicious. "Oh, yeah?" I was torn between the desire to be among single men and the deep-rooted belief that Renee was up to something for her own good.

"Yeah. Now, why don't you do something with that hair tonight? We got places to be tomorrow." She drained her glass of wine, stood up, and looked at her watch. "Gotta late date. Gotta shuffle. Thanks for the grub." She strode toward the living room. Girl never wasted a minute, always on the go.

I got up slowly, trailing behind her, still suspicious. "Okay, but where is it that we're going? And what do *you* mean when you say 'roll up'?"

Slinging her $400 Dooney & Bourke over her

arm, she looked back at me with a sigh. "Jewel, even *you* know what 'rolling up' means." She headed down the hallway to the front door.

I pursed my lips. "Listen here, Ms. Nightingale. I know how to roll up on a brother. But somehow I feel like my roll and yours are two different things. *Where* did you say we were going?" I stood in the doorway of the kitchen, waiting for my answer. Renee can come up with some wild-ass schemes.

At the door she turned. "To a b-ball court. Got invited to watch a game." She opened my front door and stepped outside. "I'll call you 'round noon. Dress accordingly—the court's kinda up in the hood." She shut the door and made tracks to her car.

I hopped forward, ran to the door, and whipped it open. I caught her fumbling for her keys, thereby foiling her smooth exit. "Excuse me, Miss Thing, did I hear you say we're going to the *hood*? And can you tell me why?"

"Jewellen Rose Capwell," she scolded with one foot in her new Lexus SUV, "you can't be afraid of your own people." She shut the door, turned on the ignition, and whipped out of the driveway.

"Oh, sure I can," I said aloud before closing and locking the door. I walked to the back of my safe little house and turned on my safe little alarm.

As I cleaned away the debris from dinner, I shook my head repeatedly. The hood. Color me snobbish, but I was always scared as hell of the hood. Hey, color me wimpy too. I grew up in Far North Dallas. The farther north the better.

I went to private school with two other blacks in the entire school; that meant in grades K through

12, there was a total of three. After my parents' divorce, I went to public school in one of the richest, whitest suburbs in the city. I thought a fistfight by the bike racks after school was gang violence. Caught a couple kissing under the stairway and I thought that was indiscriminate premarital sex. What did I know? You grow up and realize that the news doesn't tell the whole story, that the Northside was not without crime of its own. I also realized that guns belonged to folks of all color. Nonetheless, I always felt more in my comfort zone north of downtown.

Probably stems from an experience I had when I was sixteen. Just hanging out at a football game on the Southside with some friends. Next thing we know, someone rolls up to do a drive-by and we're literally sprinting for our lives. Spent an hour and a half hiding between a Dumpster and a parked car before we got the all clear. For weeks afterward, I was terrified that one of the shooters had seen my face and was hunting me down. Melodramatic, yes, but also terrifying. Since then, it took a major event and arm-twisting to get me south of downtown.

Don't get me wrong, I hang with "my own people." I like the music, can speak the lingo, rock the attitude, the whole nine. I can go to a Metallica concert Friday and a 50 Cent concert Saturday and never confuse the two. I watched reruns of *Friends* and *Girlfriends*. I had a lot of black friends but quite a few white ones too. I was equal opportunity.

Even dated one white boy for a little minute until I realized that my natural inclinations simply attracted me to tall Nubian princes, as Renee would say. So what if I met a great white guy and fell madly in love, I wouldn't be with him? Not sure, it would be a decision. Not that any of this matters; it had been so long since I met a male of any color that attracted me, I'd forgotten what it feels like. Apparently it was time I got out and saw what was out there . . . again.

I went upstairs, entered the bathroom, and began pulling out all the various paraphernalia I'd need to resurrect this hair and face before morning. I caught a glimpse of myself in the mirror as I turned around to look for my intensive conditioner and almond-peppermint mask.

Pausing, I took stock of what I saw. Medium complexion, somewhere between butterscotch and caramel if I was forced to narrow down the color. Features set in an oval-shaped face that has too often been called "cute." Large brown eyes with lashes that appreciated a volumizing mascara. Button nose and medium-lipped mouth that was a little wider than I would like. Shoulder-length chestnut brown hair parted sensibly on the side. It was currently in need of a trim and a conditioning rinse. Usually curled under and tucked practically behind my ears, which were pierced once and usually adorned with a simple hoop or a diamond stud.

I turned to the side and shifted my shoulders back to see how the silhouette was holding up— 5'7" on a tall day. Size 8 from the waist down, 10 across the chest. I inherited my grandmother's body—small bones, top heavy, narrow waist, no hips or ass to speak of, thighs that required weekly aerobic maintenance atop admittedly great calves and size 7 feet. Speaking of feet, it couldn't hurt to touch up the toenail polish and do a quickie manicure.

It was entirely possible that I had let a few things slide during my dating hiatus. How did I let Renee sucker me into this mess? I had about ten hours to turn myself from Hilda the hausfrau to Fiona the fly girl. It ain't gonna be easy.

More from Michele Grant

Heard It All Before

Accustomed to living the high life in Dallas, everything Jewellen Capwell knows about the hood comes from the movies. So when she agrees to accompany her best friend, Renee Nightingale, to a Southside ball game, her only concern is keeping her cool around the peeps. She's not there to ogle guys—until she spots Roman Montgomery. When it comes to men, Jewel's heard it all before, but Rome's working from a whole new script . . .

Sweet Little Lies

Christina Brinsley is that girl. You know the one: a little bougie, a little opinionated, knows it all, has it all, and is a total perfectionist. But when her latest assignment leads her to sizzling, hot professor Steven Williams, the one man who sees through her efforts to outsmart and outmaneuver her way through every situation, Christina can't believe she's falling for a man who may be a key player in the scandal she's investigating. . . .

Pretty Boy Problems

Responsible, mature, employed . . . everything Avery Beauregard Montgomery is not. Instead, Beau is a natural-born charmer. He has breezed through life on his dazzling looks, six-pack abs, and sparkling personality. But when he meets Belle, his sister's new business partner, he's ready to give up his trifling, pretty boy ways . . . but what will it take to get Belle on the same page?

Available wherever books and ebooks are sold.

In this thrilling debut novel from
Carrie H. Johnson, one woman with a
dangerous job and a volatile past is feeling
the heat from all sides . . .

HOT FLASH

Coming in June 2016

Chapter 1

Our bodies arched, both of us reaching for that place of ultimate release we knew was coming. Yes! We screamed at the same time . . . except I kept screaming long after his moment had passed.

You've got to be kidding me, a cramp in my groin? The second time in the three times we had made love. Achieving pretzel positions these days came at a price, but man, how sweet the reward.

"What's the matter, baby? You cramping again?" he asked, looking down at me with genuine concern.

I was pissed, embarrassed, and in pain all at the same time. "Yeah," I answered meekly, grimacing.

"It's okay. It's okay, sugar," he said, sliding off me. He reached out and pulled me into the curvature of his body, leaving the wet spot to its own demise. I settled in. Gently, he massaged my thigh.

His hands soothed me. Little by little, the cramp went away. Just as I dozed off, my cell phone rang.

"*Mph, mph, mph,*" I muttered. "Never a moment's peace."

Calvin stirred. "Huh?"

"Nothin', baby, shhhh," I whispered, easing from his grasp and reaching for the phone from the bedside table. As quietly as I could, I answered the phone the same way I always did.

"Muriel Mabley."

"Did I get you at a bad time, partner?" Laughton chuckled. He used the same line whenever he called. He never thought twice about waking me, no matter the hour. I worked to live and lived to work—at least that's been my story for twenty years, the last seventeen as a firearms forensics expert for the Philadelphia Police Department. I had the dubious distinction of being the first woman in the unit and one of two minorities. The other was my partner, Laughton McNair.

At forty-nine, I was beginning to think I was blocking the blessing God intended for me. I felt like I had blown past any hope of a true love in pursuit of a damn suspect.

"You there?" Laughton said, laughing louder.

"Hee hee, hell. I finally find someone and you runnin' my ass ragged, like you don't *even* want it to last. What now?" I said.

"Speak up. I can hardly hear you."

"I said . . ."

"I heard you." More chuckles from Laughton. "You might want to rethink a relationship. Word is we've got another dead wife and again the husband swears he didn't do it. Says she offed herself. That makes three dead wives in three weeks. Hell, must be the season or something in the water."

Not wanting to move much or turn the light on, I let my fingers search blindly through my bag on the nightstand until they landed on paper and a pen. Pulling my hand out of my bag with paper and pen was another story. I knocked over the half-filled champagne glass also on the nightstand. "Damn it!" I was like a freaking circus act, trying to save the paper, keep the bubbly from getting on the bed, stop the glass from breaking, and keep from dropping the phone.

"Sounds like you're fighting a war over there," Laughton said.

"Just give me the address."

"If you can't get away . . ."

"Laughton, just . . ."

"You don't have to yell."

He let a moment of silence pass before he said, "Thirteen ninety-one Berkhoff. I'll meet you there."

"I'm coming," I said and clicked off.

"You okay?" Calvin reached out to recapture me. I let him and fell back into the warmth of his embrace. Then I caught myself, sat up, and clicked the light on—but not without a sigh of protest.

Calvin rose. He rested his head in his palm and flashed that gorgeous smile at me. "Can't blame a guy for trying," he said.

"It's a pity I can't do you any more lovin' right now. I can't sugarcoat it. This is my life," I complained on my way to the bathroom.

"So you keep telling me."

I felt uptight about leaving Calvin in the house alone. My son, Travis, would be home from college in the morning, his first spring break from Lincoln University. He and Calvin had not met. In all the years before this night, I had not brought a man home, except Laughton, and at least a decade had passed since I'd had any form of a romantic relationship. The memory chip filled with that information had almost disintegrated. Then along came Calvin.

When I came out, Calvin was up and dressed. He was five foot ten, two hundred pounds of muscle, the kind of muscle that flexed at his slightest move. Pure lovely. He pulled me close and pressed his wet lips to mine. His breath, mixed with a hint of citrus from his cologne, made every nerve in my body pulsate.

"Next time we'll do my place. You can sing to me while I make you dinner," he whispered. "Soft, slow melodies." He crooned, "You Must Be a Special Lady," as he rocked me back and forth, slow and steady. His gooey caramel voice touched my every nerve ending, head to toe. Calvin is a singer and owns a nightclub, which is how we met. I was at his club with friends and Calvin and I—or rather, Calvin and my alter ego, spurred on by my friends, of course—entertained the crowd with duets all night.

He held me snugly against his chest and buried his face in the hollow of my neck while brushing his fingertips down the length of my body.

"Mmm . . . sounds luscious," was all I could muster.

* * *

The interstate was dark, unusual no matter what time, day or night.

In the darkness, I could easily picture Calvin's face, bright with a satisfied smile. I could still feel his hot breath on my neck, the soft strumming of his fingers on my back. I had it bad. Butterflies reached down to my navel and made me shiver. I felt like I was nineteen again, first love or some such foolishness.

Flashing lights from an oncoming police car brought my thoughts around to what was ahead, a possible suicide. How anyone could think life was so bad that they would kill themselves never settled with me. Life's stuff enters pit territory sometimes, but then tomorrow comes and anything is possible again. Of course, the idea that the husband could be the killer could take one even deeper into pit territory. The man you once loved, who made you scream during lovemaking, now not only wants you gone, moved out, but dead.

When I rounded the corner to Berkhoff Street, the scene was chaotic, like the trappings of a major crime. I pulled curbside and rolled to a stop behind a news truck. After I turned off Bertha, my 2000 Saab gray convertible, she rattled in protest for a few moments before going quiet. As I got out, local news anchor Sheridan Meriwether hustled from the front of the news truck and shoved a microphone in my face before I could shut the car door.

"Back off, Sheridan. You'll know when we know," I told her.

"True, it's a suicide?" Sheridan persisted.

"If you know that, then why the attack? You know we don't give out information in suicides."

"Confirmation. Especially since two other wives have been killed in the past few weeks."

"Won't be for a while. Not tonight anyway."

"Thanks, Muriel." She nodded toward Bertha. "Time you gave the old gray lady a permanent rest, don't you think?"

"Hey, she's dependable."

She chuckled her way back to the front of the news truck. Sheridan was the only newsperson I would give the time of day. We went back two decades, to rookie days when my mom and dad were killed in a car crash. Sheridan and several other newspeople had accompanied the police to inform me. She returned the next day, too, after the buzz had faded. A drunk driver sped through a red light and rammed my parents' car head-on. That was the story the police told the papers. The driver of the other car cooked to a crisp when his car exploded after hitting my parents' car, then a brick wall. My parents were on their way home from an Earth, Wind & Fire concert at the Tower Theater.

Sheridan produced a series on drunk drivers in Philadelphia, how their indiscretions affected families and children on both sides of the equation, which led to a national broadcast. Philadelphia police cracked down on drunk drivers and legislation passed with compulsory loss of licenses. Several other cities and states followed suit.

I showed my badge to the young cop guarding the front door and entered the small foyer. In front of me was a white-carpeted staircase. To the left was the living room. Laughton, his expression stonier than I expected, stood next to the detective questioning who I supposed was the husband. He sat on the couch, leaned forward with his elbows resting on his thighs, his head hanging down. Two girls clad in *Frozen* pajamas huddled next to him on the couch, one on either side.

The detective glanced at me, then back at the man. "Where were you?"

"I just got here, man," the man said. "Went upstairs and found her on the floor."

"And the kids?"

"My daughter spent the night with me. She had a sleepover at my house. This is Jeanne, lives a few blocks over. She got homesick and wouldn't stop crying, so I was bringing them back here. Marcy and I separated, but we're trying to work things out." He choked up, unable to speak any more.

"At three a.m."

"I told you, the child was having a fit. Wanted her mother."

A tank of a woman charged through the front door, "Oh my God. Baby, are you all right?" She pushed past the police officer there and clomped across the room, sending those close to look for cover. The red-striped flannel robe she wore and pink furry slippers, size thirteen at least, made her look like a giant candy cane with feet.

"Wade, what the hell is happenin' here?" She moved in and lifted the girl from the sofa by her arm. Without giving him a chance to answer, she continued, "C'mon, baby. You're coming with me."

An officer stepped sideways and blocked the way. "Ma'am, you can't take her—"

The woman's head snapped around like the devil possessed her, ready to spit out nasty words followed by green fluids. She never stopped stepping.

I expect she would have trampled the officer, but Laughton interceded. "It's all right, Jackson. Let her go," he said.

Jackson sidestepped out of the woman's way before Laughton's words settled.

Laughton nodded his head in my direction. "Body's upstairs."

The house was spotless. White was *the* color: white furniture, white walls, white drapes, white wall-to-wall carpet, white picture frames. The only real color came in the mass of throw pillows that adorned the couch and a wash of plants positioned around the room.

I went upstairs and headed to the right of the landing, into a bedroom where an officer I knew, Mark Hutchinson, was photographing the scene. Body funk permeated the air. I wrinkled my nose.

"Hey, M&M," Hutchinson said.

"That's Muriel to you." I hated when my colleagues took the liberty to call me that. Sometimes I wanted to nail Laughton with a front kick to the groin for starting the nickname.

He shook his head. "Ain't me or the victim. She smells like a violet." He tilted his head back, sniffed, and smiled.

Hutchinson waved his hand in another direction. "I'm about done here."

I stopped at the threshold of the bathroom and perused the scene. Marcy Taylor lay on the bathroom floor. A small hole in her temple still oozed blood. Her right arm was extended over her head, and she had a .22 pistol in that hand. Her fingernails and toenails looked freshly painted. When I bent over her body, the sulfur-like smell of hair relaxer backed me up a bit. Her hair was bone-straight. The white silk gown she wore flowed around her body as though staged. Her cocoa brown complexion looked ashen with a pasty, white film.

"Shame," Laughton said to my back. "She was a beautiful woman." I jerked around to see him standing in the doorway.

"Check this out," I said, pointing to the lay of the nightgown over the floor.

"I already did the scene. We'll talk later," he said.

"Damn it, Laughton. Come here and check this out." But when I turned my head, he was gone.

I finished checking out the scene and went outside for some fresh air. Laughton was on the front lawn talking to an officer. He beelined for his car when he saw me.

"What the hell is wrong with you?" I muttered, jogging to catch up with him. Louder. "Laughton, what the hell—"

He dropped anchor. Caught off guard, I plowed into him. He waited until I peeled myself off him and regained my footing, then said, "Nothing. Wade says they separated a few months ago and were trying to get it together, so he came over for some making up. He used his key to enter and found her dead on the bathroom floor."

"No, he said he was bringing the little girl home because she was homesick."

"Yeah, well, then you heard it all."

He about-faced.

I grabbed his arm and attempted to spin him around. "You act like you know this one or something," I practically screeched at him.

"I do."

I cringed and softened my tone five octaves at least when I managed to speak again. "How?"

"I was married to her . . . a long time ago."

He might as well have backhanded me upside the head. "You never—"

"I have an errand to run. I'll see you back at the lab."

I stared after him long after he got in his car and sped off.

The sun was rising by the time the scene was secured: body and evidence bagged, husband and daughter gone back home. It spewed warm tropical hues over the city. By the time I reached the station, the hues had turned cold metallic gray. I pulled into a parking spot and answered the persistent ring of my cell phone. It was Nareece.

"Hey, sis. My babies got you up this early?" I said, feigning a light mood. My babies were Nareece's eight-year-old twin daughters.

Nareece groaned. "No. Everyone's still sleeping."

"You should be, too."

"Couldn't sleep."

"Oh, so you figured you'd wake me up at this ungodly hour in the morning. Sure, why not? We're talkin' sisterly love here, right?" I said. We chuckled. "I've been up since three anyway, working a case." I waited for her to say something, but she stayed silent. "Reece?" More silence. "C'mon, Reecey, we've been through this so many times. Please don't tell me you're trippin' again."

"A bell goes off in my head every time this date rolls around. I believe I'll die with it going off," Nareece confessed.

"Therapy isn't helping?"

"You mean the shrink? She ain't worth the paper she prints her bills on. I get more from talking to you every day. It's all you, Muriel. What would I do without you?"

"I'd say we've helped each other through, Reecey."

Silence filled the space again. Meanwhile, Laughton pulled his Audi Quattro in next to my Bertha and got out. I knocked on the window to get his attention. He glanced in my direction and moved on with his gangster swagger as though he didn't see me.

"I have to go to work, Reece. I just pulled into the parking lot after being at a scene."

"Okay."

"Reece, you've got a great husband, two beautiful daughters, and a gorgeous home, baby. Concentrate on all that and quit lookin' behind you."

Nareece and John had ten years of marriage. John is Vietnamese. The twins were striking, inheritors of almond-shaped eyes, "good" curly black hair, and amber skin. Rose and Helen, named after our mother and grandmother. John balked at their names because they did not reflect his heritage. But he was mush where Nareece was concerned.

"You're right. I'm good except for two days out of the year, today and on Travis's birthday. And you're probably tired of hearing me."

"I'll listen as long as you need me to. It's you and me, Reecey. Always has been, always will be. I'll call you back later today. I promise."

I clicked off and stayed put for a few minutes, bogged down by the realization of Reece's growing obsession with my son, way more than in past years, which conjured up ugly scenes for me. I prayed for a quick passing, though a hint of guilt pierced my gut. Did I pray for her sake, my sake, or Travis's? What scared me anyway?

Grab These Novels by
Zuri Day

__Bad Boy Seduction	978-0-7582-7513-4	$6.99US/$7.99CAN
__Body By Night	978-0-7582-2882-6	$6.99US/$8.49CAN
__A Good Dose of Pleasure	978-0-7582-7512-7	$6.99US/$7.99CAN
__Heat Wave (with Donna Hill & Niobia Bryant)	978-0-7582-6543-2	$6.99US/$7.99CAN
__Lessons from a Younger Lover	978-0-7582-3871-9	$6.99US/$8.99CAN
__Lies Lovers Tell	978-0-7582-2881-9	$6.99US/$8.49CAN
__Love in Play	978-0-7582-6000-0	$6.99US/$7.99CAN
__Love on the Run	978-0-7582-7511-0	$6.99US/$7.99CAN
__Lovin' Blue	978-0-7582-5999-8	$6.99US/$8.99CAN
__The One that I Want (with Donna Hill and Cheris Hodges)	978-0-7582-7514-1	$6.99US/$7.99CAN
__What Love Tastes Like	978-0-7582-3872-6	$6.99US/$8.99CAN

Available Wherever Books Are Sold!

All available as e-books, too!

Visit our website at **www.kensingtonbooks.com**